CW01655563

DEEPFADED

CRAIGSON PALMER

Copyright © 2025 by Craigson Palmer

All rights reserved. No part of this publication may be reproduced, stored in retrieval system, or transmitted, in any form or by any means, electronic, mechanical, photocopying, recording or otherwise, without the prior permission of the copyright holder.

No portion of this book may be reproduced in any form without written permission from the publisher or author, except as permitted by UK copyright law.

For permission requests, contact: craigson.com@gmail.com

ISBN 978 1 9193771 0 0

The story, all characters, and incidents portrayed in this production are fictitious. No identification with actual persons (living or deceased), is intended or should be inferred.

Cover Illustrator: Sashee Jade Sandoval

BEFORE YOU READ!!

Despite only being a teenager when I wrote this story, this book may contain sensitive scenes that include: Strong language, violence, mental illness, eating disorders, neglect, self-harm, suicide, grief, alcoholism, and implied assault. Therefore, I recommend not reading this if you get triggered easily by any of those topics.

Disclaimer - You may also look like this once you've finished this book:

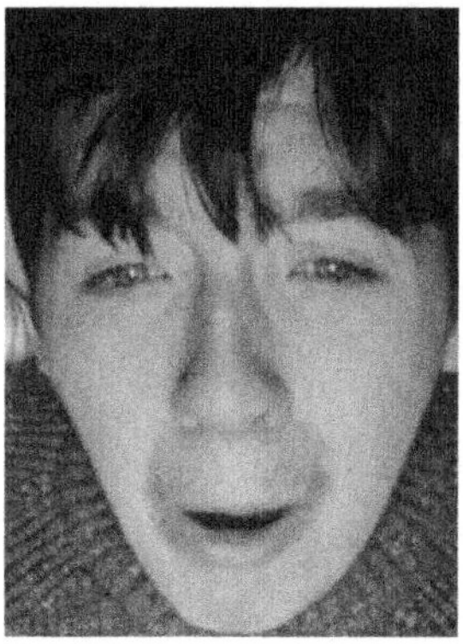

PLAYLIST: TRACK 1

Alien Horizon| Oliver Taylor

I'm growing up too fast| redhead

Alien Blues| Vundabar

Ghosting| Mother Mother

We're Going to Be Friends| The White Stripes

Noise Cancelling Headphones| Sylvia Daley

Prom Queen| Beach Bunny

Overwhelmed| Royal & the Serpent

Penny Lane| The Beatles

Reflections| The Neighbourhood

I Can't Handle Change| Roar

Death with Dignity| Sufjan Stevens

Linger| The Cranberries

Oh Daddy| Fleetwood Mac

I need to be alone.| girl in red

Zombie girl| Adrianne Lenker

It's My Party| Lesley Gore

Die Your Daughter| Susannah Joffe

Kids| Current Joys

Pretend| Alex G

TV| Billie Eilish

Weird Girl| Mommy Long Legs

Fifteen on a Skateboard| Diners

Family Line| Conan Gray

Secret| Orchestral Manoeuvres In The Dark

Plasticine| James Marriott

PLAYLIST: TRACK 2

My Girlfriend Is a Witch| October Country

I Kissed A Girl| Katy Perry

Drunk on Halloween| Wallows

Last Christmas| Wham!

Please, Please, Please, Let Me Get What I Want| The Smiths

My Alcoholic Friends| The Dresden Dolls

Deceptacon| Le Tigre

Appointments| Julien Baker

She Knows| J. Cole, Cults, Amber Coffman

Mastermind| Taylor Swift

No. 1 Party Anthem| Arctic Monkeys

Destroyed Myself Just For You| Montell Fish

ARE WE STILL FRIENDS?| Tyler, The Creator

Don't Let the Sun Go Down| George Michael, Elton John

Slipping Through My Fingers| ABBA

Daddy Issues| The Neighbourhood

I Bet on Losing Dogs| Mitski

Chamber Of Reflection| Mac DeMarco

Little Dark Age| MGMT

Daddy Dance with Me| Krystal Keith

Video Games| Lana Del Rey

Back to the Old House| The Smiths

If We Have Each Other| Alec Benjamin

Don't quite belong| dodie

Man's World| MARINA

PLAYLIST: TRACK 3

Sun Bleached Flies| Ethel Cain

Garbage| Twenty One Pilots

No Surprises| Radiohead

Remember You Omnichord| Trillian

Lights Are On| Tom Rosenthal

Francis Forever| Mitski

Funeral| Phoebe Bridgers

Space Song| Beach House

Queen of Noise| The Runaways

Take A Slice| Glass Animals

Labour| Paris Paloma

FOR ALL THE TANCAN'S AND TAYLOR'S OUT THERE.

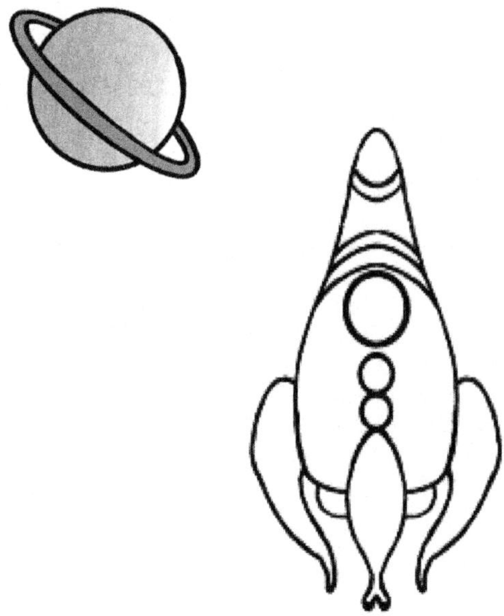

Art by Riley

Prologue

March 21st 2016 - 2,124 days before he destroyed himself.

Melissa Milten knew she was going to die that day; what she didn't know was that her murderer would be her ten-year-old son.

Stripping gaudy paper from his mountain of gifts, Tancan buried the cream carpet underneath a rainbow of ribbons. His blue eyes glistened as he tore an envelope, unleashing a bank of dancing notes, each one fluttering like a butterfly.

"£50! Thank you so much, Mum. I think I have enough to buy my rocket ship! Can you order it for me, pretty please?" he begged, jumping up and down. "Or can I open my big present now?"

"Slow down, little munchkin," said Melissa. "You still need wait for daddy to finish writing his emails before you even think about touching that. You know he doesn't like it when you don't wait for him."

A trail of space-themed wrapping paper led to a metallic bow tied across a cardboard box. The box balanced on

Tancan's kneecaps. His hands hovered over the edge of the paper, itching to tear a corner off. As his nail dug into the seam, a distant chair scraped its feet against the kitchen's sandstone tiles.

He tilted his head towards the kitchen.

His dad was sitting alone at the dining table, stroking his fingers along the sharp edges of a dwelling tower of documents. The top page boldly stated: **Autism Spectrum Report**

"Dad, I've finished opening my presents! You can come and watch me open my main present now!" he called, hoping he could distract him from whatever daunting sentence he had read.

Felix lifted his head and smiled. "Okay, sweetheart." He stood up, placing the letters aside, although his eyes remained fixed on the top page.

The wrapping paper tugged away in handfuls, each rip revealed something big. A box bigger than Tancan's head. "My LEGO rocket ship!" he gasped, running his fingers over the image and rotating the box at every angle. "Woah, it even comes with mini astronauts to sit inside!"

He wrapped his hands around his dad's neck. "Thank you!" he muffled into his chest, before throwing himself towards his mother, squeezing her just as tightly.

"Look at this, Finn!" Tancan hopped towards his younger brother, drumming his fingers along the package. "Five hundred and eighty-six pieces!"

"No way!" Finn skipped around the back of the box. "It says it's aged six plus, so I can help you build it too!"

Tancan ignored him. It was a better option than getting told off for telling Finn that he couldn't help. It was his gift and he didn't want any of the pieces to get lost.

His flapping hands yanked open all the numbered plastic bags, the same hands that took ten years to notice. He aligned each individual brick, categorizing them into sectors of colour. He knew what he was doing. To him, this wasn't a toy; this was a trophy.

After rummaging in the attic, Felix pondered downstairs carrying a dusty case. "I have one last surprise to show you," he said, crouching down beside him.

"Oh, I wasn't expecting anything else," Tancan mumbled, worrying about the case taking up a lot of space in his bedroom. He wasn't being ungrateful, but he didn't add that item to his list and hadn't prepared a reaction for whatever was hiding inside.

Felix unlocked the padlock and pulled out an old *gun*. The rusted *weapon* was *loose* in the living room. In the same room as two *children* and a crying ten-month-old *baby.*

Tancan's hands trembled as his dad placed the cold, heavy object in his possession. He hadn't wanted to touch it, not even look at it, but now the weight was on him. This wasn't some historical object that was passed down by his ancestors; it was a machine. A killing machine that didn't belong to him. "Dad, I'm scared," he murmured, holding himself as still as a statue.

"It's not going to hurt you, honey. Stay still so I can take a photo."

"But what if it's loaded? I don't want it. Please take it away!"

Felix unlocked his phone. "Tanks, stop being silly, it's not load—"

Tancan's fingers loosened, and in the split second, the weapon slipped out of his bare hands. He tried to catch it, but it was too late. His finger had caught on a piece of steel alloy.

Bang!

His hands recoiled. The gun clattered onto the golden-oak floor.

Melissa screamed in *agony*.

The photo frames that ran across the walls stretched and shrunk. He couldn't move. His hands, his legs, nothing worked. The echo of the gunshot pierced through his ears, and his dad's shouting only rippled through the holes.

"Get me a cloth, anything!" Felix pressed down on Melissa's dress, blooming with maroon paint. A fragment of metal had struck through her chest, yet her pupils were still conscious.

Melissa's hands reached for her husband's face, brushing against his stubble. "Felix!" She took her final breath. "Take care of my babies," she pleaded, her blood splattering on Felix's plain-white shirt.

*

Sirens screamed outside, painting the tinted windows blue.

The paramedics barged into the living room. One knelt, attempting to feel her pulse, but the bullet had already ripped right through her heart. There was nothing they could do.

The other medic took their gaze away from her body and locked eyes with Felix. "I'm so sorry," they said. "Your wife is *dead.*"

Felix's head melted into the ground, scraping his nails through the carpet. He sat up and snapped his attention towards his twitching child. "What did *you* do?" he roared before collapsing against the surrounding floral wallpaper. He held the cloth to his chest, using the unstained corner to soak up his tears. "I'm so sorry, baby; it's not your fault. Don't worry, we'll be okay."

But Tancan wasn't okay. He would never be okay. His mum was dead, and it was all his fault. He was a child *murderer*.

1: Regret

March 23rd 2021 - 296 days before he destroyed himself.

Dear Star Diary,

I hate birthdays. A few days ago, I turned fifteen, but I still feel like I'm nine.

It was Mum's fifth anniversary too, and the thought of her being trapped underneath a chalky white sheet makes me dig my rocket-shaped pen into my legs. It hurts. It really hurts, but at least a pen is softer than a knife. I know she wouldn't want me to, but I can't stop. Every time I hurt myself, I seem to forget what happened, even if it is just for two minutes.

I think my dad must be hurting more; he's overflowing the bin with cans again. I don't understand how he gets so angry; he never used to be. I guess he uses alcohol as some sort of coping mechanism. The more beer he consumes, the angrier he becomes. Today, it lasted a whopping two hours and twenty-eight minutes.

I trust he won't harm me on purpose, but I fear he might do something stupid one day. Like when he frightened

Sapphire into my room after he smashed a plate across the kitchen.

Whenever he drinks, it's always my responsibility to keep Finn and Sapphire safe. They are like my babies. They will sit in my room and watch the swirling blobs levitate to the top of my lava lamp for an entire hour, or however long it takes for Dad to calm down. And I'm supposed to be the only autistic in the family?

Dad has hardly attended any of Sapphire's ballet rehearsals this year, but I haven't missed any. There is something about seeing her face light up whenever she spots me in the audience. I'm glad she appreciates me. She always runs over to me and hugs me at the end of the show. "Did you see me twirl all by myself?" she will say with a huge grin on her face.

Dad forgets other things too. The amount of times he's forgotten to pick me up from school is insane, so I am glad me and Finn are now in secondary school and can walk home together. Dad also forgets to cook dinner, so we end up eating leftovers most nights.

Some days I choose to starve myself because the texture of rice goes icky after being left in the fridge. I'm used to it by now.

If Dad gets very cross, I will text his best friend. I have known Stephen since I was born, and he visits us most days. He was the one who bought me my navy-blue alien hoodie, and I've worn it every day since my birthday. The hoodie I've desired for months is finally mine, despite Dad's moaning about the cost.

Stephen's support has been like a lifeline for Dad after he lost Mum, even if he always rejects every penny that Stephen slides into his pocket.

As much as I trust him, I haven't told him about the plate incident. I don't want him to worry about us even more than he already does, but I don't know how much longer my patience can put up with this.

Like every day, I plan out my entire schedule, then suddenly, boom! Dad's drunk again. Great. He always leaves his half-empty cans in the most random places, forgetting he literally has a five-year-old daughter who will play with anything she can get her hands on. It drives me crazy, that man honestly has no common sense sometimes, and by the next morning, he's magically back to normal like nothing happened.

Maybe if I hadn't gotten diagnosed so late, Dad would've given up by now.

— Love your favourite space nerd, Tancan :)

2: Toxic

March 24th 2021 - 295 days before he destroyed himself.

Felix clinked a spoon against his mug's ceramic walls, watching the coffee whirlpool as the steam curled into his nostrils. "Seriously, Tanks, skipping another day of school? I thought we'd spoken about this?" he said, wiping his thick-rimmed glasses with a microfiber cloth.

“But... I’m tired,” he mumbled.

“Well, you should’ve gone to sleep earlier, then.”

“No, I’m the emotionally drained kind of tired. I don’t think I can cope with another day of busy corridors and loud classes. It's not like I'm going to miss anything; I don't have any friends at all, and I can't even concentrate in that manic classroom."

"That's not the point, sweetheart." He sighed. "Your school has sent me many emails concerning your poor attendance. You know I care about you, but it's hard being a single dad and looking after three kids by myself. Do you think you could try going in tomorrow, for me?"

Tancan nodded, gripping the sleeve of his hoodie as he crept towards the front door.

"Where are you going this early?"

He gazed at the time on his phone. "I, uh, need to go for a walk since I've been feeling quite stressed lately, just to clear my head a bit."

"Alright." He smiled. "I'll still be here once you get back if you want to have a proper chat later on."

Tancan smiled back before closing the door behind him. He released a sigh of relief and checked the time again, adjusting his headphones. Step one completed.

***

His pace slowed as he neared the park. Beyond the gate, a weathered statue walked beside him. Its worn face made it seem almost alive from being exposed to a variety of weather. He had reached an old oak tree. His shoes crunched over the fallen leaves as he approached a boy sat on a bench.

"Finally, what took you so long?" the boy said, rubbing the back of his buzzed hair, a vape clenched in his hand.

Tancan's tongue stroked the roof of his mouth. "Sorry, my dad wanted to chat."

"Yeah, yeah, whatever. Just make sure nobody knows about this. I don't want any of my guys finding out I'm hanging with the only other gay boy in Audresbury. So... I was thinking that today we could try—"

He shook his head. "Owen, I need more time."

"Just because you have *autism*, doesn't mean you can avoid this *forever*."

He sighed. "I don't feel comfortable even thinking about that stuff yet, plus it would feel weird since you're seventeen, and I literally just turned fifteen a few days ago."

"If you want to date me, you actually need to be intimate with me." He held Tancan's hand. "Just *try*."

"My dad would flip if he found me with an older boy, I'm still not out to anyone either. I... I'm not prepared."

Owen leaned forward, pulling Tancan towards him. "I never wanted to date you in the first place. I asked you out as a joke. Just look at you: shaggy hair, oversized hoodie, you look *homeless*. Nobody else will ever love *you*, Tancan. But if you want me to love you, you'll have to do whatever I tell you to do.

He Jolted back, tossing Owen's hands off of him. "I don't want to *kiss* you!"

Owen scoffed. "What's your plan, then? I didn't walk all the way over here for nothing."

"We could... go back to my house and play video games?"

***

Felix was still sat in the exact spot, switching his attention from his true crime magazine. "Who's this then?" he asked, raising an eyebrow.

The lie balanced on Tancan's tongue like ash, and it didn't help that Owen's eyes were beading him like a hawk. "Just a friend."

Felix chuckled. "Didn't you just tell me that you had no friends?"

Halfway upstairs, Tancan tilted his head over the banister. "Yeah, but he doesn't go to my school."

With a grin, Tancan pushed his bedroom door open. "Look at my solar system poster! I also collect—"

Owen's face flushed with laughter, his eyes flickering across all the toys displayed on shelfs.

Why's he laughing? Did I say something funny? Tancan thought. His finger pointed to the other side of his room. "And that is my sensory—"

"What are you... Five years old?" He took out his phone and began recording.

"Wait, please don't post it anywhere!"

He smirked. "Too late. It's live."

Within minutes, hundreds of people were watching, commenting with phrases like 'space geek,' and spamming the chat with laughing and skull emojis. Tears streamed down his cheeks, faster than the rain splattering against the widow. Despite his attempt to hide his face under his elbow, the spotlight had still managed to hold him captive.

Owen slithered his arm towards the rocket perched on the shelf behind him.

Tancan barricaded it with his arm. "Don't touch it!" he cried, yet Owen's hand had already swiped the model, an "oops" escaping his lips as the ship plummeted into millions of microscopic pieces.

His fingernails dug into his knees as throbbing sobs drowned him deeper in the sea of bricks. White, red and oranges clenched in his hands.

Felix launched himself upstairs. Two at a time, barely bouncing off each step. He had heard *everything*. He pinned Owen with his pupils. "Get out of my house *right now*."

“You think you can intimidate me when you raised a son like *him*?” He left with a wider smirk, pursed lips, and a side-eye, but the thick air refused to leave with him.

Felix crouched down, stroking his palm across his son's head. "I'll help you rebuild this," he said.

Tancan shook his head; the words spun at the back of his throat. "It's ruined. I can't even remember what order the astronauts were sitting in." He slumped his posture deeper into the floor. It was too much effort to lift his arm. Gravity had already compressed his tear-filled eyes shut. Something had broken him, as well as the toy.

"Would you like anything to eat?" asked Felix, scooping the pieces into a random container.

"I'm not hungry," he said, knowing he would not eat for the rest of the day.

"Okay, there are still some leftovers in the fridge if you do later on."

Tancan nodded, but as Felix went to walk out the door, he looked up. "Wait, Dad. Please, can I have a hug?"

"Of course, sweetheart," he said, crouching down again. "You don't need to ask, just hug me whenever you need to." *As if it was that easy.*

3: Trap

Owen: Hey Tancan. I'm so sorry about earlier. I feel awful after what happened, and I think I should apologize to you properly in person. Can you meet me at the park again at 10pm?

YOU DELETED A CHAT

Owen:

???

I know u saw the message.

Me:

Sorry, I can't. It's too late.

Owen:

Pls Tancan. I feel like a bad person.

Me:

That's because you are. You destroyed the last gift my mother gave me before she died. My social battery is drained, so just leave me alone.

Owen:

If u bail on me, I'll make sure everyone knows that ur gay and I'll tell them that you've sent me nudes.

Me:

What! Owen, listen to me. You can't lie about those sorts of things. I would never take a pic like that in my life, but rumors spread around my school like wildfires. Most kids already think I'm a freak after you exposed my bedroom to thousands of people. I'm begging you, please don't ruin my life any more than you already have.

Owen:

I will be waiting.

Minutes flickered into seconds as the clock hands continued their dance. Every second was like a decision creeping towards him. Every time the cogs churned, his heart pulsed. Tancan skimmed hundreds of online posts; each one rotting his brain with random memes until the endless loop of what-ifs had vanished. He had never snuck out before; he never even wanted to, but if he didn't, he would have to isolate himself in his room forever. He glanced at his phone.

21:52

Right as his hand grazed past the doorknob, a voice whispered, "Where are you going?" Finn leaned against the radiator. "Are you sneaking out?" he asked.

"Shush!" With a finger pressed to his lips, he opened the door. "I'll be like ten minutes. Don't tell Dad."

“Fine. But I get the last mars bar!”

***

Tancan's twitching fingers grasped his phone. *It's just anxiety; it's literally just anxiety.* A small artificial glow from the device briefly lit his path; then darkness returned around the corner, swallowing all the stars.

Okay. The park is at the end of this road. We're almost there. He continued to mosey down the path, checking behind every two seconds.

He paused.

A figure shuffled down an alley. The streetlight behind them only revealed half of their silhouette, but they appeared to be facing in his direction. A Nike Tech tracksuit, the same one that Owen wore, became visible.

Tancan crept forward. "Owen, is that you?" he whispered, hoping it wasn't some random drunk man chilling in the alley. "I thought we were meeting at the park?"

"Yeah, it's me, come closer," said the voice, still lurking in the shadows.

He froze, wondering if it was him, or just a mimic trying to lure him into the abyss.

"I'm not going to bite you, Tancan."

He trod forward, pinching his nose to avoid the waft of cat pee drifting through the air. The wind had stopped thrusting at his neck, and as he turned around, a mob of kids, none older than sixteen, had caved in behind him.

They stood shoulder to shoulder, forming some sort of barrier at each end of the alley.

His whole body tensed, his back arched and fingers curled. "C-Can you all step away please, I'm starting to feel a little claustrophobic."

They giggled, puffing their vapes into his face.

"Guys, don't get too close, or you might catch his disease," Owen warned, pretending to cough.

"I'm autistic. I don't have a disease. What did I do? Please tell me what I did! I'm sorry if I upset any of you. I just want to go home." An uncontrollable shaking seized his body, as though he was being tossed around inside a broken washing machine.

Owen pulled out a knife. "Oh, Tancan, you are so *gullible*, aren't you?"

4: Rescued

Tancan's limbs locked in place like solid stone. His forehead sweltered, but he didn't dare wipe the sweat away. One wrong move, and then he was gone.

The other teens' trainers scraped against the gravel.

Owen held the knife steady, no smirk, only a hard stare. He wasn't joking anymore. But before he could act, an ominous shadow sauntered across the wall.

Shrinking to five foot six, the creature ripped off its hood, revealing a head of bleached-blonde hair. She was a girl.

As she emerged from the darkness, the moonlight glistened on the glint of her nose stud, illuminating her face in front of Owen. "Oye!" she yelled. "What do you think you're doing?"

"Nah." Owen lowered the knife, a dry smirk tugging at the side of his mouth. "Man thinks she's talking to me."

"Yeah, smartass, I am talking to you." Her hand clamped around his wrist, cranking it like a balloon animal.

"You're a psycho!" he screamed, yanking his arm away.

She released her grip from Owen's arm. "Who's next?"

Nobody moved, spoke or flinched; only the rubber bike tires had enough courage to make a single screech.

The girl raised her skateboard in the air. "If any of you even thinks about intimidating this kid again, I will bash every single one of your heads until blood gushes out of your mouths."

They all scurried away.

She lowered herself to Tancan's level, where he remained cocooned on the damp gravel.

He held himself, rocking within his own universe, the words caught between his thoughts and his tongue.

"Hey, you alright, mate?" she asked. "Do you know where you live?"

He wrestled a pack of communication cards from his pocket; his head aimed at his lap as he pointed to the house card. The other side displayed a sticker with his address printed in faded black ink.

"Do you want me to walk you home or something?"

He nodded. Something in the girl's presence seemed comforting to him, at least compared to the 'vape squad.' The way she sat calmly with him must've connected some type of circuit inside him. He stood up like a newborn doe testing its legs, although the rest of his body pleaded to remain grounded.

She walked ahead. Tancan followed close behind, his steps mimicking hers.

"Thank you," he mumbled, wiping his sleeve across his face.

"Right... so you do talk, then?"

"Only when my brain lets me." He stared at her layered wolf cut, not knowing how he was supposed to keep the conversation going. "I, uh, like your hair," he stated, avoiding walking through the dark in silence.

"Ew, creep. Thanks, I guess?"

"..."

"I'm Taylor, by the way."

"My name is Tancan."

"Is that like your *actual* name?"

"Mhm... I think it's uncommon; my mum wanted to pick something unique."

"Tell her I think it's a cool."

"Oh..." He dug his hand in his pocket. "She *died* five years ago."

"Aw, sorry to hear that, dude."

As they trudged forward, the wind steered icy rain into their faces, each exhalation forming a cloud of white breath against the deep sky. Appearing as if they were both smoking, yet Taylor was the only one carrying a lighter in her pocket. Tancan's hood thickened with moisture, but Taylor remained dry.

The further they walked down the never-ending road; fewer houses dotted the landscape.

"Umm... my house is that way," he mumbled, pointing in the opposite direction that they had walked.

"I know," she said. "I'm taking you to my home first."

"What! I was supposed to be home ten minutes ago, and my dad doesn't even know I snuck out!"

"Don't worry, we'll be quick!"

The muddy pathway croaked beneath their feet as Taylor led him through an endless field.

"This is my home," she said.

"You live here?"

"That's not what I said. This is where I spend most days. It's safer here. I call it 'trauma dump field.'"

"There is nothing here though?"

"That's the point. You can scream anything as loud as you want out here." She placed her skateboard on a dry-ish section of grass. "I'll go first. Count me down."

"Okay. Three... Two... One—"

"I HATE SEAN MAXXIE!" She exhaled, letting the wind absorb through her nostrils. "See, it felt amazing. Try it!"

"Uh, are you sure nobody will hear us out here?"

"Yeah. Go on!"

Tancan's tongue curled around the top of his teeth, his eyes scanning in every direction he could reach. He lifted his shoulders and inhaled a gulp of the crisp air. He couldn't do it. But the quicker he did, the sooner he could go home and snuggle underneath his fresh covers. He took one final breath before blurting out, "I DON'T BELONG ON THIS PLANET!"

"Woo Hoo!" She clapped one hand on her skateboard and used her other pinkie finger to wipe her smudged eyeliner.

“That felt so good! Wait.” He paused, looking closer at her face without making eye contact. "I feel like I've seen you before. Aren’t you in Mrs White's class?"

"You go to Audresbury Academy too?"

"Yeah, but I hardy attend school."

"How come I've never seen you?"

"Most people don't see me; I'm usually zoned out at the back of the classroom. I’m just there, observing over everyone."

"Well, I *see* you now," she said.

5: Home Sweet Home

Tancan stumbled onto the porch, his dripping clothes clinging to his skin. His frozen fingers fumbled for his house keys, swinging his moon-shaped keychain against the handle. But before he could even insert the key, the door swung open.

Felix slid his phone into his pocket, steam gargling inside his nostrils. "Where were you? I was worried sick! I've tried calling you *several* times. It is almost midnight."

"Sorry, my phone died."

"That's not good enough, Tancan. How many times do I have to tell you that you're not allowed to leave this house by yourself unless your battery is fully charged? Where on earth did you go at this time of night? You could've gotten yourself killed!"

If Taylor hadn't been there, then his dad's anxieties could've been right. All he could picture was him answering that haunting call.

Felix rested his hand on his shoulder, feeling the shivers that ran through Tancan's body. "Hey, did something happen to you?"

"Owen and bunch of mean kids tried to... hurt me, but I don't know why."

"What kids? Tell me everything."

He could barely remember it, as if nothing had happened. Using the details he was certain about, he managed to piece together his side of the story.

"Owen, again? That little *sick bastard*."

Tancan's head nodded to every sentence escaping from his dad's mouth, without even processing the information. "He messaged me. He wanted to apologise for breaking my rocket ship, but when I got there, random kids started circling me, until Taylor saved me."

"Who's Taylor?" he asked.

Tancan glanced out the window.

She was still there, waiting outside the doorway, under a small area of shelter.

Felix rushed to reopen the door. "Please come inside; it's pouring out there."

The checkered rug welcomed her into their home, as if the house itself was waiting. She slipped off her shoes, holding her trickling hair above her forehead.

"I'm so sorry; I didn't notice you there. I would've invited you in if I had." Felix handed them both a towel. "Here," he said, "I don't want either of you getting ill."

Taylor hovered over the settee, glancing up at Felix, "You sure?"

"Of course, it'll dry. Sit down, make yourself at home."

Tancan tangled the corner of the towel around his finger. "What's going to happen now?"

Felix sighed, rubbing his hand over his cheek. "Well, first I want you to charge your phone and show me the messages. Then, I will probably have to contact the police. That boy is *dangerous*; you're probably not the first he's targeted."

Tancan's anxiety didn't fade; it only bubbled in his chest. Owen hadn't hurt him, not physically at least. There was no way the police wouldn't believe him without evidence. Nobody *ever* believed him. There was no way he could relive that day. He didn't know what terrified him more: Owen's smirk or the images the sirens would flicker back into his head.

Felix took Tancan into kitchen. "Sweetheart, look, I know how vulnerable you can be, and some people take advantage of your disability. It's a *hate crime*," he said, scooping a spoonful of cocoa powder into a mug.

"*Okay,*" he agreed, even though he heard nothing, apart from the whistling kettle. "But I'm not talking to the police." He held down the power button for a few seconds until his phone revived.

The messages were gone.

He refreshed the page. Still nothing — no threats, taunts or lies. No matter what he tried, the inbox remained empty. Panic sliced through him like katanas. It was the only evidence he had, and the judge would only use Owen's wrist against him.

Felix rolled his eyes. "Alright, I won't call them, but you are not leaving this house alone again without *my* permission, do you understand?"

Tancan nodded.

Felix placed two mugs of hot chocolate on the coffee table.

"Thank you," said Taylor, tugging down her sleeves.

The one covered in tiny planets was Tancan's special mug. Only he could drink from its rim, and it had to be made his dad's special way, otherwise he couldn't drink it.

Taylor took a few sips before setting the cup down.

"Done already?" Felix's giant, *man hands* reached over. "Let me help you take off your soaking jacket."

She barged her elbow into his arm. "Oh my gosh, I am so sorry. My reflexes snap when anyone touches me." She adjusted her jacket's position. "Do you mind if I keep it on?"

"Of course. Whatever makes you feel comfortable." He picked up his car keys. "Would you like me to drive you home?"

Taylor shook her head as she stood up. "It's okay, I'll walk."

He clinked his keys against the window. "Walk? Alone? In this?"

"I do it all the time, I'll be okay."

"Why don't you stay here? Just for the night. I can't let you go back out there after what just happened to you guys."

A small grin formed inside her cheek. "Really?"

"Just make sure to message your parents; I bet they're worried sick."

"I know they're not."

"Well, do you want me to call them for you?"

"No, thanks." She stood up, gripping the sleeves of her jacket. "Is it okay if I use your bathroom?"

"Sure. It's the first door on the right."

"Thanks." She placed a Sylvanian Families elephant on the coffee table, holding a miniature custom-made skateboard. “Tancan, can you watch Herbert whilst I’m gone? He’s my emotional support critter.”

“Yeah.” He chuckled. “You named an elephant ‘Herbert’?”

“Bro, shut up! Your dad is literally called ‘Felix.’” She looked over at him. “No offence, Mr Milten.”

He placed his hand on his heart, an amused expression on his face. “None taken.”

She left the room.

“Funny girl, I like her.” Felix tapped Tancan's arm. "Is it okay if she stays in your room tonight?"

He clenched his teaspoon tightly. *I just met her, and she's going to sleep in my safe space?* He couldn't say no, not after what she did for him. "Uh, okay."

"You're a good kid, Tancan; don't get into any shenanigans, alright?"

"*Ew*, Dad!"

"I mean it."

*

The flickering glow from the bathroom spilled onto the dark landing. Through the gap, Taylor faced herself in the mirror, carefully unravelling the bandages on her arms. Inch by inch.

Eyes were watching her, but they didn't belong to Tan-can.

6: Sleepover

Tancan glided the back of his fingers between his cat's ears; the soft fur velveting against his skin. With each stroke, his kneading fingers massaged through her silky Bombay fluff.

He paused.

The bathroom light switched off.

Taylor knocked on the door.

A silent scream clogged his throat. "Come in," he murmured, memories of Owen's taunts flooding his head.

She scanned across the categorized toys lined across Tancan's shelves, each display representing a fandom he belonged to. She had nothing to say apart from, "Who's this?" pointing towards his lap.

"That's Starla."

"Cute name. Did you name her?"

"Yeah, she's my therapy cat — she's a rescue."

Starla sprang from his lap, her whiskers twitching as they lightly grazed Taylor's ankles.

"Why is she sniffing me?"

"She's finding your scent. I think she likes you."

“I guess you must be some sort of ‘cat whisperer’ too.” Taylor tugged at the hem of her soaked baggy jeans. "Kinda random, but do you have any long-sleeved pyjamas I could borrow?"

"Yes." He pulled open a middle oak drawer. "All my pyjamas have planets and aliens on them! Well actually, I have some with bunnies on, but I only wear them around Easter."

"I meant, like... *normal* ones?"

"They are normal pyjamas, what do you mean?"

"Like plain ones without images or symbols?"

"Oh! You should've said that. Well, I don't, but my dad does, and they probably stink like his crusty armpits."

She rolled her eyes. "Fine, I'll just go for the bunnies."

*

After Taylor changed inside the bathroom, she sank into the plush face of an alien-shaped beanbag, the beads swallowing her whole as she leaned her head back. "So... is it just you and your dad living here?"

"Nope, I have a five-year-old sister, and my brother is turning twelve soon. Who do you live with?"

"Just my brother, Sean—he's a dick."

"How come?"

"Look, I only just met you, and I'm not in the mood to explain my entire life story, okay?"

"Oh... sorry."

Glow-in-the-dark stars shimmered along the ceiling, their pale light creating a celestial pattern only Tancan could see. He ran his fingers over his moon-embroidered blanket. "Taylor?"

"Yeah?"

"Do you think my room is *childish*?"

"It's very different from mine, but it's not childish either. If you like it, that's all that matters. I like the vibe in here; it's cool."

"You think my room's *cool*?"

"Yeah, I do. Why'd you asked that?"

“I don’t know. At first, you didn’t really seem like the type of girl to carry an elephant figure in your pocket. ”

“A lot of people think that. Groups of teenagers will take one glance at my black nail polish and eyeliner and scream ‘emo’ at me. I usually just walk away laughing at the fact that they don't even know the definition of that word. It only annoys me if they ask me to roll up my sleeves and I shout, 'piss off' and go and hide somewhere. Sorry, I've started to rant too much, you just seem so easy to talk to, and you're... actually *listening* to me."

"You're easy to talk to, too. I always stutter when I try to have a full conversation with my dad." He rubbed his arm. "I really like your style, it's nice seeing people customising their avatars more. People just seem to follow fashion trends all the time." He swirled his tongue around his cheek. "I wish I could be as confident in my appearance as you, I just wear jogging bottoms and a hoodie every day."

"I'm nowhere near *confident* in my appearance, but I'm starting to find myself." She reached into her black, over-shoulder leather bag and pulled out a stick of eyeliner. "Stay still."

"Why? What are you doing?"

She moved it towards his eye. "Giving you *guyliner*."

"Wait, you're going to poke my eye out."

"I will do if you don't stop twitching." She wiped a smudged area with the corner of a tissue. "Okay, there we go."

"Ah, I can't blink!"

"Give it a few seconds to set."

He walked into the bathroom, keeping his eyelids forced open, and gazed at himself in the mirror. "Oh, wow, I look..."

"*Hot*?" Taylor suggested.

"Yeah... You could say that."

Dear Star Diary,

Turns out there are actually some good people in this world. I just don't understand why Owen wanted to hurt me. I haven't upset him, have I? He is... I don't even know how to describe him, but I never want to see his smug face again. Ever.

On the other hand, I made a new friend today, well; I hope she considers me as one. I often struggle knowing whether someone is a friend or a 'friendly acquaintance.' Although I've never had a proper friend before, apart from Finn, but he's my brother and I don't know if that counts.

There's this guy I play *Space Tycoon 2* with online. We only use the text box in the game, so I have no idea how old he is; he could be like sixty for all I know.

So, It actually is kinda nice to talk to Taylor, since most kids at my school avoid me because I'm 'different.' Like I'm sorry I don't enjoy tackling balls from the 'lads' or suffocating my eyes in fake eyelashes. I'm just not like that.

My therapist keeps telling me I should talk to someone when I start feeling depressed, but the teachers never seem to care, and when I get home, my dad is always too busy or too pissed to talk to me.

My mum had always been the person I would talk to the most. She was a very religious woman; every night she would read me a story about Jesus and mark a cross on my forehead.

Even though Dad's never been religious himself, he still tries to teach Sapphire Mum's traditions and doesn't seem to bother with me and Finn anymore. I wish he did. After she passed away, he briefly started attending communal worship on Sunday mornings. That didn't last long before the drinking begun.

I've started reading the *Bible* since I'm worried that my relationship with God isn't strong enough. Mum always taught me to love everyone, and that's what I do.

The problem is, I committed a grave sin. I murdered my mother, and now I'm going to hell and will never see her again. If I had just kept still, I could've saved her, but no, I let go.

I've prayed and prayed for God to fix me, but who am I to ask him to mend his creation? If I had no purpose in life, I wouldn't be here right now. I just want her to come home, but I know that is something I can't pray for. If only I could tell her how sorry I am, then I might start feeling happy again. She'd understand me better than Dad does.

I heard him watching TV with Stephen the other day, and they were watching this series about a gay man living in London. I remember one of them saying something like, "How ridiculous is this?"

What if they both think I am ridiculous too?

— Love your favourite space nerd, Tancan :)

7: Moody Mornings

March 25th 2021 – 294 days before he destroyed himself.

Taylor was already sat at the dining table, drumming her knuckles onto her knees. "Oh, hey sleepyhead, you're finally awake. Your dad has great taste in music, by the way."

Tancan's fingers tangled through his messy dark hair before he slipped onto the chair beside her. "Yeah, he likes to play my mum's favourite songs in the morning whilst he cooks breakfast."

Felix gently stirred porridge with a wooden spoon. “Hey, Taylor, I'm about to fry up some juicy bacon, want some?"

"No, thanks. I don't eat bacon."

"More for me then, Tancan doesn't eat it either." He flipped a fresh strip into the pan, the sizzling muffling his voice. "Did you guys have fun last night?"

“Yeah,” said Taylor, scratching off her cracked nail polish. “We made out whilst watching *My Little Pony*, you should join us next time.”

“I love that show!” expressed Tancan’s little sister, Sapphire, standing in the doorway. “Can I join?”

"That's why you shouldn't make adult jokes in front of five-year-olds," stated Tancan.

"You know what, I think I'll pass that offer." Felix glanced at Tancan's face. "Tanks, are you wearing... eyeliner? "

He shot his head towards Taylor. "I thought you said it disappears overnight?"

"Yeah... About that... You really shouldn't believe anything I say, dude."

Felix took a bite of his bacon sandwich. "You know, back when I was your age, I wore eyeliner to a rock concert—"

Tancan rolled his eyes. "Oh, here we go again..."

Taylor set her phone down on the far side of the table. Lost in Felix's awful dad jokes and long stories from his childhood, she failed to notice her phone vibrating. **How many calories are in one slice of bacon?** lit up on screen.

Tancan's eyes flickered between the accusing screen and Taylor's unreadable face. He turned in the opposite direction, pretending like he hadn't seen anything. He then got up and poured himself a bowl of star-shaped cereal.

"Why are you eating cereal without milk?" asked Taylor.

"Because it makes the stars go mushy and gross," Tancan responded.

"Weirdo."

"Dad! Did you hear that? She just called your son a 'weirdo.'"

"Well, she's not wrong," Felix mused.

"Wow." Tancan scoffed. "You guys are assholes."

"Language!" Felix warned, wiping his hands with a tea towel. "Stephen will be here later to watch the game, so don't freak out if we get an unexpected knock at the door."

"What time?" Tancan asked.

"Probably after lunch."

"Yeah, but what *time*?"

"I'll let you know when he's on his way."

*

Sprawled on the sofa, Taylor scrolled through random posts. "I'm so bored, let's do something!"

"Like what?" Tancan sat opposite her, rocking back and forth cross-legged.

"Literally anything. We could maybe go shopping?"

"I don't know; I'll have to ask my dad first," he said, knowing this was the closest he'd ever get to saying 'no,' even if a tiny part of him actually wanted to go too.

He dragged his feet back to the kitchen, his gaze gripping on the floor as he loitered behind a dining chair. "I know—"

"Wait a minute, let me finish writing this," Felix said, his hands glued to his laptop.

"Oh... Sorry."

After ten years of keyboard clicks, his dad gave him the *nod.*

"Okay, I know my allowance isn't due until next week, but please can I have it early? Taylor wants to go shopping, and I kind of want to go too."

"Since when do you ask to go shopping?" He removed his glasses, placing them on top of a pile of envelopes. "I'm still disappointed in you for sneaking out last night, but you know what, sure." He reached into his wallet, pulling out a few notes. "Here's an extra fifty. Just spend it wisely, okay? And be home before 6:30."

As the money he didn't deserve landed in his palm, his semi-closed eyes widened in disbelief. "No, Dad, that's too much. You can barely afford the bills."

"You've been through this week. Treat yourself, sweet-heart."

He chewed on the inside of his cheek. *The rest of the money will get wasted on beer, anyway.* "Are you sure?"

"Yes. I just need you to promise me you'll be safe with Taylor and that you won't be meeting up with Owen again."

"I'm not, I promise."

"Alright then, have a nice time." He smiled, placing his glasses back on his face. "Oh, you got another letter in the post."

"Thanks." He pulled an envelope from the Jenga tower of pizza pamphlets. *There better be a gift card in here.* He flipped the sheet of paper, revealing the most useless words he's ever read. "Seriously, another questionnaire? Are they trying to make me want to unalive myself?"

"Tancan! Don't joke about things like that."

Mental Health Survey

Child's Name: Tancan Milten

Date: 25/03/2021

I typically get along with other kids my age.

yes mostly sometimes rarely never

most days I feel?

Very sad sad Neutral Happy Excellent

When I get angry I sometimes hurt myself or other people.

strongly agree agree somewhat agree disagree strongly disagree

Thank you for your feedback! :)

8: The Beginning

Tancan halted in his tracks. His hand frantically patted each pocket. "Shoot!"

"What's wrong?" asked Taylor.

"My lanyard's gone! I must've left it at home."

"It's not a big deal. You'll survive without it."

"It lets people know I have a hidden disability. I don't want everyone looking at me like I'm crazy if I have a melt-down."

"Trust me, some people in our society don't care about a laminated card, and it won't magically stop them from being ableist."

"I know." He tugged tighter on his backpack. "At least they're aware. It's essential to me."

She turned around, immediately pointing at his face. "Bro! It's literally around your neck, you absolute donut!"

He looked down, making sure she was telling the truth. "Oh. Oops. Sorry for the panic."

Taylor reached into her jacket pocket, the zipper cold against her fingers. "Before my mum left, she gave me this

Build-A-Bear voucher, but I never got around to using it. Figured I'll give it to you since you seem to be into that stuff."

"Really?" He flapped his arms. Thank you so much! It's not expired, is it?"

"Nah. It says it's valid until the '25th of March 2024.'"

"Maybe we could get matching ones!" He hesitated at the zebra crossing, the oncoming traffic roaring at him as cars shot past. The signals drummed in his ears, each beep clashing like cymbals.

"Dude, what are you doing? Just cross!"

"I'm waiting for all the cars to stop completely," he said, his shoulder hugging a lamppost. A van driver blared the horn. Tancan sprinted across the road, his head hung low, without thanking the driver like he always did. Tears filled his eyes. "Did I do something wrong? I was just trying to be sensible."

"Don't cry. You did nothing wrong; men are just impatient, grumpy idiots. These sorts of things happen to me all the time; stop taking everything so personally. Sorry for being snappy, but I am desperate for the toilet, and we still have to walk all the way up this road!"

***

Glaring into the restroom mirror, Taylor scrubbed plaque from underneath her fingernails. No matter how hard she tried, it wouldn't wash away, staining her deeper than any soapy water could reach. And until her hands were spotless, she couldn't leave. Silent tears dribbled down her cheeks. If she stayed with Tancan any longer, she would hurt him.

*

Outside, Tancan rummaged through his pin-covered bag, searching for his noise-cancelling headphones. They muffled the surrounding cacophony, but nothing was ever silent. What was he supposed to do? Stand there like an awkward statue? And if he zoned out, he risked locking eyes with a stranger, giving them an unintentional death stare. It was like being thrown onto a stage, alone, in front of an audience that wasn't even looking, but somehow, they could still sense his every movement.

He continued to stand against the wall, rocking back and forth on his heels. People poured out of the toilet block in waves, spawning as if it were some sort of simulation. He scanned their heads, but Taylor never appeared.

More teenagers strolled past, their eyes lingering on him for a second, before whispering in their little friend groups. They all walked towards him, their fingers pointing, calling his name, but he didn't dare to look up. His vision droned into every somewhat space they could occupy, but the lighting was his biggest obstacle. The floor was the only place he could look without being judged, trapped inside the capsule toy vending machine beside him.

She had been in there for twenty-two minutes, and it wasn't like he could casually walk into the women's restroom to see if she was okay. There was hardly any signal inside the building, and if he stared at his phone for too long, he could miss her. It was 14:17. He was supposed to be at the bookstore by 13:55. The routine he had planned was already a crumbling mess.

Taylor stepped out at last, unplugging her fingers out of her ears as she escaped the blaring hand dryers. Her knuckle dabbed her eyes before she zipped her jacket up to her chin.

"Are you okay?" he asked.

"Yeah, I'm fine." She scoffed. "You stand so nonchalantly." She opened the camera on her phone, checking her appearance. “I look okay, don’t I?”

“Yeah, I was just worried about you because you were in there for so long... I thought you might’ve abandoned me.”

“I would never abandon someone that easily,” she said.

Tancan's eyes widened as he glanced through a bookstore window. "Look! This place also sells Jellycats!" He bounced toward the non-fiction section, running his hands along the neatly stacked books until one caught his eye. **How Rocket Ships Are Designed.** He flipped through the pages, reading over facts he already knew. Before he could check the price, a red sign with bold white writing caught his attention: ***Spring Sale! Buy any book and receive a FREE packet of glow-in-the-dark star stickers!***

He headed to the register, his anticipation fuelled by the thought of the book sitting in his collection.

The cashier scanned the book. "That'll be 15.99 please." That wasn't right. Someone must've placed the wrong book down. He couldn't just say he didn't want it anymore; he didn't have the confidence; they'd probably think he was being difficult. After receiving the receipt, he jammed the book into his backpack before bolting out of the shop, mumbling, "social anxiety will be the death of me," through his teeth.

"That was boring, there was hardly any Yuri in there." Taylor sat on the bench outside of the entrance, her hand pressed against her brow. "I feel dizzy. Mind if we grab a little snack?"

"Sure, there is a corner shop at the end of this road."

Taylor drifted through the narrow aisles, stroking various objects. She latched onto a packet of Monster Munch. Her fingers traced the crinkly edges as she read the ingredients, before putting it back down.

The moment he noticed she had left with just a pack of gum, Tancan bent down and picked up the crisps, staring into the taunting monster's eyes. Once he paid, he took a pen from his pocket and scribbled over the nutritional details on the back. He couldn't bear to look at her like that, not after everything she's done.

He hid the packet behind his back as he walked towards Taylor, who was sitting on a patch of grass. "I've got a surprise for you."

"You'd better not have wasted your money on me."

He nudged the bag toward her. "Not wasted at all."

She sighed. "I told you, I'm not *hungry* anymore."

"Turn it over."

As soon as her eyes landed on the scribbles, she wrapped her arms around him, squeezing him like a child hugging their favourite character at Disneyland.

"Please, can you let go? You're kinda squeezing my organs out."

"Yeah, sorry, dude, I don't know what came over me."

"I used to check the ingredients for my mum because she was allergic to nuts, and I also struggle with food sometimes, but I know whatever you are going through is completely different, and I am not trying to compare myself with you, but I can somewhat understand how you feel."

"You don't have to make an entire monologue explaining yourself; I understand what you mean."

"Sorry."

She popped open the bag, slipping the corn snack onto her fingertips, as if she was connecting with her inner child.

He didn't comment on how brittle she seemed. He had no right, even if he wasn't that far behind.

After swallowing one claw, she folded the bag, as if a teaspoon of mashed potatoes could cure her hunger. "Do you think I'm cute?" she asked.

"Uh, yeah... Why?"

"Like, do you think I am *attractive*?"

"Umm... Actually—"

"I know you're *gay*."

"Wait, what! How did you know?"

"'Sexy male astronauts.' Maybe close your laptop before you sleep, you absolute weirdo. But, say you weren't, would you find me attractive?"

He clenched a handful of grass, ripping it from the ground, now worrying if he forgot to turn off his laptop and his dad seeing his concerning search history. "Why are you asking me this?"

"Since you're the only person who makes me feel *real.*"

"If you want my honest opinion, I think you're one of the most beautiful people I've ever met, and any guy who doesn't think you are pretty is a complete idiot."

"Call me that again, and you will end up like Owen." She chuckled, a genuine smile crept onto her lips. "You know, it's not just boys I like."

"You like girls too?"

She stood up, leaving her phone on the ground as she wiped grass off her knees. "I'll let you work that out."

"Who's that on your lockscreen," asked Tancan, pointing to a selfie of Taylor doing the peace sign next to a boy with dark brown natural locs that barely reached his shoulders. In the photo, he also wore an oversized grey hoodie, similar to the one she carried in her backpack.

"Uh, just an old friend," she said.

9: Changes

A wave of nostalgia washed over Tancan as he entered Build-A-Bear. Six years had passed, but everything remained the same, well, almost. He reached into a pit of unstuffed bodies, pulling out an alien-bear with holographic eyes.

"That one looks kinda dirty; pick a different one," advised Taylor, rubbing its stained foot.

He clutched the alien-bear to his chest. "This one chose me. I can't abandon him; we're literally bonded now."

"But they're all the same."

Tancan pouted his lips and twisted its head towards her. "Look at his little face and tell me he doesn't look as happy as the rest of them."

"Alright, fine. Get the *depressed* alien."

"Alien-bear," he corrected, excitement draining from his face. Groups of people had swarmed into the shop. He stumbled backwards, squeezing his eyes shut, seeking a place to hide.

Taylor weaved past him. "I'll join the stuffing line before more people flood the shop."

His grip tightened on his bear's antennae as more people caved around him. *Just leave me to stand here and die, why don't you?* His eyes scanned every corner, hoping to locate a somewhat quiet spot. He glanced at the sound booth. *Hmm, there are only like two people near there.*

After placing a sound chip inside the glowing white circle, he opened his camera roll. Guilt taunting him as he scrolled past his mum's haunting smile. At last, he reached a video that was recorded on Christmas Day 2014. It was faint, but obvious who was talking.

Taylor approached him. "You almost done, loser?"

"I haven't even looked at the clothes yet!"

"I'm not gonna bother; it's like a *tenner* for an outfit. Frogs don't wear clothes, anyway."

"That's such a crime. At least get it an accessory to cover up its *frogussy*."

Her hand swung over her mouth. "Stop! You can't say stuff like that in here!" A mischievous grin spread across her lips. "Glad to see my humour is influencing you."

***

They wandered away from the main the shopping centre.

“I heard the new bubble tea place is good,” suggested Taylor. “Should we try it?”

“Yeah,” agreed Tancan, having no idea what he agreed to. Her voice went in one ear and out the other. He could only focus on the label of his shirt scratching the back of his neck and the person busking in the middle of the street was screaming lyrics rather than singing them.

Taylor stopped at the entrance of a secluded alleyway, the cathedral's shadow hovering over her. "Okay, the last shop is just down here."

Tancan's steps slowed. He took one glance at the alley before a disorienting blur consumed his path. The voices of passers melded into a murmur. Even Taylor's words muffled, as if he had been plunged underwater. His face turned pale. His hands pressed against his forehead as he lowered himself against a stone wall, plugging his fingertips into his ears, but that still didn't calm his raging heart rate.

She handed him his alien-bear. "You're having a anxiety attack; you'll be okay," she assured him, reaching her arm out. "Try taking some deep breaths."

"Don't touch me." He reached into his pocket, pulling out a sticky note. Written: **space video**, with a QR code printed beneath.

"First, focus on your breathing."

"Breathing is useless to me—I just... Please! I *need* the space video!" He clawed his head into his hands. Everything was spinning.

Taylor scanned the code, but it didn't load. "I think the signal is too weak," she said, waving her phone in the sky. "Just keep hugging your alien, uh, do you want me to talk about aliens or something? Tancan, you'll be okay, I promise."

He closed his eyes as if he were falling into a deep sleep. His body was still but breathing heavily. After a few minutes, his eyelids opened halfway, still glued with tears. "I want to go home."

"We will go home soon, okay?" She grabbed his water bottle from his backpack. “Have some of this, then you might feel well enough to do one more shop?"

He hugged his alien so tight that the seam across it’s back threatened to come undone. "I want my dad," he wept. "Can you call him to pick me up, please?"

"I promised him I'd keep you safe, and I meant it. I will sit here all day if I have to."

He wiped his eyes with his sleeve. "Do you promise there is only one shop left?"

"Yeah." She wiggled her Pinky finger. "I Pinky-promise."

***

Tancan kindly held open the door for the people waiting inside. One person, then another, then another four shuffled passed, and neither of them said 'thank you.' *Wankers.*

Racks of clothes stretched across a massive warehouse, reeking the scent of musky leather through the air. Aisles overflowed with a vibrant display of cotton jumpers and vintage pieces from as far back as the 1930s, folded neatly without a single tear in sight.

"What is this place?" Tancan looked up. Green vines draped from the ceiling, making the store feel like a forgotten temple buried inside a jungle.

"This is where I usually get my skating clothes from." She delicately removed a black, long-sleeved top from its hanger, clutching it while she gazed at her reflection. "I think it's time you found *your* style."

Tancan pulled down on his drawstring. "But I love this hoodie."

"We're not getting rid of it; we're just expanding your wardrobe."

"What's the point? I wear the same thing all the time."

"You realize we're starting college next year, right?"

"That's why I'm excited to ditch my uncomfortable uniform. Then, I can wear this hoodie every day!"

"You need actual outfits. Not just an oversized hoodie with an alien's face plastered on the front."

He tugged his sleeves over his hands. "I don't care; I just want to be comfortable."

"Dude, people will laugh at you."

"They *already* do." His fingers stroked across thick corduroy trousers and velvet blazers. "Everything seems so *old.*"

"No shit, Sherlock, everything in here is *secondhanded,*" she said, pulling a *Penny Lane* coat over her shoulders.

Every tag scratched at Tancan's skin, every seam pressed against his noodle arms. He pulled a sweater over his head, but the neckline felt like a noose. Each patch of fabric was a wet cloth clinging to his skin. Another jacket; another failure. Nothing in there belonged to him.

He approached a mannequin, dressed in a sage green zip-up hoodie with a design of two halves of a star that complete the image once zipped.

"Look, this is perfect!" he said, touching the fuzzy thermal lining inside. "Are we allowed to take their clothes off?"

"Poor mannequin. Maybe *don't* word it like that." She snorted, pulling the jacket off its fiberglass arms. "See, this diva ain't gonna hurt you for stealing their jacket."

He slipped the jacket on. "It's too tight around my shoulders." He flapped his arms, trying to loosen it. “Nope. Get it off. Get it off.”

"It's not tight, it's just not the extra, extra, extra—"

He ripped the sleeves of his arms, freeing himself from the straitjacket. "Alright, I get it."

"—extra-large hoodies you wear to cover up your *twink ass*."

"What else am I supposed to wear, then?"

"Literally anything that doesn't make you look like a divorced father of three." She picked up a shirt from the men's section, pushing it against her shoulders.

Tancan chuckled. “You realise that's a man's shirt, right?”

“Yeah, I'm not that stupid! It's just a piece of fabric and I literally wear boxers to bed, problem?” She glided her hands through floral dresses; the lace tickling her nose as she swooshed past.

“You seem annoyed. I haven't upset you, have I?”

"It’s not you, don’t worry. Last year, I became mates with this boy called Noah. Even though his parents were rich, they ignored him all the time, believing their wealth could solve all his problems." She wiped the dry tears from her face. "It made him feel like he didn't belong in that household anymore, and a few months ago... They moved to London, shortly after they found the binder I gave to him."

His smile faded. "I... I'm so sorry," he said, "It wasn't *your* fault, and I'm glad you were there to support him." He looked at her phone again. “Was that—"

She nodded.

10: Freedom

Tancan stopped to tie his shoe at a bench. "Are you sure you know the way back home this time?"

"Duh, I've lived in this town my whole life."

"So have I; my house is back down there." His finger pointed towards the road they had just crossed.

"We're going somewhere else first."

"No, no, no," he mumbled. "I thought we were going home. You promised me we would go straight home after that vintage clothing shop."

She cut through the park. "No, I said we've finished shopping. The day has only just begun. Don't worry, we'll still be back before six, and we didn't even plan a routine."

"I did. I planned *everything*! You keep throwing new things at me, and it's stressing me out!"

"I keep forgetting; it's just so hard for me to wrap my head around these things, you know. Plans change all the time, but I'll try to explain where we're going next time."

"What *things*, Taylor!" He rubbed his face with both hands. "Sorry that I'm a bit... Too much sometimes. I've had to mask all day; it's so tiring, but I really appreciate you trying to understand how I feel, unlike my dad."

"You're not too much; you don't need to explain yourself to me. Just make sure you share your plans with me first, so we can both follow the same routine."

He smiled, accepting her words, as much as he wanted to push her into the trash can beside them. "So, where are we going?"

She gestured ahead. "To Bunny Hill over there."

His eyes lit up. "That's where Stephen used to take me and Finn sledding when we were younger. It was so much fun! I just don't get why everyone calls it 'Bunny Hill' if there aren't any actual rabbits at the top."

*

With each step, gum wrappers stuck to their shoes as they stomped up the slope. It was like stepping through a minefield; every crushed can was deadly. One wrong move could send Tancan rolling, and Taylor stumbling after.

A spark flared in her eyes. "I should give you a nickname!" She pressed two fingers to her chin, pretending to be jammed in her thoughts. "Hmm... Maybe 'T-N-T.' Kinda sounds like a cool version of Tancan."

"'T-N-T', really? Do I look like a *creeper* to you?"

"If you dyed your hair green, then maybe you'd explode, but you looked like an actual creep when you wanted to undress the mannequin."

"Who are you to judge? You were the one who stole their jacket for me, so you are the one who will pay for their mannequinny therapy."

She burst into laughter. "Bro, we're such weirdos."

*

"Hey, look!" She ran to an old bench at the top of the hill. "Last year, me and Noah carved our initials on the armrest; someone better not have painted over them." Her fingers traced the engraving, running over the splintering grooves. The letters were still visible if she squinted. She reached into her pocket, pulling out a small packet of gum. With a flick, a tiny blade ripped out the wrapper.

Tancan's eyes widened. "Isn't that illegal?"

"Nobody will ever know." She winked, placing the knife in his hands.

He flipped it over, inspecting the handle, noticing a faint stain on the blade — a rust-coloured smear. Wood wasn't the only material it had stabbed into.

His hands wobbled as he pressed the blade to the wood, carving a single extra letter onto the bench, but all he could think about was Taylor's bandaged wrists. "Look, now it has all our initials, all three of us!"

She stepped closer, squinting at the letters. "It now spells 'T-N-T.' Stop! That's the nickname I Literally just gave you."

He shuffled next to her on the damp grass, scrunching his knees to his chest. *Maybe in another universe, I would be a part of an actual friend group.* He fell onto his back. "Noah might be looking at the same duck-shaped cloud as us right now."

"Nah, that's not a duck, it looks like your mom—shit. Sorry. I didn't—"

"You know... It kind of does look like her. I see her smile beaming at us from heaven."

"How do you she's there, Tancan? Like there are so many possibilities that could happen once we die. What if we get reborn as different people or just fall asleep forever?"

"I just know that I'm going to see her again one day. Do you believe in God?"

“I don’t know. I’ll never end up in heaven anyway,” she said, brushing grass from her jacket. She sat up and hit shuffle on her playlist. "Join me!" She jumped onto her feet, waving her arms around like an inflatable tube dancer.

“I can't," he muttered. "I don't know this song."

"Just dance with me, loser!" She dragged him onto his feet. The faint sunlight casting him as the star of their tiny, makeshift stage.

They both grabbed the paws of their Frog and Alien, grinning as they linked their stuffed animals' hands and spun in circles. The more they danced, the more feathers flew off their arms. He was an astronaut; she was free. They were two seven-year-olds, making daisy chains, pretending that time didn't exist anymore.

As they continued to dance, the sun faded behind the clouds. Peering over rooftops, the pale sky had blended with the sun, merging into ripples of purple.

"Wait." Tancan fumbled for his phone. "What time is it?"

"Calm your tits, it's only like six-ish. We still have like half an hour."

"What! We have to go, now! it will take that long to put everything back in our bags and walk home!" He checked his messages. His dad would've usually been spamming him with calls, but there wasn't a single text.

Taylor peered over his shoulder. "He probably hasn't noticed the time. Busy doing whatever middle-aged men do in their free time, like plucking his eyebrows?"

"Why on earth would my dad be plucking his eyebrows?"

"I dunno," she said. "Just a guess."

11: Stars

They walked side by side down the hill. The sky above them had faded into a pale shade of blue, dotted with a couple of pink gumdrops.

"Your time blindness is worse than mine. Do you think my dad will be mad?" asked Tancan.

Taylor brushed her hair back, a single strand of fusilli pasta dangling over her eye. "Nah, your dad seems chill."

"Not always; he rarely cooks breakfast — only for Sapphire — he put on one of his little shows for you. It's like he wears this mask that makes him a completely different person, especially when Stephen comes round. I just don't get it."

***

Taylor opened the front door. A man stood in the hallway, turning his oblong face towards her.

"Can I help you?" he asked, his forehead wrinkling.

She stepped back, checking if they were at the right house. Before she could respond, Tancan bolted past like a gazelle, launching himself into the man's arms.

"Stephen! You're here!"

"Ah, there's my amazing Godson!" The back of his hand stroked Tancan's new jacket. "Not wearing your alien hoodie today, then?"

"I did, but it's still in my backpack." He grabbed his new book, pulling out the stickers compressed inside the first page.

Felix stood further back, his hands outstretched, gripping the chipped wood of the doorframe above his head. "So, you walk in and hug Stephen before your own papa bear? How rude." A true smile on his face, his teeth visible, not the tight, blank expression he always wore. "My boy is finally getting out of the house. I'm so *proud* of you, honey."

Tancan paused. *Proud?* Stephen must've fed him too much sugar since it was a sentence he hadn't heard his dad say since he won an egg and spoon race in Year 2. He wrapped his arms around Felix's white cotton shirt, his fore-head pressing against the greying strands of his stubble.

He couldn't let go, as much as he wanted to; his hands weren't releasing. His head drifted onto his dad's chest. The day with Taylor was great, but too much, and for once he could get close to his dad without roaring beer breath shoving him away. *Had he really been sober all day?* At first, it was a happy thought, until it wasn't. He was out all day; it wasn't the grief making Felix drink; it was him. He wasn't his son; he was the alcohol. Felix missed the alcohol; not *him*.

His hands slipped off his dad's shoulders, watching Taylor sat alone on the bottom step. Neither of them was her family; they only belonged to him, but she belonged to him too. He tapped her shoulder. "Would you like to help me stick the stars across my ceiling?"

"Sure." She stopped midway, glancing at a framed photo on the wall. "Is that your mum?"

He nodded.

"She was *really* pretty."

"Yeah, she was. She was *perfect*... So, I know this might sound kind of weird, but do you ever look at your bedroom and think 'Wow, I designed this place!' It's like a museum where I display every item I have ever owned in my life."

She shrugged. "Not really, unless you call empty Monster cans 'collectibles?'"

Felix called upstairs. "REMEMBER WHAT I SAID, 'KEEP THE DOOR OPEN.'"

"YEAH, I KNOW!" He jumped on his bed, stretching onto his toes as he scattered the glow-in-the-dark stars above his bed, some slightly crooked, but that didn't matter if they weren't falling into the overflowing swamp of scrunched up clothes on the floor. "I guess the cans count. I used to stick empty packets of Magic Stars into my diary."

Taylor's attention flickered towards the neon signs hung on the other side of the wall. "I bet your electricity bill is high."

"It is. My dad used to be the manager of a restaurant before Mum died. After that, he couldn't cope anymore. We've been living on benefits for the past few years, but Stephen has helped us out a lot. How come you can afford all your skating gear if you don't live with your parents?"

She closed the door shut, fully, holding her wrist to her chest. "I kind of already have a job."

"I thought you were only fifteen?"

"I'm still fourteen; my birthday is in June."

"Oh?" He sat down, dangling his feet off the edge of his bed. "So where do you work?"

"All over town; my brother sends me to deliver packages to people."

"So, you deliver people's mail?"

"No. These are *special* packages."

"Like for birthdays?"

"I deliver *drugs*," she whispered, "*illegal* ones."

He must have misheard it. "You're just joking, aren't you?"

"I wish I was." She slumped onto the beanbag. "It's the only way I can get money without stealing from Sean's stash, but you can't tell anyone this now that we're mates, alright?"

"So, would you consider me as one of your friends?"

"Duh. First of all, I *saved* your ass, then I realised you were different from most of the boys in this shitty neighbourhood. Why would I ask to hang out if you weren't?"

"Does that mean you trust me?"

"I don't rely on trust." She scoffed. "Every single person I have ever trusted has let me down, and I'm not even going to try anymore."

*

Whilst she was in the bathroom, Tancan reached into his bag and pulled a handful of essentials he bought for Taylor: Toothbrush and toothpaste, a packet of milk chocolate buttons, a roll-on deodorant, her own pair of plain long-sleeved pyjamas, her own sage green fluffy blanket, a mixture of different pads and tampons, whatever she preferred, and an elephant-shaped water bottle because they were her favourite animal.

He could've spent the rest of his money on his special interests, but he chose to spend it on her because she mattered way more than a new space magazine. She needed those items; Tancan didn't.

"What's all this?" she asked, tying her hair out of her face.

"I, uh, wanted you to feel safe in my room."

She picked up the pack of tampons. "Ugh, I can't stand the texture of these ones, but thanks for trying, I appreciate it. You're honesty so lucky you never have to experience periods, they literally ruin your entire week, like you'll never have to experience the nausea running to the toilet as soon as you wake up and flushing out all the old blood and discharge—I'm oversharing again, I'll stop, sorry." She let out an awkward laugh. "I need to learn how to filter myself."

"It's okay," he said. "Girls get it much harder than boys do."

She picked up his laptop, noticing his Pinterest board was still open. "I don't know if I should be concerned... Do you really have some weird astronaut kink?"

"Hey! Stop snooping my laptop!"

She clicked on his YouTube search history. "Let's see how educated you are. *'Last to stop eating carrots,'* Seriously, dude?"

"Okay," he said. "If you think mine is so random, why don't we look at yours?"

"Nah, mine is just full of *Ellie Williams* edits, but you're not 'woke lesbian' enough to understand. How can people only be attracted to males? It is so baffling."

"Wish I wasn't."

Dear Star Diary,

Today, I got to see a completely different side of Taylor. She's like the complete opposite of me: she drinks, she vapes and knows how to ride a skateboard, but at the same time I see so much of myself in her. I've asked so many questions, and I'm surprised she doesn't hate me already. Maybe I need practice being the 'therapist friend.'

No clue when she's going home, but it better be soon. I need my privacy, and if she snores like she did last night, she's getting dragged into the bathtub. She sleeps like my forty-three-year-old dad.

I'm fully convinced that she must've cloned him or something since 'Mr Smiley Pants' has been acting so odd all day. That 'two-faced drunken panda' only ever seems to care about watching sports, always blocking me from talking whenever his favourite team is playing. I stand there like a lamppost, waiting for years until it ends. You know when it does because him and Stephen will either yell, 'Go on!' or swear their heads off.

Maybe I am just an object to him, but at least I have a purpose when I'm with Taylor.

I've always wondered why a handful of middle-aged men are so obsessed with watching people kick around a ball on the screen. I told this to Taylor, and she replied, "Me too, sounds a bit zesty. I can't really say much though, since I watch women's rugby." She winked. "But for other reasons."

I didn't ask any further.

She then opened the cabinet underneath my tv and said, "Oh, you still own DVDs? Let's see what films you have."

"I don't really watch movies," I admitted. "My dad's the film nerd, not me. I either watch space documentaries or animated web series."

"That tracks. I've never heard anything more autistic in my life." It's fun when she jokes about autism because it makes me feel less alone, but I wish she could understand how it really feels, other than only noticing my quirky side. She pulled out a 2017 copy of *IT*. "You don't seem much of a horror guy."

"I'm not," I said. "I watched *Killer Klowns from Outer Space* two years ago and got fixated on clowns for months. I concluded that *Pennywise* may also be from whatever planet they came from and ended up writing a fanfic about it. I tried reading the book, but it had like a thousand pages and my attention span is awful."

"Have you ever watched *Skins*?" she asked.

"Yeah," I lied, wanting to seem cool in front of Taylor.

"Oh really? Didn't seem up your street. It's one of my favourite shows. A bunch of college kids in Bristol, so not that far from us. I watched it when I was eleven and probably shouldn't have."

"Oh," I said, "I'm still trying to grasp the fact that I am almost a college student. I know we are still in Year 10, but it's like my childhood is flying past before I even have the opportunity to appreciate it."

— Love your favourite space nerd, Tancan :)

12: Exposed

April 1st 2021 - 287 days before he destroyed himself

Finn burst into Tancan's bedroom, his knees trembling.

"What's wrong?" asked Tancan, tossing his duvet away from his feet.

"Dad and Stephen are arguing!"

He rushed to the top of the stairs, his heart pounding as he peeked over the railing. Below, the men stood apart, but close enough to inhale each other's breath.

"You have to quit drinking!" Stephen yelled, "No wonder your kids are afraid of you!"

"Bullshit!" claimed Felix. "Don't tell me how to raise my children, especially not from someone who isn't even capable of making their own!"

Stephen pulled a wrinkled piece of paper out of his pocket. The edges tore as if someone had ripped it out a diary.

Dad is turning into a monster, and I don't know what to do anymore. I'm alone. I can't become the adult in this family!

Stephen slammed the paper onto the counter. "Explain this, Felix. You promised me you wouldn't do it when they're in the house."

Tancan's head shot towards Finn and Taylor; only they knew which drawer the diary was hidden in. "Who was it?"

"I'm so sorry, Tancan," admitted Finn. "I was afraid; he's getting worse, and I needed to tell someone. We are just kids ourselves, and we can't spend our entire childhoods being locked inside your bedroom until he calms down. I only ripped that page off, I swear, then I put it in Stephen's coat pocket when everyone was asleep."

No matter what he said, it would not restore that page. A chunk of his diary was gone. "That's my *private* journal! It wasn't yours to destroy. Now Dad is going to know all the messed-up things I wrote about him. Thanks a bunch, Finn. He has been sober for an entire week, and now his streak is probably going to end. I understand you were trying to help, but I promise you he will get better if we just give it some time."

"It's been five years! Sapphire has never even seen what he was like before. He needs help from a professional.

You've known him longer than I have, don't you see he's getting worse?"

Sapphire opened her bedroom door; her fingers plugged in her ears. "Why is everybody shouting?"

"Don't worry, Saffy," assured Tancan, "Finn has just made a silly mistake. Why don't you show Taylor inside your princess castle?"

Finn barged into his room, slamming the door shut.

Tancan tightened his grip on the banister, the distant echo of the argument still ringing in his ears. *Dad is going to hate me now.*

Taylor approached him, holding Sapphire's plastic teapot. "We could head for a walk and blow off a bit of steam if you'd like?"

"Taylor!" Interrupted Sapphire. "Have you filled up my teapot yet?"

"Almost!" she answered. "Anyway, Tancan, how does that sound?"

"To be honest, anywhere is better than this house right now."

""Just to let you know, I'll need to stop at my place on the way home. I need to grab a few things."

"Don't you think it might be a good idea to go back now? Sean is probably getting worried about you."

"Trust me, he's not. He's probably out getting high and celebrating the fact that I'm gone. But you're right; seven days is pushing it."

Tancan creaked down the stairs, his hands hidden in his sleeves.

With a scrunched page in his hand, Felix glanced at him, rubbing the back of his neck. "I'm sorry you had to hear all that, Stephen stormed off in one of his 'man tantrums;' he'll be back soon."

"No, Dad, look, I should be the one apologising. I didn't want you to—"

"It's fine," he said in a blunt tone. "I'm not in the right headspace to discuss anything right now."

"Okay, me and Taylor are going out, I'll see you later."

He sighed. "I know what you're like; you'll end up being burnt out tomorrow, then you will be rotting in bed all day. Why don't you and Taylor just stay here and watch another movie or something?"

"She says everything I watch is boring, plus you always say I spend too much time in the house and need to go out more. I'll be back before dinner."

"She was peeking into the spare room last night. Make sure the door is *locked every time you go upstairs*. She's still a stranger, remember? We can't trust *anyone snooping* around your mother's stuff, understood?"

Tancan nodded.

13: The Wreckage.

"What was your mum's name again?" asked Taylor, her feet dragging across the pavement.

"Melissa," he said. "But everyone called her Missy. One time Dad called her 'Missy Pissy' and Finn thought it was the most hilarious thing in the world. What's your obsession with my mum? You've asked about her like five times within two days; are you supposed to be my secret sister or something?"

“Such an obvious trope.” She crossed the road without even checking for traffic. "I wish you were though. I'd much rather have you as a brother than Sean. My mum left about a month after my ninth birthday, and I think I've just become attached to the thought of having a mother figure around, you know?"

"Welcome to the club." He passed inappropriate graffiti plastered across a garage door. "What about your dad, or was he absent?"

She pointed down at the end of the road. A dilapidated slum of flats grouped together, each one displaying the personality of its owners. "That's my place," she said, dodging his question. "Ours is the one on the second floor."

I'll take that as a yes then. He eyed the apartment, then glanced at Taylor's bandaged wrists. "Your windows cracked!"

"Yeah, Sean has a habit of punching *things*," she whispered. "Don't worry, he's usually out around this time of day, so we should be safe."

Entering the doorway, he pinched his nose, holding his breath in case he accidentally inhaled any of the cannabis in the air.

"Relax, dude, it's just weed."

"You don't smoke it, do you?"

"I tried it once. Hated it."

Piles of untouched dishes, stacked on the draining board, dripped onto the crumpled clothes laid across the wooden-planked floor. Mould climbed on the walls like an army of ants, trying to reach the remains of roasted meat still clinging around the stove.

“Does he ever clean this place?” A gagging sensation took control of Tancan’s throat. "I think I’m about to be—"

Heavy footsteps thumped up the stairs, each creak inching below them.

"Shit," Taylor hissed. "Hide!"

Tancan scrambled into a closet, holding himself within his own shadow, daring to peek through the narrow gap.

A muscular man with tattoos sleeved up his arm barged through the door. "Where the *hell* have you been?"

She swallowed. "I just went for a skate."

"Overnight? Don't *lie* to me." His tone sharpened. "I know when you're lying."

"I stayed at my friend's house, that's all."

He scoffed. "Like anyone would want to be friends with you."

"He's nice."

"'He?' You're staying over with the boys now? You little dirty—"

"No, Sean, it's not like that... He's—"

"He's *what?* You better not tell me he's one of those *fags*!"

She snapped her head toward the closet door, checking if Tancan was too visible. Before she could take another step, Sean's hand clamped around her wrist, yanking her back into the somewhat of a living room.

"You do *not* walk away from me when I'm talking to you!" he roared.

"I'm sorry, Sean."

"What was that?"

"I said I was sorry, Sean."

"Say it again."

"Sorry, Sean."

"Louder."

"I'm *sorry!* Alright?"

Satisfied, he released her, picking up what seemed to be a plastic sandwich bag filled with a salt-like substance. "Clean all your *shit* out the living room. The boys are round later, and you better be out of our way."

Once he left, Tancan slowly opened the wardrobe door, his heart racing.

He followed Taylor's scent into her bedroom. It wasn't a scent; it was a smell, like cannabis, mildly sprayed with vanilla perfume. It was the first thing he had noticed when they met, but he didn't want to offend her. Was there even a way to tell someone they stank politely? At home, the smell had disappeared, but now it was back, and stained on his clothes too. Yuck.

Her room wasn't much of a bedroom either, only scraped up walls covered in band posters. She slept on a double mattress on the floor and the only functioning item in there was a drum set in the far corner.

"Wow, I was right. You're a massive music nerd."

"Shush! Anyway, this is my actual home *sweet* home," she said in a sarcastic tone, scooping her belongings into a woven shopping bag. "Sorry about him." She reached for a flannel shirt hung on the back of her door. As she ripped it off the hanger, her jacket tugged, revealing a bruise on her upper arm.

"Is he always like that?"

"Yeah, but I'm used to it now."

He gazed at her cracked mirror. "Did Sean smash that too?"

"Nah, that was me."

"Make sure to grab everything you need."

"It's not like I'm moving in with you; I just needed a break from this place."

He nodded, knowing whatever he had agreed to wasn't true at all. She couldn't come back here, not after what he had saw. She didn't deserve that; nobody deserved that. He peered out the window, hoping to find at least one pleasant thing in the neighbourhood.

A boy walked past wearing a burgundy knitted jumper, an AirPod in his right ear.

"Stop spying on my neighbours, weirdo."

"I'm *not*."

"That's my new neighbour. Poor guy. There's a shortcut through Trauma Dump Field behind this house. I see him walking over there quite a lot. Wait, you think he's cute, don't you?"

"No, I don't! Shut up!" he said, his eyes still following the boy's dark curls draping over his forehead.

"I've never spoken to the dude, but I'm pretty sure he's straight. Sorry, man, I can be your boyfriend instead; just give me time to grow a dick first."

"After Owen, I doubt I'll ever get another boyfriend. Ugh, I *hate* boys."

"Me too, girly."

"Look, on a serious note, I know that Sean—"

"Tancan, I don't want to talk about it. He's just a prick sometimes."

"No, this is serious. You're fourteen, Taylor; you're still a *child*. He is supposed to take care of you, never mind whatever that was. When we get home, I'll talk to my dad, and he will call social services for you, ok?"

"No! You can't! I am not going through that *again*! It's fine. I'll stay here. You don't know what that man is capable of."

"I am not leaving you in this shithole with that *monster*! Okay, sorry, I say we go back, not breathe a *word* to my dad, and handle this ourselves, as long as we're gone before Sean returns, deal?"

"How do I know you're not tricking me? Today is literally April fools and I've seen this all before."

"I am not *lying* to you. I swore on my mother's grave that I would never *lie* again."

“What have you lied about before?” she asked.

“I can’t say.”

14: Out

Stephen's car still hadn't returned.

"Are you sure Sean doesn't know where we live?" asked Tancan.

She shook her head; a tatty pillow stuffed under her arm. "He hates this side of the neighbourhood; he calls everyone around here 'snobs.' Are you sure your dad is okay with me staying longer?"

"I don't see why not. I'll just make something up without mentioning Sean. Also, you can dump all your things into Finn's room. I'm sure he won't mind, just like he didn't *mind* reading my diary and ripping *two* pages out."

“I’ll find somewhere else. I’d rather not get involved in your ‘sibling rivalry.’”

*

Felix arranged his record collection in the living room. Mostly British rock groups, like *The Smiths* and *The Beatles*.

"Do you know when Stephen is coming back?" Tancan Asked.

"Hopefully soon so he can defend you from your 'raging alcoholic' father."

"Dad, I didn't write that against you; I'm just worried."

"Honey, you shouldn't be worrying about me; you're my *child*. Anyway, let's forget about all that for now." He picked up a *Tears for Fears* album, his top teeth peeking through his salt and pepper stubble. *"Head Over Heels,* what a throwback. This was your mom's favourite song."

"Never heard of it."

He gasped. "If you don't know that song, you're *not* my son."

"I guess I'm adopted then. It's not my fault I listen to the same five songs on repeat."

Felix scooted himself on the sofa, admiring the face that was much more valuable than his entire collection. "So, did you make any more friends today?"

"You know I can't just walk up to someone and start small talk."

"I'm sure you can if you practised. You could ask if they play that game you like, '*Roadblocks*'—if that's what it's called?"

He sighed. "I've already tried that, and they all laughed at me."

“I dealt with many jerks in Oklahoma when I was your age. They thought I was insane for wanting to study at a film school in England, but it was the best decision I have ever made." He stood up, placing his coffee mug in the sink. I can't believe my oldest is already fifteen. I got my first girlfriend at that age, you know, and I have noticed you and Taylor have gotten quite close lately.”

"I don't—"

"No, come on, I saw that grin on your face. Do you think she likes you back?"

"Dad—"

"She has a great sense of humour, I like her."

"Dad! Taylor is a *girl.*"

"I know that. Oh, I see. Does she use those ‘pronoun’ thingies?"

"No, Dad... I like boys. I... I'm *gay,* and I'm sorry I didn't tell you sooner, but I just couldn't. I didn't want to give you another reason to be ashamed of me... I was scared to tell you because I thought.... And—" His voice cracked. "I'm so *sorry,* Dad."

He raised his arm.

Tancan flinched.

But instead of throwing an imaginary beer can at him, Felix pulled him into his arms, whispering, "Hey, hey, hey... listen... It's okay. I'm not *ashamed* of you; I *accept* you." He held his head up. "I *love* you, and that will never change; I'm your dad."

Tancan sniffled, his face rubbing against his dad's chest. "So, you're not mad?"

He shook his head. "Honey... Why did you flinch like that? Did you really think I would hit you?"

"I don't know." He dropped his head back into his arms, but Felix didn't catch him that time.

"Tancan..." The word dissolved on his tongue, both hands cupping over his face. "I'm trying. I'm *trying* my hardest." He stormed out of the room. "I'm going to bed. Good night."

"Dad, wait! Please!" He reached his arms out. " I know you would never hurt me."

He didn't respond; he kept walking.

Tancan dragged himself upstairs. *I can't go one day without upsetting someone, can I?*

"What's up, pussycat? Did you ask your dad if I could stay longer?" asked Taylor, stretched on the beanbag, that she now claimed as her own.

He exhaled, wiping tears from his eyes. "I completely forgot to ask, sorry."

"Dude, you look like you got punched in the face by an onion, you good?"

"No, not really. I just came out to my dad, and he *hates* me now."

What! There's no way he's homophobic! He sounds like the fruitiest straight man ever."

“No, he's not. I actually think he's an ally."

"Oh, slay! Why would he hate you then?"

"Because I basically couldn't keep my thoughts to myself."

"I know lying is bad, but sometimes you've got to hold things back, so you don't hurt people's feelings."

"I just thought, maybe if he knew how worried I was, then maybe he would stop drinking so much."

"Life doesn't work like that, unfortunately."

15: Paralysis

The house had drowned into darkness. No power, only a pyramid of beer cans, lit by six candles on top of the dining table. Tancan pulled Finn and Sapphire underneath, silencing them with a finger on each of their lips.

"They must play this game a lot. Hmm... I wonder where they could be," chirped Felix, a playful tint in his voice.

"Tancan, do you think Daddy will find us under here?" whispered Sapphire.

He shielded his arm around her. "That man is not *your* dad."

"Oh, Sapphire, my little princess," he cooed. "I give up, you win. You can come out now!"

She wriggled out of Tancan's arms. "Okay Daddy!" She crawled under the tablecloth.

Tancan lunged after her. "Sapphire, no! He's not—"

Too late.

A veiny hand with withered fingers yanked her by the hair, swinging her like a rag doll, and tossed her into a glass cabinet.

As if it were a feather, Felix flipped the wooden table, his sharp fingernails piercing through the linen. He gripped Finn's jaw, pressing two fingers behind his teeth while the rest curled around his chin. "What's the matter, Finn, is Daddy pressing too hard?"

Tancan bolted, scraping his bare feet across the blood-stained carpet. He tripped. Slowly, he turned his head. Starla's decomposed body sprawled across the floor — split clean in half like a butcher's knife had sliced through her fur. Her chatoyant eyes stared up at his panting lips. He leapt over her, tilting his head from the ground.

As he neared the top of the stairs, he was met with a familiar fragrance. No, it couldn't be. "Mum!" Tancan cried.

She was alive, wearing the same outfit she had died in. Her Primark beige jumper, Matalan jeans, and necklace engraved with her wedding date: **26/05/2005.**

She reached for him, her semicolon tattoo still inked on her wrist. "Baby," she rasped. "Please—"

Just as Tancan's fingertips brushed against hers, she crumbled, dissolving into a sand-like substance.

"No, Mum! I'm sorry! I'm sorry! I'm sorry, please, don't *leave* me!""

Felix, now parked on the eighth step, crushed a beer can in one hand. "Step closer, sweetheart. I don't bite."

"YOU'RE NOT MY DAD!" he screamed, peaking over the top step.

His grin widened. "You're right, I'd much rather have a daughter like Taylor than a *retarded* son like you." He climbed another step, his empty eyes full of hatred. His lips curled, revealing rotted teeth. "You *murdered* my wife; you little *dirty* shit." He preached on the final step. "My life would be *perfect i*f you never stepped foot in it." He leaned in, breathing scolding air into Tancan's ear. "You can cry all you want, but nothing will *ever* stop me wishing that the bullet ripped through your little *worthless* heart."

Tancan slowly backed away, his nails curling into his stiffened palm. "What are you?"

The creature, still wearing Felix's skin, placed a mirror in front of him. "Look." A much older version of himself reflected through the glass. He was about his dad's current age and had a can of beer moulded to his hand, but the wrinkled eye-bags made him appear more like a sixty-year-old.

He ran his hand through his hair. "No!" he said. "This can't be real; I've never even tried alcohol!" Was this some sort of sign? One of his biggest fears was staring right at him. He was the spitting image of his dad — a much more obnoxious version.

He blinked.

He was back in his room. His eyes snapped awake, but his body didn't. He was frozen, apart from his eyes.

Creak.

Noodle-like fingers webbed around the edge of the doorframe. The door continued to groan until he saw it. Red, beaded eyes drilling into his soul.

He blinked again.

Now it was on top of him.

Bowling balls pressed down on his shoulders, pinning him in place, as if the rest of his room was being sucked into a vacuum.

He blinked again.

Taylor nudged his shaking shoulder. "Tancan! You, ok?"

He scrambled upright, gasping for air, his heart hammering against his ribs. The door, Shut, just as he left it. "Taylor!" he cried, “Can you get my dad, please?"

Before she could, Felix had already burst into the room, throwing on his dressing gown.

Tancan grabbed his dad's hairy wrist, shielding his reddened knuckles over his face. "Sweetheart, what happened?" he asked, sitting on the edge of his bed.

His lips parted, but only fractured words slipped out. "Beer. Mum. Blood," his voice wavered as if he was almost chanting something.

Felix wrapped an arm around him, pressing a kiss to his cheek. "It's okay, I'm here," he said, shushing him. "Don't worry, you're safe."

"I want Mum."

"I know, baby." His thumb spiralled across Tancan's forehead. "How about I read you an alien story until you fall asleep?"

He shook his head. "Can I sleep in your bed tonight?"

"Sweetheart, you're getting a bit too old for that." He sighed. "I mean... I'm a grown man, and you're a teenager. It might seem—"

"Yeah, but you're my *dad,* not some random weirdo. You and Mum always let me."

Felix ruffled his hair. "Alright, come on then, *space ranger*."

"Please can we keep the big light on?" he asked, picking up his diary from his bedside table.

"How about we leave the bathroom light on and keep the door open?"

"Ok."

Felix stretched out his arm on his Queen size bed, sliding underneath Tancan's neck. A familiar melody hummed through his nostrils — the same lullaby he used to sing when Tancan was little, the nostalgic rhythm clinging to him like tiny sloth claws.

Tancan gripped his dad's grey sports shirt and rested his head on his chest. "Dad... if I weren't autistic, would you still drink?"

Felix's arm tightened around him. "Don't be so ridiculous; you being autistic has never interfered with my life," he said. "Your mom would've said the same."

He snorted. "Your *'mom,'*" mocking his American accent.

"Come on, Tanks, I'm trying to have a serious conversation here. Me and her did everything we could to get you your private assessment, and I don't regret a single penny I've spent."

Felix fell asleep; Tancan remained awake, spooned inside his dad's arms. Who could sleep after a nightmare like that? Most dreams vanished within seconds, but this one was still vivid, more like a memory than a dream.

He pinched his thigh in silence, making sure he was awake this time, and that the man sleeping next to him really was his dad. He closed his eyes, recalling everything he had ever read about the *butterfly effect*, *chaos theory* and *alternate universes* — they were all patterns, which all led to truths.

16: Marshmallow Man

April 2nd 2021 - 286 days before he destroyed himself.

Dear Star Diary,

It is currently 5:23 AM. I still feel the same paranoia I felt before I fell asleep. I've switched the light on now, and Dad is still sleeping. The door is closed. The curtains shut. TV is switched off. I'm safe.

Most nights I play calming space ambience music to distract me from hearing footsteps creaking up the stairs or gentle knocking sounds against my window. I can't tell if they're real, but I stay still just in case.

It feels so wrong sleeping on this pillow; Mum should lie here, not me. I haven't slept in this bed since I was nine, and whenever I had a nightmare, I'd fall into the gap between them both. Dad would kiss me before rolling to his side, but she would stay holding my hands until she knew I felt safe again. I wish I were still small enough to fit through the gap.

I'm now at the age where I am constantly being told that I am too 'old' for stuff, but still too 'young' to do other things. Dad has stopped tucking me into bed every night and doesn't even try to comfort me after I graze my knee anymore. I don't know why he stopped; I never asked him to.

Maybe he loves Sapphire more than me because he hasn't stopped for her.

The older I get, the further he seems to drift away from me, and I can't tell if it is me or the alcohol that is the problem.

He has been sober for nine days now; his record is twelve. I doubt it'll last if I continue to annoy him any longer. Every birthday, I wish for him to stop forever, but, as usual, my wishes never come true. Maybe for my sixteenth, he might let me have a birthday where I don't end up crying for once. Even if I show him all the scars on my legs, it still won't be enough evidence to prove to him how damaged I am.

On his bedside table, Dad has a picture of himself inside his childhood home in Oklahoma. He looked exactly like me; it's scary. He seemed so happy and innocent back then. How did he end up the way he is today? Maybe my dream was a glance into the future after all.

At the top of his chest of drawers, he made an entire shrine dedicated to me: my baby hand impression moulded into air-dry clay and my christening outfit folded neatly on top. Mum made him stop collecting records shortly after I was born. It must've been tough having to prioritise me over the things he loved more.

If I labelled myself as vinyl, would he listen to me?

I know how much he loves me, but I don't think he likes me very much. Not as much as he used to, at least. I hope he knows that my heart will always have a dedicated spot for him, even when he is acting more like a monster than the big marshmallow he is being right now.

— Love your favourite space nerd, Tancan :)

"Did you dream about your mum last night?" Taylor asked, grabbing herself a single banana for breakfast.

Tancan raised his submerged head from his chocolate star-shaped cereal. "No," he lied. "What made you ask that?"

"I heard you mumbling her name before you woke up."

Tancan's phone buzzed. A text from his dad flashed at the top of his screen: **I didn't want to wake you. I'm at the dentist with Finn and Sapphire xx**

"Who's that?" she asked.

"Just my dad, we've got the house to ourselves."

"Cool. I'm going to attempt a 360 on the halfpipe today. You can come and watch if you'd like."

"I'm not really in the mood, sorry."

"Come on, I've been practising for weeks!"

"I said no!" The words snapped out sharper than he intended. "Sorry," he muttered. "I didn't mean to be rude. It's just... everything's been so daunting after last night. I need a day staying in my pyjamas, eating my comfort foods, and binge-watching my favourite space documentaries."

"Fine," she said, taking her skateboard from beneath the coat rack. "Someone better be recording me if I land it." She slammed the front door behind her.

Tancan was left alone with his anxiety perched on his shoulder. Scenes from his nightmare flooded his mind. Everyone had left him, including Starla, who had disappeared out of the cat flap. He closed his eyes tight, hiding from whatever creature was lurking upstairs, because he knew it was waiting for him.

The doorbell rang.

He froze. Somebody was about to kidnap him.

The doorbell rang again.

He ran to the nearest blind and peered through the narrow gap. Stephen's car was parked on the drive. Thank God.

"Hey, buddy," Stephen said, "is your dad home?"

He shook his head.

"I just wanted to discuss something with him. I'll be back a bit later. See you soon."

"Wait, no!" Tancan grabbed his hand. "Please don't *leave* me."

He stepped into the house, placing his palm on Tancan's shoulder. "What's wrong?"

"Everyone hates me." He sobbed, tears drooling down his face. "Yesterday I upset dad and today Taylor is mad at me because I didn't want to go to the skatepark with her."

"*Hate* is a very strong word. Everyone gets a bit frustrated at people sometimes, but that doesn't mean they *hate* them."

"And then you ditched me after I wrote that dumb note in my diary that caused an argument between you and Dad. No matter what I do, I always end up hurting people."

"Hey, come here." He cradled him in his arms. "You're one of the nicest kids I know, and I am honoured that your dad chose me to be *your* Godfather. I would never *ditch* you, Tancan."

"I know. I've just been so worried lately, and I don't know why."

"How about we order some pizza for lunch? Your dad should be back by the time it arrives."

***

Tancan picked all the pepperoni off his pizza, placing it on the edge of his plate. "I'm never sleeping in Dad's bed ever again. Last night he let out the most disgusting fart when he was lying right next to me. I actually almost died; it was *that* lethal."

Sapphire chuckled; a *well-done* sticker stuck to her dress. "Daddy farted on Tancan!"

"Don't listen to him. He's making it all up," added Felix.

They all laughed apart from Finn, who abruptly left the table.

Stephen, still chewing, asked, "Where are you going? You've hardly touched your pizza."

"I'm not hungry," Finn muttered, disappearing upstairs.

Tancan set the last slice aside for Taylor, knowing she'd probably ignore it too.

17: Torture Chamber

April 19th 2021 - 269 days before he destroyed himself

Dear Star Diary,

Today was my first day back at school after Easter break; it sucked.

Finn walked ahead of me and Taylor, pretending like he didn't know us. He's been avoiding everyone for the past few weeks. It's so weird. At least Taylor seemed okay with me for once.

As I entered form, I saw the most dreadful thing on the board: a seating plan change. Most kids complained to the teacher because they preferred sitting at the back where they could mess around, whereas I just wanted to stay in the same spot where I always sat.

As usual, the kid next to me yelled across the classroom, "nah Miss, why am I sat next to Tancan? He's so weird!" which made the entire class burst out laughing. I've never even spoken to half of them, so I have no idea why they all think that.

Compared to them, I would be the normal one. All they are interested in is starting rumours about people and launching pens across the room. I must admit, sometimes the jokes they make are kinda funny, but when I attempt to join in, they will look at me like I'm being 'childish,' and when I ignore them, they act like I am too 'serious.'

I left class five minutes early to avoid being trampled by the kickable Year 7s with backpacks bigger than their bodies. As usual, a few kids moaned to the teacher about it being unfair that I get to leave early and gave me death stares as I walked out of the room.

Walking through the corridor was like stepping through a minefield. A random teacher asked me to do my top button up. I nodded, pretending to do it until he walked away. I don't understand how kids can cope like that; it feels like you are being strangled, especially with the tie too.

I met up with Taylor outside my science class, the only lesson that is kinda bearable. Mrs White could actually teach, unlike most teachers. I wouldn't say she was my favourite teacher, but she was the one I liked the most. Her lessons weren't too fast paced and were somewhat enjoyable. She's a lot more patient than a lot of the other teachers. Although when she lost her temper this morning, she yelled at a kid so sharply that it made me feel like I was the one being yelled at.

Taylor asked her if she could sit next to me.

Mrs White nodded, looking very confused. "I didn't know you and Tancan were friends," she said, but also seemed pleased that I wasn't sitting in the classroom corner doodling over my hands.

I thought sitting next to Taylor would be fun; turns out it is a nightmare. She kept whispering to me when we were being lectured about our GCSE exams for the hundredth time. Since primary school, we've been taught not to talk when the teacher is talking, so I didn't get why Taylor wasn't obeying this rule. I kept my mouth shut, slowly nodding to everything she said.

For most of the lesson, I gazed out the window wondering why teachers stopped students from using the toilet. They have no right to. It's not fair that young girls must come to school on their periods, sit in pain on low plastic chairs, and wear uncomfortable uniforms.

The way most boys view periods is the same way most neurotypicals view neurodivergents. They can only possibly know how it feels to a certain extent but can *never* understand how it actually feels.

When I say I want to be like everyone else, I don't mean being popular or any of that cliché crap. I want to start conversations with anyone and stop walking around like a complete dork with my head buried in my shoulders. I can't even understand social cues or know when it is my turn to join a conversation because nobody ever takes my struggles seriously.

During break, I handed out invitations for the lunar eclipse party I had planned to throw on May 26th. I had been looking forward to it all year. Taylor told me there was no point in inviting kids from our year since they would just laugh at me. But I did it anyway because I didn't want anyone to feel left out. Most of the kids ignored me; others laughed, and a few of the nicer kids told me they were busy that day. There were a handful of 'chavy' kids who took the invitation and said they would love to come and called me their 'bestie.'

Maths was probably the most stressful lesson because there were a group of kids sat behind me and Taylor, whispering about us the entire time. One girl tapped me on the shoulder. "Are you dating?" she asked.

"No," I mumbled, in quiet voice, so the teacher couldn't hear me.

"Just ignore them," Taylor muttered.

"Oh?" the girl said. "'Alien boy' and 'emo girl' can actually talk." She turned towards her squad, laughter hidden in her voice. "I thought they were both 'non-verbal.'"

"Can you mind your own business?" Taylor shot back, like she was about to throw a chair at her. She's became very defensive whenever someone comments about my autistic behaviour. Glad to see someone actually caring about me.

"Is there a problem, Taylor?" the teacher questioned.

She jumped out her seat. "I can't do this; I'm going for a break."

"Uhm, excuse me!" The teacher pointed at her seat. "No, you're not."

Taylor stormed out the class, leaving me to look after her bag. I wanted to check on her, but I knew she needed her own space and time to calm down. I didn't see her for rest of the day.

At lunch, invitations I had handmade with my foam planet stickers had been tossed in the trash. Five hours wasted. I knew those kids were just messing with me, but I still had hope. I didn't want them to come anyway, but they should've just handed them back to me instead of throwing them away. I'll probably cancel the entire party and just watch it from my bedroom window. Why are teens so mean?

I tried not to cry as I walked down the corridor, looking only at the floor. Then, a pack of boys pushed past me, barging me into the wall. I said nothing because I didn't want to start a fight. If someone hit me, I wouldn't hit them back and would start crying instead. That's why Dad always tells me to 'man up.'

Everything went all blurry, and my heart was pounding. I balanced myself, but I was too dizzy and sat between two lockers.

I sat there for a few minutes, crying, all disoriented. About ten teachers had ignored me as they walked past before I heard a voice running towards me.

"Tancan!" Finn cried, holding out his hand for me to grip onto. "What happened?"

I wasn't in the right state to talk. It was ironic that only one Year 7 had noticed me, a kid from the youngest year group, which showed how untrained teachers are.

They will watch me sitting at the back of the classroom, silently sobbing my eyes out, and act like they don't see me when they obviously can. Maybe I should try screaming instead. I've been told I can approach teachers when I feel upset, but none of them don't get why I can't do that so easily. Then, they have the audacity to write, 'They're a pleasure to teach, but they need to participate in class more,' on my report card.

I still wasn't talking, so Finn took me to reception. The receptionist offered to take me to the 'sunshine room.' The room is supposed to be a quiet room for anxious kids like me to calm down, but instead, it's unsupervised and full of boisterous kids who want to skip class. I would've much rather hidden in the toilets, even if I'd had to deal with Year 9 boys trolling me again.

I had English last, and it felt like I was in there for five hours. Once I had completed the work, I spent the rest of the time glancing at the clock and daydreaming until I could leave. We had a supply teacher, so I was one of the few who actually did some of the work; most of the kids spent the lesson hiding their phones underneath the table.

Taylor received an hour of detention for calling a teacher something I won't repeat after she left maths, so I handed her bag into reception, and walked home with Finn instead.

"How was your day?" I asked. It felt like forever since I've had a proper chat with him.

"It was okay," he replied. "We practiced writing poems in English."

I looked down. He was clenching a sheet of paper.

"Ooh!" I snatched it out of his hand. "What's this then?" I said, holding it above my head where he couldn't reach. "Is it a love note?"

"No! Shut up! Give it back!"

That's what he deserved for tearing my diary. I unfolded the paper, and to my surprise, it was a poem he had written for Mum.

My Mother's Grief – Finn Milten

You used to stroke my hair until I fell asleep,

But now I spend most nights trying not to weep.

Dad told us we'd be fine, and that the pain would start to fade,

Then he spilled beer all over the love you made.

My older brother Tancan, he tried his best,

But your affection would never rest.

If I asked about you, he'd refuse,

Only because he was still bruised.

Sapphire played with her ponies, full of innocence.

Nothing was as pure as her adolescence.

I asked her, "Are you okay?" but she just shook her head.

"All my friends' mummies are alive — why does mine have to be dead?"

Then Taylor came along and took your place.

She piled the house with her junk, taking away all your space.

She seems like a good friend to Tancan, which I hope will last,

But nothing will ever be able to mend my family's past.

I wish I had thought of you while staring at the flowers,

But today, when I accidentally called a teacher "mum," I lost all my powers.

I was so young when you passed; I didn't even know how to pray.

I love you so much. I wish I had told you more on your last day.

"Oh wow," I said, wiping my tears away. "Finn, that was beautiful."

"Really?"

"Mhm. Also, I want to thank you for what happened at lunch. I don't think I could've survived without you."

"Well, you survived the first three years alone." He chuckled. "Sorry I haven't been myself lately. I got a little upset after Dad told me you slept in Mum's bed after your nightmare. Sometimes I wish I weren't the middle child, you know?"

One of my biggest worries was Finn to becoming a 'glass child.' I had to make something up. "Dad was talking about you a lot that night. He said that you've got a lot of her features. He was telling me about the time I used to growl at him whenever he picked you up as a baby; I wanted you all to myself."

"Growl?"

"Yeah, didn't you know that I'm the big bad wolf? And I think it's dinnertime!"

He ran, and I chased him all the way home, howling, "Awoo!" and it made me realise how much I had missed playing with my brother.

As usual, I had a nap as soon as I got home. I get drained after masking all day, so much that I lose motivation to do literally anything. Countless kids constantly asking me why I get it so easy, but they've never had to stay awake crying, ruminating their existence.

— Love your favourite space nerd, Tancan :)

18: Princess Party

May 15th 2021 - 243 days before he destroyed himself

A unicorn-themed tablecloth covered the dining table, piled with an assortment of sweet treats. Outside, a rented princess carriage bouncy castle, finished with an inflatable slide, sat on the patio.

Like a pack of ninjas, a group of wild six-year-olds charged through the carriage flaps, where Felix was already twirling wands around with the birthday girl.

Taylor adjusted the wig Sapphire forced her to wear. "Your dad is literally a 'man-child.'"

"Honestly," Tancan said, watching Felix attempt to somersault to impress a bunch of hyper kids. "His big ass is going to end up squashing a sugar fairy."

"I wonder how long it's going to take until he has had enough and goes back inside for a drink," added Finn, sliding a brownie onto his plate.

Tancan pointed to the food table. “By the way, Taylor, my dad told me to inform you to not take any of the Quorn nuggets since some of Sapphire’s friends are Vegetarian and Halal, so he bought those specifically for them.”

“Hate to break it to you, mate, but the ‘dumb blonde’ stereotype is *fake*. I can read a damn *sign*, you bloody idiot!”

The deafening pop music, the giggling that sounded more like hyenas—everything was too much. If Tancan was six, then maybe he could've borne a bit longer. He stepped back, but everything seemed to get closer. He bit his lip, bouncing his fingertips against his leg until the sensation was the only thing he could focus on. His surroundings became fuzzier, yet he knew that if he vanished, his dad would complain. He couldn't spoil Sapphire's birthday.

Stephen approached him. "Buddy, we're about to do the cake now, so if it is too overstimulating for you, then you're welcome to go back upstairs."

***

He had made it past two hours. That was an accomplishment, right? He glared out the bathroom window, spectating over the party that he was no longer a part of. He missed out on musical chairs, but he couldn't mask any longer.

Everything was going well until it was Taylor's turn at the pinata. Her knuckles reddened around the bat, swinging it at the cardboard unicorn and smacked its face with full strength. She didn't just smash it; she obliterated it, beaten until sweets poured out of its decapitated head. Her princess wig hung off her head, the blindfold halfway down her face.

By the time Tancan made it outside, it was too late. She had *euthanized* the unicorn.

She swung the bat again, crushing its horn into mush. “Your dad probably loves you right now, but he won't forever!" The words exploded from her lips. "Wait until you become a teenager, then you'll understand what I mean!" she darted her sight towards Sapphire before collapsing onto the grass.

The partygoers circled her, the sunlight glinting off their plastic tiaras.

She shot up, wrapping her arms around Felix. She cried into his shoulder, in a voice so desperate that he could barely hear, "Please take care of your daughter."

Felix crouched, stroking her hair as he let her sob into his shoulder. "Tancan, can you take Taylor up to your room?" he asked.

He nodded, a sickening taste slithering up his throat. She had never acted that way towards his dad before. *Is that all you have to say to me? So no, 'hey sweetheart, are you doing alright?' because obviously she matters way more than your own child.*

***

"Uh, so... Taylor," Tancan began, closing his bedroom door. "Do you ever cut yourself when you feel upset?"

"What the hell! What's wrong with you? Why would you even ask that?"

"Oh, it's just..." He glared at her wrists. "I haven't seen you change your bandage, and don't you need to keep the wound clean, so it doesn't get infected?" He rolled up his leg cuffs, revealing his scarred over-knee. "It's okay, I used to as well, but I've stopped now. Please don't tell anyone. I have enough people worrying about me as it is."

"You won't understand what I'm going through, just leave me alone!" She stormed into the bathroom, slamming the door behind her. Bathrooms were always the nearest space she could isolate herself in.

Felix knocked on Tancan's door. "I've wrapped up two slices of cake for you and Taylor," he said, placing a lump of tin foil next to the TV, his fingernails covered in Sapphire's nail polish.

"Where are the party bags?"

"There were a few extras, but one parent asked if they could take some home for their other kids. I assumed you wouldn't mind, so I gave them away."

"No," he murmured, shaking his head. "No, Dad, you always save me a party bag."

"Honey, it's just a little bag full of silly plastic toys and candy. You're turning sixteen next year. It's not the *end* of the world."

He knew the dumb plastic toys would just end up being stuffed into a box and never picked up again; that wasn't the point. It was a tradition, and his dad still couldn't see how much it mattered to him. Maybe Felix had stopped viewing him as a child after all.

19: Claw Machines

May 22nd 2021 - 236 days before he destroyed himself.

Dear Star Diary,

Something's wrong with me, but not the same feeling I usually feel, something 'weirder' if that is even a proper word. I've been cutting my leg again, and I don't know why because Dad hasn't drank for almost two months. I should've started feeling happy by now, but I still carry guilt over my shoulder every day.

Ever since Sapphire's sixth birthday, Taylor has been avoiding everyone, especially Dad and Stephen. It's like something had snapped in her brain. She's hardly ever in the house anymore; it's strange, like she will disappear all day then sneak back into my room in the middle of the night. This morning, I asked her if she wanted to come on our yearly trip to the *Space Dome Play Centre,* and she said, "I would rather die." Her loss, I guess.

I dashed towards the desk as soon as we arrived. The nice, sweet lady, that had worked there since I was little, must've retired because there was a new lady sat at the main desk. This new one looked miserable, as if someone had forced her to do that job.

She stamped Sapphire's hand. "So, is it just the little girl?" She asked.

My dad furrowed his eyebrows and said, "No, all three of them."

She scoffed, looking towards Finn. "The younger one might make the cut." She then pointed at me. "But definitely not 'that' one.'"

"Oh..." I said, as the sensitive person I am, when in my head I was saying, *'Seriously, love, I am standing right next to you and you're just embarrassing yourself.'*

Dad's tone changed to the voice he used when he's trying to have a serious discussion with someone. "Listen, my oldest has special needs and has loved this place since he was a toddler." He leaned over the counter and whispered, "Please, I will pay extra if I have to."

The woman glanced at me as if she was about to eat me. "He doesn't look disabled," she said directly in my face, *cheeky bitch,* like she wanted me to hear it myself. "Do you think letting a teenage boy like him run around with a bunch of infants is safe? It's against our policy to let a child over twelve years of age into our facility, unless they're an adult supervising a child," she added.

Before Dad unleashed his inner 'male-Karen,' I had left. I ran to the back of the building and hid behind a Monster Drop machine. I couldn't understand anything. Did that mean I could never go down the black hole slide ever again? In that moment, I could've written an entire essay trash-talking her, but staying silent was the best option.

Neurotypicals often talk to me like I am a toddler, and it is so frustrating. Like I will ask someone to clarify the instructions they gave me, then they get annoyed and start slowing it down like I can't understand English. They also use this tone in their voice, which makes them sound like they are dumbing it down as if I don't already know what sound a cat makes.

I get it, some people think it's immature to watch cartoons or play with toys over a certain age, but I can't just suddenly stop liking the comfort that I grew up with. The thought of people judging me makes me cringe so bad, I actually want to chop my head off."

Most of the time I won't mention that I am autistic, especially if we are already deep into a conversation, because they automatically shift like they aren't talking to the same person anymore.

Places always advertise that they are supportive of all disabilities, when most of the time they are only referring to the wheelchair ramp, they added to the entrance of the building.

Okay, back to what happened: I get where she was coming from, but she didn't have to be such a bully and make me think I was doing something wrong when I clearly wasn't. Thanks to her, that memory will float around my head for the next twenty years.

Most people will laugh it off in seconds, but for me, being told off is the worst type of punishment. I will worry about it for the rest of the day, then drag it around in my mind for weeks. It never disappears. Some days I will be lying in bed and then my brain will start replaying the most humiliating scene in my head that happened when I was five. I am always awake throughout the night trying to make these memories disappear, but they never do.

People usually get told off if they do something wrong; I am doing something wrong.

I walked past the security guards roaming freely around the building. Each time they passed me, I worried they were going to arrest me, even if I hadn't done anything. I looked so suspicious for no reason.

Stephen found me wandering around the coin pushers. "I know you are feeling overstimulated," he said. He says that word a lot; so does Dad. I know they don't mean any harm, but I don't think they actually know the definition and just found it on one of those autism blogs run by non-autistic parents.

All the machines had been altered since my previous visit. Why was the big spinning wheel near the door now? It made no sense. As I was about to return to Dad, a claw machine caught my eye. It was full of cats wearing different costumes. There was even an astronaut kitty.

I sprinted to Stephen, begging him for money in the same way that Dad used to beg him when he first lost his job. I felt bad. I didn't want to take his money; it wasn't mine to have. He gave me a few coins, and I was sure I was going to win that darn cat.

Every time the claw grabbed, the cat fell everywhere apart from the shoot. Now I understand why people call them 'rigged.'

"We could just find the same thing online for half the price," Stephen blathered. Every second, more money dissolved out of his pocket, and he told me I'd had enough after already spending a tenner trying to grab the dumb cat.

Then, it happened. On the last go, the claw got jammed into the helmet and tossed it into the shoot. I jumped up and down, flapping my hands. Stephen high-fived me. I finally won at something. At least I thought I did.

— Love your favourite space nerd, Tancan :)

20: The Truth

Felix reclined on the sofa, scooting over for Tancan to join him. "I'm so sorry about earlier, sweetheart. Your mom would've hated seeing the disappointment on your face."

"Do you ever miss her?"

"Of course I do. Your mother was an amazing woman."

"You always say 'was,' but she still 'is,' right? She's still looking down on us?"

"Yeah... She sure is."

Tancan's heel got caught on the cuff, absentmindedly pulling up the leg of his pyjama pants. The more he repeated the motion, the more satisfying it became. He continued to roll the fabric, and then it was too late. His scabbed-over wounds were exposed, painted across his knee.

Felix bent over, hovering his hand over a scab. "Sweet-heart... What happened?"

In an instant, he yanked his leg away, a nervous grin tug-ging at the corners of his lips. He let out a small, awkward chuckle, tilting his head down to hide his face.

Felix stood up, his tone growing firmer. "Tancan, what happened? This is very important. Did you do this to yourself, sweetheart?"

He nodded. He couldn't deny it; the truth was already out.

"Why... Why did you do this to yourself, baby?"

"I don't know..."

"Alright, I think it would be best if I cancel your space magazine subscription until this stops."

Tancan shot out of his seat, eyes widened. "What! Why are you punishing me? You're supposed to help me; this is exactly why I never wanted you to find out!"

"Every time you harm yourself, I will do the same thing to myself. Do you understand?"

"I hate you!"

Felix paused. "Does Taylor do this too?" he asked. "Did she encourage you to do this to yourself?"

He shook his head. "No, Dad, I started when I was eleven, and I tried to stop, but these outbursts keep coming back. I can't control this!"

Felix pulled Tancan into his arms. "I know, baby. I'm so sorry if I ever made you feel like this."

"You didn't cause this; I just keep blaming myself for what happened to Mum." His throat tightened. "And It's like I'm a burden in everyone's life, and it's exhausting trying to constantly explain myself over and over, just for people to never get it."

Felix gently stroked his son's forehead. "I'm trying, Tancan, I'm trying my best to understand you," he said, brushing his hair out of his eyes. "Tell me, why do you blame yourself?"

"Why shouldn't I?" he said. "I was the one who pulled the trigger."

"What trigger?"

"The gun you gave me on my tenth birthday. I pulled the trigger and *killed* her, didn't I?"

He dragged his arm away. "Tancan, you know that's not what happened; don't be so *stupid*." He stood up and treaded toward the kitchen. "I can't believe this," he muttered.

"Dad, wait!" He trailed behind him. "What's wrong?"

Felix turned, placing a gentle hand on his son's shoulder. "Why would you *lie* about her *death*? That's sick. You don't believe that's what happened, do you?" He pulled out a chair, watching Tancan's blank stare. "Guns are illegal in England. You know that don't you? Sit with me at the dining table."

Once he sat, Felix leaned forward. "Do you remember when the police officer knocked on our door? He told us that your mom's body had been found in a field a few blocks away. They sat at this very table, displaying photos of her to verify her identity. You tried to look, but Stephen took you and Finn out of the room. Do you remember any of that happening?"

Tancan sank into the chair, the wood chipping him as he sank further. His voice trembled. "Dad... Why are you *lying* to me?"

"I'm not. Nobody knows how she died, but someone must've seen what happened."

"So... You're saying someone else could've killed her?"

"I don't know, honey. The police stopped the investigation years ago."

He wrestled himself out of his dad's arms. "No, no, that didn't happen!" he denied. He bolted from the table and ran upstairs.

***

Felix stepped Stephen outside. "I'm worried about him. He thinks he *killed* Melissa. Apparently, I gave him a *gun*. He said he accidentally *shot* her in the living room. His face, I've never seen him look so serious in his life. I found scars on his legs. He's been cutting himself, Stephen, carrying the guilt of her death like he *caused* it."

"We should take him to see a psychiatrist; anything could be going through his mind right now."

He rubbed his hand across his face. "You know he won't open up to a stranger, and I don't want them putting him on any medication — he's much too young for that."

“Okay,” he assured. “let’s keep an eye on him for the next month or so, and if we notice any changes in his behaviour, we will get him seen as soon as possible.”

21: Records

June 7th 2021 - 220 days before he destroyed himself

Dear Star Diary,

My entire family has gone insane!

Dad and Stephen both keep giving me strange looks, acting like I am a completely different person. Who's telling the truth? It's like everyone around me is lying to my face.

I've spent two weeks trying to remember exactly what happened that day. It's like a short film reeling through my head; each scene is exactly how I remember it.

Dad has directed his own adaptation, and there are a lot of scenes he has cut out.

If I never killed her, then who did?

A few nights ago, I caught Taylor roaming around the house. She kept glaring at my old family photos, wiping the dust from around Dad's face. She must've seen him stuffing Mum's mail underneath the cabinet because she was there too, rummaging through letters addressed to 'Melissa Milten.'

I asked her what she was doing, and she replied with, "Nothing." So, first she was acting all clingy around my dad, now she's looking through my dead mum's mail? She never even knew her.

she was searching for something specific, scanning her eyes across each document.

I helped slip all the paperwork into the corresponding envelopes, but I must've done something wrong since she shoved the letters further into the drawer and said, "Go back to bed."

I don't get it. Some days she acts like I'm her best friend; other days it's like I'm just there, blocking her way. In class she will yap all lesson, then will pretend she doesn't know me as soon as we step into the corridor. What if she's embarrassed of me?

She's hiding something from me. I know she is, if not multiple.

— Love your favourite space nerd, Tancan :)

22: A True Friend

June 27th 2021 - 200 days before he destroyed himself.

As Taylor left the house, Tancan handed her a birthday badge, the same one he wore three months ago. "You're old like me now," he said, "halfway to thirty," which sounded much better in his head.

"Thanks, dude." She clipped the badge onto her loose flannel shirt. "You sure you don't want to join me?"

"I'll meet you in like an hour. I have a few things I need to finish first."

***

After she arrived at the skatepark, Taylor slid the badge into her pocket. She rested her board against the curb, her silver chin dangling over her nose as she laced up her worn-out Converse.

Tancan snuck behind her, balancing a cardboard box in his arms. "Surprise!"

"Oh... You made me a cake?" She asked.

"Yeah, well, kinda. Dad bought it from Tesco." He lifted the lid. "You have to light the candles yourself because he doesn't trust me to use lighters safely."

She forced a plastic smile, curving a wooden knife through the white chocolate stars. "Think you could handle the first slice for me?"

He nodded, shovelling a small triangle into his mouth, bordering his lips with a chocolate residue. "Give yourself a treat day. Even if you ate the entire cake, you'll still be able to skate."

She closed the lid, placing the cake aside. "I'll have some later."

Tancan reached into his pocket, pulling out a lilac drawstring pouch, inside: a bracelet, customised just for her. A tiny skateboard charm dangling alongside a miniature barrel of T-N-T. "Sorry it's not much, it took me hours trying to find the right charms online."

"Oh, wow," she said. "I haven't gotten any birthday presents in *years*."

"Really? Do you like it?"

She rolled up her sleeve and slid it on her wrist, lifting the elastic cord over her bandages. "Yeah, of course, thank you so much."

“Of course. I wanted to get you something you could carry with you everywhere you go, like you carry Herbert and your gum-disguised pocketknife to keep you safe.”

“Shh!” She took off her flannel top and tied it around her waist. “Being on Sertraline during a heatwave is *not* of the weak.” She gulped half of her water in one sip. “I feel like I am about to die.”

“You take antidepressants?”

“Yeah. Sucks not being allowed grapefruit.”

***

A brown envelope stuck through the letterbox. Someone must’ve placed it there moments before they got home. Tancan snatched the edges, pulling out a simple card. The front was generic, a cheap design that appeared like it had been grabbed last-minute. Most of the card was blank. No name, no message, only a single line, scrawled in the top corner.

I know youre here.

A chill crawled down his spine. He skimmed the street as if he were being set up by a television crew, but the road was empty.

"What's that?" Taylor asked.

He stuffed it into his pocket. "Ten percent off at that Chinese restaurant that opened in town. Don't worry, it's not addressed to my mum this time."

"Bro, will you let it go!"

"First of all, I am not *Elsa*. Second of all, no, I will not."

"I wasn't even reading her letters; I was trying to look for something *private* I'd lost, and I found it."

23: Wave Pool

July 4th 2021 - 193 days before he destroyed himself.

Soaked tiles smudged beneath Tancan's toes as he navigated his way through the maze of pool lockers. He was trapped. Tugging down polyester swim shirt, he rubbed his finger over the embroidered aliens on his trunks. Most of the cuts below his thighs had scabbed over. Nobody would notice.

After years of curving around each corner, he eventually found his way to Taylor.

She stood underneath the waterfall, her fingers stroking the raindrops as they splattered on her plain-black shorts. She wasn't alone.

Someone had followed her.

As Tancan moved in her direction, he noticed Sean creeping behind an artificial palm tree, watching Taylor through tinted sunglasses. He dragged his feet through the shallow water, positioning himself directly in Sean's line of sight before he checked over his shoulder. "Sorry to be 'that guy again,' but the waterfall is way too loud. Is it okay if we move towards the wave pool?" It wasn't like he was lying; it was loud, but that wasn't the only problem.

"Dude, you are literally shaking. We can get out if it is too busy for you."

"I'm fine; it's just a bit echoey in here, and I probably should move about more before I freeze."

"Seriously, summer has only just started. We can come back here another time when it isn't so manic."

"But I promised my dad I would have fun this summer and not spend all day in bed playing on my iPad."

As he said that, Felix and Stephen strutted towards them, both wearing matching flamingo swim trunks. "

Every muscle in Tancan's face drooped. "You've actually got to be kidding me."

She whispered in Tancan's ear, "Now those are some hot dad bods."

"Shut up!" he mouthed.

"Looks like somebody's excited to see me," Felix said, scratching his hairy chest.

"Dad, what are you doing here? I thought I was supposed to be here alone with Taylor to help me build my confidence."

"After dropping Sappy at her friend's house, me and Stephen thought we'd come for a splash too. I've read about this place on Facebook. Seems fun. We were your age once, too, you know."

Of course it was Facebook. "Yeah... Like thirty years ago. Have fun *playing* with Stephen," Tancan said, walking away in embarrassment.

**

Five hundred steps later, Tancan and Taylor joined the line at the top of the stairs.

"Okay." Taylor halted at the last step. "Hear me out. Stephen's arms are kinda—"

"Can you actually stop calling my dad and Stephen attractive? It's so weird!"

“Jeez, I’m just messing with you. You’re the gay one anyway.”

“Yeah, but I don’t get turned on by men in their *forties*, especially not my *flipping* Godfather!”

“Says the guy who has an *entire* collection of *Jonathan Bailey* edits in their camera roll.”

“I saved *one* edit. And he is only *thirty-three*.”

“Whatever you say, homo.”

Two girls in front of them turned around, holding in their laughter.

Tancan leaned against the rail, looking down on the three main swimming pools. Sean walked around the edge of the wave pool; his eyes fixed on the slide tower. "Taylor, are you seeing this?"

"Bro, we're next!"

"No; come here, quick!" He blinked. Sean had vanished. Was he imagining stuff again?

"We've lost our place, so this better be something urgent. Are you checking out all the cute boys and want me to approve?"

"No, Taylor, I saw someone."

"Like who? Oh? Wow! I think I know who. It looks like there might be a bit of chemistry between them."

"No, that's not who I mean—wait, what?" He scanned the Olympic pool. His dad's hands gripped Stephen's shoulders. "Don't worry, they're always like that. They've been obsessed with each other since Uni."

She pulled down her swim shirt, similar to Tancan's, hiding her exposed wrists. "I love it when straight men act gay for each other. As soon as we get home, I am writing a fanfic about them whether you like it or not."

"I am *so* done with you."

"In that case, why don't you go and join your *DILF* with his water yoga, or whatever he is doing over there?"

"Excuse you! My *what*?"

"Your dad. What else do you think I said? You must be mishearing things, dude."

24: Teenager

July 13th 2021 – 184 days before he destroyed himself.

Dear Star Diary,

I think I'm in love with Taylor; it's hard to describe the exact feeling, but it's like I always want to be wherever she is. I've only ever felt safe locked away in my room, which is strange because I have felt safe in whatever building she is inside of. I see her more as a sister than a friend, and I think that's why I always treat her the way I wish my dad treated me.

I'm still trying to wrap my head around the fact that she chose *me*. Nobody ever choses *me*. *Me?* Out of all the other 120 kids in our year group. What's so special about *me?*

Even if there were kids at my school who also liked Aliens, I would still pick her because whenever she's with me, I somehow feel normal. If someone had told me five years ago that I would have a friend like her, I would've spat water in their face. She's like the complete opposite of me, and I think that's why I sometimes I'm get tired of her.

She keeps trying to embarrass me wherever we are, like I don't already feel insecure enough in public. She's started making these sexual jokes about everything — I hate it. I keep telling her to stop in the nicest way possible, but she just carries on, and I don't want everyone in public thinking I am weird for other reasons.

The idea of making love to someone just feels wrong and gross. I've tried talking to Dad about it, and he just tells me I'm too young to know how I feel. He says that it will change when I'm older; I never see that happening. I'm only certain that I'm not attracted to girls, and every gay boy I've met online immediately blocks me after finding out I'm autistic or that I'm not interested in meeting up for a shag. Maybe across the universe there are other boys like me.

I have a few online friends who are just as obsessed with space theories as I am, but they don't know me like Taylor does. She always calls my facts 'dumb,' but I know that's just her humour talking because she's one of the few people who listens to the garbage rambling out of my mouth.

I wish she got my references, although I have a habit of gatekeeping and get annoyed when someone knows a fact that I don't or states that they love my special interests more than me. Those documentaries are my entire life. I have all the official merch and make my own custom room decorations. I try to mention them in every conversation; it's the only way I can engage for a long period. Then I will probably go quiet again. It's like posting on social media and getting thousands of views and zero likes every time I open my mouth.

Whenever I try to start a conversation, people always assume that I am bragging because I switch the topic to myself. I don't mean to come across as selfish; I just try to be relatable since most people don't get my humour, and I don't get theirs either. It's like my brain must translate everything, and nothing is ever accurate.

Maybe I should stop talking completely.

I also need to stop relying on Taylor to help me do the simplest tasks. I'm always asking her to tell me when it is ok to cross a road or help me order at a restaurant. How come people can do those things so easily? She will ask me if I am doing alright and I will probably nod my head because I don't know how to explain that I am freaking out about some fake scenario in my head about my house catching on fire whilst I am out and not being able to rescue Starla or my comfort items.

If Taylor was a boy, we'd probably be married by now. I just need a proper boyfriend, and then maybe I will be fixed.

A boy who will take me on cute, romantic dates to small, independent cafes or pretty Japanese restaurants. That's all I want.

Whenever Dad and Stephen take us out for dinner, they always pick the worst places. It's always pubs. I hate pubs. They are always full of loud, drunk men shouting at a TV that only plays one channel. The tables are sticky, and all you can hear are glasses clinking together behind the bar.

Dad will tell me and Finn to go find a table whilst he heads straight to the bar with Stephen. I can't do that! How am I meant to know if a table is taken already?

They both usually order sizzling steaks or gigantic burgers, but I can only ever seem to find things I will eat on the children's menu. Dad usually orders for me, making the waiter assume my meal is for Sapphire, when she's the one having the adult portion of mac and cheese.

I bring my own cluttery too. It feels disgusting eating with pieces of metal random strangers have shoved in their mouths, and I can't monitor the cleaning process either.

It's annoying because no matter how hard I try to explain myself, Dad still doesn't get me, and I don't think he ever will. He's been making me, and Finn do so much lately, all because he wants to slump in the living room with Stephen. At least that's better than drinking.

After Finn gets home from school, he will disappear into his room. He always used to ask me to play video games with him, but he doesn't even bother anymore. He's been my best friend since he was born, and now I feel like I'm losing him too.

On the bright side, I only have three and a half weeks left of year ten, and I'm honestly so glad. Before I befriended Taylor, the teacher would tell us to get into groups, and everyone immediately ran to their friends' tables, and I would just stand in the corner looking into space until someone approached me.

Of course, nobody wants to talk to the quiet kid, so I would wait until the teacher came over and randomly put me into a group. Most of the time I would just sit there brainstorming ideas in my head, not getting involved. Whenever I did, kids ignored me, like I was invisible to them.

On the topic of school, Dad was called into my and Finn's old primary school. Sapphire has been repeating inappropriate words that she overhears Taylor say. I mean, I found it hilarious that she called her male teacher a 'masc lesbian,' but the school thought otherwise. Maybe Taylor isn't the best role model after all.

— Love your favourite space nerd, Tancan :)

25: Blinded

After forgetting to stay hydrated all day, Tancan tiptoed downstairs. Taylor was still out on her midnight walk or whatever she did. The living room door was slightly ajar, and the light hadn't been switched off. As he got closer, soft music danced out of the room. He leaned forward, poking his head between the gap.

An emotion surged through his skull, one that felt unfamiliar, but still hurt. Denial pinged through his mind, whenever his dad spoke to other women; a constant fear nibbled at his knees. *What if he fell in love again and forgot about her?* Now, that fear stitched across his face in broad daylight. He was never allowed to kiss another woman, but that was exactly what he was doing.

Except the woman wasn't a woman at all.

Stephen and Felix clenched each other's shoulders, fumbling with the zips on their jackets as their lips locked in place. Felix's short beard scratched over Stephen's shaven stubble, his hand holding his cheek as their noses clinked together. Felix's head twisted, avoiding colliding his thick glasses against Stephen's bridge.

Unable to process what he was looking at, Tancan couldn't take his gaze away. As much as he wanted to, he remained stationed. He saw everything: the way they gazed into each other's eyes, the muffled whispers tickling their ears. Then, the name, "Melissa," slipped through Felix's lips.

Stephen jerked away, huffing his hands to the side, and peeled his jacket back on. His back now facing the door, unaware of Tancan's disgusted eyes. However, Felix was staring right at them.

Tancan flinched, closing the door fully before bolting upstairs and shutting himself into his room. Using all his strength, he pulled the beanbag in front, gripping the handle closed and barging any escaping air.

Each step moaned louder, creeping towards his door. Tancan held on to his door tighter, like Blu Tack holding up a poster.

Felix knocked. "Tancan, please can you let me in?"

After moulding his hand onto the door, he let go, letting it swing open.

Tancan rammed his head into his dad's torso, shoving him out his room. "Go away!"

"Tancan, listen to me." He steadied himself. "You can't tell anyone what you saw."

He couldn't push him anymore. He collapsed on his bed, staring at the man who wasn't his dad anymore. Felix had already met his dream girl and promised Stephen a lifetime of friendship, not whatever that was. Women had always attracted him. So why... Why did he look at Stephen like that?

Felix sat on the edge of his bed, running a hand through his hair. "Look, sweetheart. When I was your age, being anything other than straight was far from normal. And even now, it's still not completely accepted. I knew I was attracted to women, and I still am. When I first met Stephen, I felt attached to him. I knew I wanted him in my life forever, but it wasn't until this year, I realised how much I *needed* him."

"So, you never *loved* her? The woman you *married* and had children with? My mother *loved* you!"

"Melissa was a very special woman. She brought so much joy and comfort to my life, and I will always love her." He rested his arm against the bed frame. "She's not *alive* anymore, Tancan. You need to realize that. It's time to move on. I'm struggling to take care of you all on my own."

Tancan's fists clenched the edge of his blanket. "But you're still *married* to her. You're *cheating* on her. Taylor's right. All men are pathetic. How could you do this to her!"

"When a loved one dies, their spouse becomes a widow. That means I became single once she passed; it's like a divorce, even when you both still love each other."

Tancan shook his head. "No, you're broken. I heard you say her name. You're not even over her yet. You need time to just—"

"Just *what?*"

"BE MY FUCKING DAD!" he screamed, yanking the covers over his head.

26: Fantasy

July 21st 2021 - 176 days before he destroyed himself.

Dear Star Diary,

I don't want to talk about what happened, because it still doesn't feel real. My dad's not gay or bisexual; I know he's not.

I haven't spoken to Felix or Stephen for the past few weeks, and yes, I am referring to him as 'Felix' because he no longer deserves my respect to call him my dad.

I've spent a lot of time in Sapphire's room. She gets me, even if she understands nothing I ramble on about. We play with her dollhouse, and I usually get assigned to the male dolls she likes the least, which is great because I pretend they are Felix and Stephen and push them down the stairs.

She keeps asking what Mum was like; it hurts me to think that she can only ever remember her through photos and not through her own memories. I hope they can reunite in heaven one day.

I spent my entire childhood looking up to Stephen as a second father figure, but I never thought this would ever happen. He was the best man at Mum and Felix's wedding, and the babysitter whenever they went out for dinner. Sometimes I even wished he was my real dad. He was there when I was born; I took my first steps towards him, and I don't think he's ever spoken sharply to me like Felix does.

Before I was born, Stephen dated this woman who immediately left him after she found out he was infertile. He hates it when I ask about her; it's the only time I can ever hear the sadness in his voice. I remember he took me and Finn to a science museum once; it was the best day ever. I asked him about ever wanting his own children. He ignored me at first, but then he told me something that I don't think I will ever forget.

"I could have twenty children and none of them would be as special as *you*." Years later, I'm still wondering what he meant by that.

I thought he stayed around to protect me; guess I was wrong. Maybe it wasn't about me at all. I can still see them snogging in my mind; it's gross. Maybe if Mum had just divorced Felix, then it wouldn't hurt this much because she would've *chosen* to split from him, but she lost her life instead. She had no *choice*.

This morning, a morbid thought sunk into my mind, and I can't let it go. I keep thinking about Felix telling me how Mum 'actually' died, and as much as I believe it or not, I have noticed certain similarities between our stories. One of the major differences is the presence of Stephen. He wasn't there in my memory, but Felix said he took me and Finn out of the room. It doesn't make sense.

What if he had something to do with Mum's death because he was jealous of her relationship? No! I hate myself for even thinking that. He was good friends with Mum too, so he would never do that. Stephen wouldn't hurt a fly.

There must be some things that Felix isn't telling me. I often wonder what is going on inside his head that makes him act out the way he does, finding a cheap shortcut out of every problem he has. He probably thinks the same about me.

I've created a fantasy in my head where everything is perfect. I fear I may become too delusional and eventually disconnect from reality, being hooked to this fake persona of mine. I've read about these sorts of things, and it never ends well. It is like a drug. At first, it feels amazing, and the more I explore, the more addicted I become.

In my fantasy land, my dad never gets drunk, my mum is still alive, Taylor feels safe and I am an astronaut who flies around the solar system. Sometimes I forget it is just in my head. I'm getting lost; it's like a labyrinth. I can control who comes in and out of my life. I am the president, and I have authority.

In this reality, I also have 7 cats instead of just Starla, and whenever someone asks how many pets I have, I will tell them about all 7 of my cats. I have told nobody about my other world yet, and I'm not planning on it either. They will worry about me more than they already do. My fantasy land has made me feel happy for the first time in years. Hopefully, the next time I visit, my cats won't try to sew buttons on my eyes.

— Love your favourite space nerd, Tancan :)

27: Summertime Funshine

August 13th 2021 - 153 days before he destroyed himself.

Dear Star Diary,

Today is Friday the 13th; let's hope Taylor doesn't try to kill me. Last week, she took me to the pride festival because she wanted me to feel 'alive,' and I did. But I think we both interpreted that phrase differently.

She danced through the stalls as if she were the one singing on stage. Then there was me, checking behind me every five seconds because the sensation of being watched was heavier than ever. Nobody was looking at the pride pin on my shirt; they were looking at me. Just because I was in a 'safe place' for my sexuality, didn't mean I could stop masking my traits.

I tried my best to avoid looking at all the trinket stalls because most of them were cramped and crowded. Wherever I stood, I was blocking someone's way. I'm always blocking the way, wherever I go. Somebody would bump into me, and

I would be the only one who says 'sorry,' when they are the one who barged past me in the first place.

I thought most of the people there would be teens my age, but a lot of them were around the same age as Felix and Stephen. I don't think I could ever have imagined either of them dancing around with an army of drag queens; I guess I don't know what to expect from them anymore.

We passed this cookie stall where each cookie was wrapped in funny quotes.

Taylor read one out, "'I'm so hungry I could eat a fem-boy.' Real."

I almost chocked on my slushy. "I beg your pardon?"

She winked. "Don't worry, you're safe."

"Aren't you a lesbian?" I asked.

"Mostly. I just say I'm a lesbian, so I don't confuse people because I feel attraction based on personality rather than their appearance and whatever lives between their legs."

As we ventured further towards the main stage, Bella-joules stood in front of us with a lesbian flag tied around her neck like a cape.

"No way, she's gay!" Taylor whispered into my ear in the same excited voice she used after Bella-joules asked to borrow her pencil in art. I couldn't hear what she said after since there was a man in a rainbow tutu singing his heart out to *Lady Gaga* on stage. She always gets so defensive whenever I joke about them ever dating because I know she has feelings for her, even though she will never admit it.

Outside the gate, this random woman approached me, ranting about how God was going to send me to Hell because I had a bit of glitter on my face. "Repent your sins!" she yelled, not knowing I already do and ask God to look after my mum every night. I don't get humans sometimes. I wonder how God would feel about her trying to scare literal children. At the time, these questions weren't twirling around my head because I was too busy sobbing.

Before Taylor escorted me away, she sandwiched the woman's head between her hands and kissed her cheek. "Looks like you're joining us too," she said. I wish I had the courage she does. She's my guardian angel that Mum must've sent down to me.

It wasn't until the bus home that I realised Taylor wasn't as confident as she acted to be. She stepped on first and took a seat.

It took me a while to find my bus pass, and an old man behind me started huffing and puffing. "Hurry up," he groaned. "I have places to be too!" Once I found it, I scanned it the wrong way because I was stressed. The driver was a prick too and commanded me to do it properly, then started to speed off before I could find my seat. Men are so misera-ble.

I sat next to Taylor. She seemed quiet. I still felt pretty anxious myself, so I stayed quiet too, until I noticed some-thing that made my blood boil.

Taylor's expression faded. She was wearing a red pleated skirt, and sitting across to the side of us was a man. He was holding up his phone, directing it towards her. At first, I thought he was just watching a video or something, until I heard the click of the photo button.

I don't think anyone else heard it, but I sure did. I turned around and called him a "disgusting pervert" to his face and told him if he didn't delete the photos, I would "grab his wrinkly old balls and twist them until they turned blue!" Not my proudest moment, but I have no re-grets.

I watched his every movement. I wasn't leaving the bus until he did what I ordered him to do. It was my turn for once. I threatened someone after spending my entire life feeling threatened by everything. I saved Taylor, like the many times she had saved me before. Where on earth did my social anxiety go? It was like we had switched bodies because she was sitting silently, pulling her skirt over her knees, and I was the one who let out what Taylor wanted to say, but couldn't.

Now I can see why she always wears baggy jeans.

Once we jumped off the bus, I asked her if she was okay. She nodded, remaining silent. I think she was used to things like that happening to her. I don't understand why someone would ever think of doing something as disgusting as that. Even if she had told him she was fifteen, it wouldn't have stopped him from doing what he did.

Whenever I am on the bus, I usually put on my headphones to block out whatever is around me, but I couldn't that time. Everything is a pin, and I am a half-deflated balloon; one minor incident and I pop. If Taylor's situation happened to me, I would never step foot on a bus again, but Taylor is much stronger than I am.

— Love your favourite space nerd, Tancan :)

28: Unforgiven Truth

August 14th 2021 – 152 days before he destroyed himself.

"Hey, Mr. Sleepy Pants, you haven't given me a hug in ages!" said Stephen, pouring himself a coffee.

Tancan brushed past him. "Maybe next time, don't lick my dad's face off. I don't know what parts of him you touched. You might need to look in a mirror, see if you have any of his nose hairs jammed in your teeth."

"Okay, Tancan. That's *enough!*" warned Felix, raising his voice.

"Oh, how rude of me, sorry 'sperm giver.'"

"It's alright, Felix. Let him express his emotions." Stephen's smile faltered, darting his eyes towards Felix, before placing his soft hand on Tancan's shoulder. "Buddy, me and your dad are sorry you had to see us like that. It was just a kiss—I promise."

He dropped the sarcastic tone, his voice filling with sadness. "It's not even about that." He sniffled. "I need my mum back."

"I know, buddy. I would never try to replace her; she's your mother, and she always will be."

"Why can't things just stay the way they were?" Tancan wiped his face with his sleeve. "You're my dad's best friend... You're not even a part of my family," he spat.

Stephen leaned against the kitchen counter, wiping his eyes with the bottom edge of his shirt. He didn't wipe his tears away, only smudged them. He scratched a tea towel across his forehead, like someone who had their heart shattered.

Crap. What had Tancan done? Did he have a habit of destroying other people's lives, as well as his own? He didn't mean any of it, but now it was too late.

His dad gave him *the look* whilst rubbing Stephen's back, the same one he always gave him whenever he's a *disgrace* to the family.

29: Roller Coaster Ride

For the next two weeks, Tancan refused to be a part of this so-called 'family' of his. Everyone had died and been reborn with actors owning names of people they had no right to. They weren't his blood; they were cold-blooded amphibians.

Most nights, he stayed awake sketching, smothering his blood over drawings of fantasy-like portraits of the family he had lost. The real ones. The ones that lived in his head. The people who hadn't been sucked up a vacuum. Of everyone, Finn was the only one who stayed the same. He was the only member without an expired passport.

Finn began offering to watch space documentaries with him, but, for the first time in his life, his older brother shook his head. None of Tancan's special interests seemed as interesting as they once were. Illustrating his delusions became much more important. Space theories had always been his greatest passion, something he could write a thousand essays on, but now he refused to even look through a screen.

Tancan kept deteriorating. His weight was dropping by pebbles every hour, and his skin blanched. Refusing to bathe, although he regularly brushed his teeth and any other hygienic treatment that would let him stay in the same worn-out pyjamas.

He had stopped existing in the present altogether. Sat on his bed, staring at his blank wall, the wall covered in posters that he couldn't see anymore. Every hour he built new land-marks out of miniature bricks, reaching into his LEGO box and building his fantasies in real life. Models circled his room, forcing Taylor to sleep in the living room. Yet, there was so much vacant land.

Finn stayed by his side, holding his hand as he played car-toons on the TV, but Tancan was still looping on the never-ending roller coaster, swerving and jolting through the depths of his mind.

"Do you know who murdered Mum?" asked Finn.

The coaster pulled into the station. Tancan collected his voice as he stepped off. He was home again, even if they're as still many prisoners trapped in the back of his mind.

He blinked. “What do you mean?"

"I don't know... Forget I said that." Finn handed him the remote. "I'll go let Dad and Stephen know you're actually alive."

Dear Mr Milten,

Over the course of the last few months, it has become blatantly clear that your son has been experiencing some challenges that may be affecting his emotional well-being and day-to-day life. While I want to respect his autonomy, I have also recognised the significant role you play in his support system.

During the span of his most recent sessions, my team and I have discovered consistent signs of social withdrawal, which appear to be impacting his ability to regulate his emotions. While these are not uncommon experiences for young people, they do require a structured plan to ensure progress and safety.

I believe your involvement and continued encouragement will be essential moving forward. With your and your son's consent, I would like to schedule a joint meeting on Thursday, September 2nd, to discuss the next steps moving forward to support his needs. In collaboration, we will be meeting with another psychiatrist who has more experience in areas that my team isn't trained in. This will be beneficial as we are a children's counselling program and Tancan may need additional support as he moves towards the adult stages of his life.

Please let me know what time would work best to schedule the appointment, and I shall send you the address via email.

Safe regards,

Emma-Jayne Norris, PsyD

Licensed Therapist| Butterfly Petals Counselling

EJayne4872@gmail.com

30: The Room

September 2nd 2021 - 133 days before he destroyed himself.

Stephen smiled at Tancan as he walked out of the kitchen. He had a white filling at the top of his left molar, but that wasn't the fakest part of his smile.

"Stephen," mumbled Tancan, following him into the living room. "I'm sorry. You're more than my family; you've always been like a second *dad* to me." He leaned forward, wrapping his arms around Stephen's neck. But he didn't hug him back.

"I hope your meeting goes well," he said, holding the same grin. Could a therapy session go *wrong*?

***

As soon as Tancan glared out the car window, he knew this wasn't his regular place; this was straight from a horror film. The outside of the building was of a damaged council estate. The roof sagged, and a heavy black door glued to the front.

Tancan gripped his seatbelt with both hands. "I thought I had another meeting with Emma-Jayne?"

Felix unbuckled his seatbelt. "We're going to meet your new therapist; he might be able to understand your anxieties better."

Every therapist he had seen before had been a woman. Even though he had spent his entire life surrounded by men, he had always found it easier to open up to females. "Why didn't you tell me this before we left? I'm not prepared. I can't go in. I planned a conversation with Emma-Jayne, not a random man I've never spoken to before!"

"It's only a quick chat this morning, nothing serious. I promise we can go straight home afterwards, but we have to go inside, okay?"

Tancan nodded, grabbing his dad's hand.

*

The reception area had a shimmering marble floor, polished to perfection. The harsh chemical smell was somehow even scarier than the building's catfishing exterior.

Tancan sat in the corner, shifting beads along a rainbow-colored activity cube. His fingers traced the loops, spiralling down until the beads clashed together.

"Tancan Milten, please." A voice called.

Tancan's head snapped up. A rocking boat had settled in his lungs. He clung tightly to his dad's hand, shaking his head.

Felix crouched down, offering his other hand. "Sweetheart, you'll be okay."

But he wasn't okay. Something about the therapist's sauntering walk made the boat jolt, like the truth was swimming beneath him.

"Would you like your dad to stay in the room while we chat?" The man asked.

Tancan's grip on Felix's hand tightened, nodding his head up to his dad's gaze.

As they entered the room, Felix let go, letting Tancan fall into a black hole. They both sat opposite each other, but Tancan could feel a glass barrier between them.

"Alright Tancan, can you confirm your date of birth for me?" the therapist asked.

He glanced at his dad, hoping he would talk for him.

"March 21st, 2006," Felix said.

"And who do you live with?".

Tancan pointed across the box-shaped room. "Him."

"Anyone else?"

His fingers gripped the edge of his chair. "I don't know anymore."

The therapist gave a small nod, writing a few notes down. "Okay. Have you seen anything lately that has made you feel particularly anxious?"

"I saw my dad and Godfather kissing. That was pretty scary."

The therapist's expression shifted, casting a brief glance toward Felix. "Right..." he said. "Do you ever see or hear things that other people can't?"

Tancan swallowed, his hands curling into his sleeves. There is no point in hiding anything; this therapist was probably going to leave him like all the others did. "For a few months, I've been having these weird dreams about my mum." He pulled down his drawstring. " And when I am awake, I sometimes hear her calling my name really faintly, or I will get this sensation that somebody is watching my every movement, and I will start seeing these shadows standing through doorways at night. I am aware it's in my imagination, but it just feels so real."

The therapist's pen stopped moving. "Does your mother ever tell you to do anything?"

"No. She only whispers my name."

He scribbled down more notes. "Tancan, I am going to take your dad into a separate room for a private chat. Will you be alright in here alone?"

He nodded.

The therapist closed the door behind him. “In the conversation we had on the phone, you mentioned Tancan believes he murdered his mother, correct?"

"Correct," replied Felix.

"I believe your son may have created a delusion in his mind in order to block out his original trauma caused by his mother's death. This is called Dissociative Amnesia, but It is possible Tancan may have also experienced a psychotic episode due to a build-up of internal stress. Primarily, psychosis is recognised between late teens and early twenties, but in some cases, symptoms can be noticed earlier on."

"What are you trying to say?"

"Tancan has also displayed signs of BPD — Borderline personality disorder. It is a mood disorder that affect how a person feels, thinks and connects with others. People develop these disorders during childhood, especially if they grew up in emotionally unstable homes where they have been exposed to constant fear."

"Was his autism diagnosis incorrect then?"

"No, not at all, and it is not rare for autistic individuals to develop mental illnesses as they transition into adulthood, which is clinically referred to as comorbid conditions. It means the individual may have multiple illnesses occurring at the same time. This leads me to my next question: Are you aware of any other illnesses that run through your family?"

"My wife, sorry, Tancan's mom *was* bipolar."

"It is possible—"

Felix looked him dead in the eyes. "He's not. I know he's not. He's too young."

"While I cannot diagnose any patients at the moment, I can begin a referral for Cognitive Behavioural Therapy; however, please be advised that significant wait times are expected."

"Okay, thank you."

"Enjoy the rest of your week and do contact me if you see any unusual patterns in Tancan's behaviour."

***

Felix hadn't turned on the radio; he always did.

Tancan adjusted himself in his seat. "What did he say?" he asked, for what felt like the hundredth time.

He gripped the steering wheel tighter. "He wants you to write down exactly what you are doing whenever you hear your mom calling your name." His voice laced with something between fear and concern. "Tancan, why didn't you tell me about this?" he asked in a profound tone.

"I don't know."

Felix fixed his eyes on the road, rubbing his fingers down the wheel. "Just tell me the truth; that's all I'm asking from you."

Tancan yanked his seatbelt. "Dad, I told you, I don't know!"

The car swerved as if Felix had shifted all his weight onto the accelerator.

"Dad! Slow down, we're going to have an accident!"

He slammed on the brake, jolting the car instantly.

"Ah!' cried Tancan. "Give us whiplash, why don't you."

Felix hid his face behind his hands. "I'm sorry. Sweetheart, I'm *sorry*."

31: Alarm

September 8th 2021 - 127 days before he destroyed himself.

Tancan rested his head against a pillar. "Yeah, my dad definitely hates me now. I should've kept my mouth shut."

"Dude, I'd be freaked out too if my son told me he keeps hearing my dead wife everywhere. He just needs time to process everything. Your mum's name was Melissa, right?" asked Taylor, opening her locker, keeping her wrist pressed against the door. "And her last name was Milten?"

"Yeah?" The image of her rummaging through the mail still lingered in his mind. "Haven't I already told you about a hundred times?"

She shut her locker, her eyes fixed outside the window, following a group of boys playing football. "Yeah, I keep forgetting; it must've been hard losing her at such a young age." As she turned her head, marks on her neck appeared slightly below the ear. It wasn't a hickey; it was a bruise.

"What's that?" He pointed.

Her hand brushed over the spot. "What's what?"

"On your neck."

"Oh... It's nothing."

"It doesn't look like *nothing.* You know you can talk to me; it's not like I will start rumours about you throughout the entire school."

"I know."

"Taylor, you need to listen to me. A teacher could see those marks and make a phone call."

"Jeez, Tancan, you're not my dad! I can handle this *myself.*"

"Yeah, well, *my* dad isn't *your* dad either!" he spat.

She narrowed her eyes. "What's that supposed to mean?"

"Sorry, I'm still not feeling like myself after that strange therapy meeting." He jogged down the stairs, ignoring Taylor's question. "Have you decided what you're being for Halloween this year?" he asked. "I'm going as an alien again, but this time, I'll be a purple one since I was a blue one last year."

"I don't know yet," she said, keeping her hand pressed over her neck. "Sean never really lets me go out on Halloween. He turns off all the lights to stop kids knocking on the door, plus it's the first day of year 11, and you're already excited for Halloween?"

"Yeah, it's my favourite time of the year! I usually start planning my costume during the summer! It's like the only day of the year where I don't feel like an outcast."

Finn trudged across the courtyard; his feet weighed down by the backpack hunched over his shoulders. "Dad told me to check on you at lunch."

Tancan groaned. "Is he seriously making you *spy* on me? I'm fine for now, but if I don't come home later, then I've probably gotten abducted by aliens."

"You haven't slept properly for a week; he's just worried about you." He placed his backpack on the bench. "Can you watch this? I'll be back in like five minutes. I'm going to grab a pasta pot from the canteen."

"Alright, I told you I'm fine. There is nothing to worry about." Tancan sat back on the bench beside Taylor, peering over her phone. "Be careful, Mr Wilson is over there, and he confiscated a kid's phone the other day."

"Yeah, whatever," she said, scrolling through text messages with her back towards him, as if a teacher wasn't the only person she was hiding her phone from. She accidentally opened the wrong tab, revealing many photos of Melissa.

Tancan snatched her phone. "Why do you have photos of my mum saved on your phone?"

"Hey! Give it back!"

"Where did you get these from? I've never seen some of these in my life."

"I found this photobook inside one of the living room cabinets." She sighed. "Well, that's the surprise ruined. I wanted to design a Christmas card for you with her face on because you always mention how much you miss her."

Tancan knew she was lying. He clicked one of the images. She appeared to be eating something in the photo. He zoomed in.

Nuts.

Fear flushed over his face. "She can't eat nuts," he mumbled.

"What's wrong?" asked Taylor.

"About a year before she died, my mum ate some peanut butter cookies and went into anaphylactic shock. She was in hospital for a while. She looked really sick, but Dad wouldn't let me and Finn see her and asked Stephen to babysit us whilst he stayed at the hospital with her.

"It was so traumatic that I developed ARFID. The thought of chocking made me physically ill. Dad had to mush up all my foods until the they became softer to swallow. I could still handle my favourite alien crackers, and that was about it. Everyone thought I was just a picky eater to begin with until I lost so much weight that I had to be hospitalized.

"The nurse recommended therapy, but my parents didn't think that was a good idea because I was only nine. I started having food exposure therapy, which led me to my autism diagnosis. Sorry for venting to you."

"It's fine, can I have my phone back, please?"

Before he handed it back to her, he swiped across to the next few photos. Each one was Melissa in hospital, looking just as terrifying as he remembered. There was no doubt Taylor was lying. Those weren't the type of wholesome photos you would put on a Christmas card.

As soon as he handed over the phone, the worst possible scenario happened: the fire alarm.

Multiple fire exits spilled with kids complaining. They would've all melted if there had been an actual fire. Usually, they would celebrate their freedom from class with cheers and shouts, but this drill was interrupting their lunch. Oh, what a bummer. This wasn't interrupting Tancan's lunch; it was destroying his entire day.

Finn sprinted to Tancan's bag, placing his pasta pot on the grass as he pulled out Tancan's ear defenders. "Here, put these on!" he said, but Tancan's fingers had already jammed his eardrums.

Kids stared at him as they shifted past. "Oh my dayz," someone said. "Nah, did I set it off in the toilets?" Everyone's voices overlapped the constant wailing of the siren, and teachers yelling everyone into single-file lines only made the music louder.

A random year 8 teacher in rugby shorts blew a whistle. "Get into your form groups!" Form groups? The form class that all hated Tancan? "Oi! You lot too!" he said, pointing toward Tancan.

"Sir, he's having a meltdown." Said Taylor.

"It's just an alarm; it will be over soon; stop messing around!"

"HE'S AUTISTIC."

Another teacher, standing further down the field, called out, "Finley Milten?" Holding a pen and clipboard, she scanned the crowd. "Has anybody seen Finn?"

He waved. "I'm over here!"

"Get back in line!" She ordered, waving the pen in the air.

"I need to stay here with my brother."

"Another staff member will sort him out."

Finn tightened his grip on Tancan's hand. No matter what the teacher said, he wasn't going anywhere.

"If you don't get here right now, you'll have an hour detention after school!"

Before she could say another word, Taylor stepped in. "If you give him a detention, then you'd better give one to me and him, too." She gestured toward Tancan, scrunched on the ground. "And I wonder what kind of reputation this school will have after punishing a child for having a disability."

A teacher wouldn't force a child in a wheelchair to climb up the stairs, so why are they doing this to him? School may feel like prison for many of the pupils, but Tancan was on death row.

32: Bruised

October 11th 2021 - 94 days before he destroyed him-self.

Dear Star Diary,

It's been a month since I last set foot in school, and I'm never going back.

Dad said, "It's your education, not mine." I've tried discussing everything with him, but him and Stephen won't listen to me anymore; they think I am a psychopath. That's why I haven't mentioned the photos that they tried to hide from me.

I don't care what they think about me, I already know what is best for me. I've written a list of my biggest fears:

- Teenagers.
- Men.
- Fire alarms.
- Crowds.
- Men.
- Fireworks.
- Dentists.

- Airports.
- That one *Creepypasta* I read when I was 8.
- Needles.
- Men.
- My dad when he's drunk.
- The texture of Mushrooms.
- The thought of Dad and Stephen making out in the living room.
- Men.
- Public transport.
- Public toilets.
- Oh, Did I mention men?

A lot of those things exist inside school. If I could learn online, it would be a lot easier.

Dad told me I can't stay home forever because it is apparently 'ruining my social life,' but school ruined my entire life. I told him that I will try again after Christmas, but I'm pretty sure he's already given up on me.

Taylor usually fills me in on all the drama. Nothing much has happened since I've been gone. She spends most lunchtimes playing football with random kids at lunch. None of them knows she's staying with me. They probably all thought she hung around with me because I had no friends.

She's filled the bathroom with cheap drugstore concealers and foundations to cover up her bruises, and I'm the only one who knows. I've spotted some fresh marks on her leg, but she claims they're from football. She doesn't even like it that much; she only joined so she could be on the same team as Bella-Joules.

I joked, if we are both still single by the time we are forty, we should just marry each other. I've never seen her look so offended in my life. She refused to marry anyone at all and had already planned to go as far away as she could, once she turned eighteen, so nobody could control her. I don't think she trusts me enough to let me go with her.

— Love your favourite space nerd, Tancan :)

33: Pumpkin Patch

October 25th 2021 - 80 days before he destroyed himself.

Tancan plodded through muddy fields, his welly boots sinking with each step, making loud farting noises as he pulled his foot out of the swamp. "Maybe I should've stayed home with Taylor and done some revision."

"Year eleven sounds so stressful," said Finn.

He sat on an old tire swing, the same one his mother used to push him on. "It honestly is. On the first day, my form tutor told us we need to revise every single day, or we will end up working as janitors."

"Oof, that's rough. I'm so glad I'm only starting year 8."

"Cherish it. As soon as you pick your options in year 9; time will fly by." He dangled his legs, his foot stroking the leaf pile below him. "Do you remember one year when Dad tripped over a pumpkin and face-planted into the mud?"

Finn chuckled. "Yeah, and when Mum tried to wipe the mud away, her boots got stuck in a puddle, so Dad had to pull her out."

He sighed. "She was the best at carving pumpkins."

Green, orange, and white pumpkins dotted the landscape like gigantic marbles. One sat alone in the centre, leaking its smushed organs into the soil. Unlike the others, this one had deflated, as if a herd of elephants had stomped on it. If Tancan didn't choose it, no one would. It would be left to rot alone.

He approached the gutted pumpkin, scooping its mushy centre into his arms and cradling it gently to the wheelbarrow.

Felix groaned. "Don't be silly, put it back."

"But I picked this one," Tancan murmured.

"We don't have all day. I still have to cook dinner once we get home."

"Dad, I feel attached to this pumpkin. I can't abandon it."

"How on earth are you meant to carve that lump of... *goo*?"

"Maybe I don't want to carve it," Tancan said. "You obviously wouldn't choose me if you placed me in a room full of *perfect* children."

Felix gripped the wheelbarrow, lifting it over a hill of mud. "This isn't about *you.* Look at your sister; she picked a regular pumpkin without any issues. And you're *fifteen-years-old;* you can't even handle a *simple* task?" he said in the most patronising tone.

"You criticise everything I do! It feels like I am the pumpkin, and you're the one carving holes into me. I get it. Sapphire looks like a mini version of Mum, and she's your only daughter, but that doesn't give you an excuse to make me and Finn feel like we must be exactly like her!"

"Buddy," Intervened Stephen, tapping his shoulder. "I'll pay for your pumpkin, but I'm more than happy to buy you another one as well."

"Okay, thanks," he said. Walking away, clutching his pumpkin tightly against his chest and made his way back to the tire swing. He sank into the rubber, letting Mother Nature rock him gently.

Finn followed, leaning his head against the rugged rope. "Don't listen to what Dad says. I think your squashed pumpkin is pretty cool."

"Thanks. I'm going to name it 'squashy.'"

***

Every night was the same. Tancan couldn't sleep. The walls cracked around him.

They always found something to argue about.

"I'm sick of you always playing the *good* parent. I am his dad, not *you*, so don't tell me I'm being too harsh on him!" yelled Felix.

"Given your behaviour, it's no surprise your teenage son is hallucinating his deceased mother. Don't let him end up like *her*."

"Why don't you just drop dead, Stephen!"

Tancan slinked downstairs, his chest rattling with irritation.

"Go back to bed. Everything is alright," assured Stepen.

"Stop fighting!" Tancan bolted out. "You've both been like this every night since my therapy appointment, and every argument is about *me*. Is something wrong? Because if there is, you should probably say it to my face!"

Felix exhaled. "You're just a little depressed, sweetheart."

"A *little?* I can't cope anymore, Dad!" He broke down into tears. "I destroyed this entire family."

"Baby, me and Stephen are trying our hardest to get you some support, but for now we are *both* here for you."

Tancan sat in the armchair, silent at first, before asking, "Do you both love each other?"

They nodded their heads in sync.

"But how did you know?"

"It's complicated," said Stephen.

"No, like how do you know if you love someone without being attracted to them?"

"Your dad and I love you and your siblings very much, but it's a feeling that I can't really explain."

"Is it like you always feel the need to protect them?"

"Yeah, kind of." He glanced at Felix. "Buddy, it's long past bedtime for me and your dad." He yawned. "You should probably come up too."

"Wait, before you go, do you think I could see you... Kiss Dad?"

"That's not really something appropriate to do in front of our child."

"I've seen it before—just one small peck on the lips. I need to know that love exists. Or just do something, anything, to prove that you will stop arguing with each other because every argument is making my home crumble."

"Okay," he agreed, turning to Felix. "I regret everything I've ever said about you."

"So do I." He placed his hands on the back of Stephen's neck, pulling him closer until their lips locked.

"Oh..." Tancan mumbled. "You're actually in *love.*"

34: Spooked

October 31st 2021 - 74 days before he destroyed himself.

The day had barely begun, yet the clock had already circled fifty times.

Finn lounged on Tancan's bed, both binge-watching Halloween episodes of their favourite shows. After what felt like an eternity of waiting, the first trick-or-treater finally rang the bell.

They both bolted, racing to grab the handle.

Finn reached the door first, releasing an exhausted sigh. "Oh, it's just *you*."

Taylor stood on the doorstep, already dressed as a witch. "Yeah, what a shame, it's only *me*."

Tancan peeked his head around the door. "Where on earth have you been?"

She shrugged, adjusting her jewel-adorned necklace. "Just went for a walk around the block, seeing if I could spot any houses that were decorated in this depressed neighbourhood."

Tancan knew that wasn't where she really went.

A chain dangled out of Taylor's left pocket. She slid it deeper, but Tancan still noticed the emerald gem dangling out of the side.

He'd seen it before, he was certain, and even if he hadn't; it was something she would never wear.

She pointed to her cauldron-shaped bucket. "Anyway, whilst I'm here, Trick—Or—Treat smell my feet, or whatever the saying is. Give me a Kinder Bueno right now! And if one doesn't get placed in my cauldron within the next five seconds, I will turn you both into frogs!"

"Stephen's not back yet, and knowing him, he's probably bought some weird off-brand version," said Finn. "Last year he bought a selection pack of palma violets, and no kids were happy at all."

"Yeah, I don't have a prince to kiss, so I'll be stuck as a frog forever," added Tancan, knowing Taylor would leave the chocolate in the cauldron to rot.

***

As soon as the sun set, Tancan was the first to bolt out the front door. He had planned the best route around as many houses as possible. "I'm so glad we convinced Sapphire that handing out sweets is more fun than trick-or-treating," he said, adjusting his headband. "She would've been a nightmare to walk around with us."

***

After three houses, Taylor led them in the opposite direction. “I have a feeling your dad is dressing in a maid costume, right now.”

“Ew,” groaned Tancan. “Why did my brain start picturing that!”

“No, but like he seems to be one of those submissive men who would whimper at Stephen.”

“Stop! My twelve-year-old brother is literally walking right behind us!”

“Yeah, but isn’t he born in like 2009? He’s old enough to get my Gen z humour.”

"Hey, wait! There's a house with pumpkins across the road!" Finn trailed behind, lifting his inflatable shark tail off the ground. "Guys, where are we going? We've been walking for a—woah!"

A massive manor, glowing with projected holograms, stood in front of them. A crowd of teenagers roamed freely around the property. The scene was straight out of an American high school movie.

"What is this?" asked Tancan.

Taylor walked ahead, bobbling Tancan's antennas. "A Halloween party, duh!"

His gut told him to turn around; this was the only night he could blend in. He would be a sixteen- year-old in five months and still hadn't even been to a proper party. He forced himself forward, slipping behind Taylor. There was no turning back now.

Finn gripped his arm. "Look," he muttered, pointing at a sign near the entrance.

No under-18s.

"Don't worry, half of the people here are underage."

Taylor dived through the crowd, abandoning Finn and Tancan to fight off the dancing zombies themselves.

Tancan gripped Finn's tail, squeezing behind the mosh pit of monsters, until they stumbled upon a small library buried amidst the chaos of the party. The dim lighting casted over the dust-coated bookshelves, trapping them inside enclosed walls.

Finn glanced up at the cobweb. "Is that real or a decoration?" He asked.

"Don't know," Tancan admitted, scanning the arranged books. "I think this place has been abandoned for years." He smirked. "What if this place is haunted by ghosts? Maybe Mum wanted to party with us?"

"I wish. She'd be way more fun than Dad." Finn glanced at an old ticking grandfather clock placed in the corner of the room. "This place gives me the creeps." He rubbed his eyes. "I think we should go. I'm already feeling tired."

"*Tired?* It's Halloween! The night has only just begun! Alright, fine, let's go find Taylor." He twisted the doorknob. "Uh oh."

"What's wrong?"

"The door! it's locked!"

*

Gummy eyeballs bobbed around Taylor's cup of cherry-red punch. She chugged it down like a vampire, nearly choking when Bella-Joules tapped her on the shoulder.

"Hey, Witch Bitch! You're the one who gave me that pencil in art, Taylor, right?"

"Uh... Yeah. Yeah, I did."

"Cool! You here alone?"

"Nope." She gulped an eyeball down her throat. "I'm with my gay-ass friend, Tancan, the one who sat next to me with an alien pencil case, and his brother," she said, staring at Bella-Joules' smudged, zombie eyeliner that somehow made her even more attractive.

“I haven’t been to a party like this since I lived in Dublin.”

“You’re Irish?”

“Yeah, only moved to Audresbury last year after my family got into a fight with a leprechaun,” she joked.

Before Taylor could even blink, Bella-Joules reached out, running her fingers over Taylor's shoulder. "You’re on the football team too, aren’t you? You scored the winning goal at the end of the game," she teased, "and not gonna lie, you looked kinda *hot*."

Every nerve in her face lit up like a sunbed, UV lighting glistening in her eyes. "Really? I saw you at the Pride festival wearing the most *lesbianistic* cape."

"*’Lesbianistic?’* Are you drunk?"

"Maybe..." She leaned onto the countertop. "You know, I'm way cooler than you think I am."

Bella-Joules picked up a neon yellow glow stick, brushing it over Taylor's golden hair. "Oh yeah? Prove it. I dare you to *kiss* me."

"That's *all?*"

She loosened her tie and undid her top button. "Mhm, bet you've never kissed an Irish girl before."

"I've never kissed any girls before." She cradled her fingertips around the back of Bella-Joules' neck, brushing her red wine bangs off her eyebrow piercing. Her lips pursed until they brushed against the soft warmth of Bella-Joules' mouth, tasting the sweetness of her cherry ChapStick. She then pulled herself back, an awkward chuckle escaping her lips before she dived in again, more passionately this time, softly biting the corner of her mouth.

Bella-joules massaged her fingers around Taylor's forehead, a hair bobble around her wrist. "I want to eat your brain," she teased.

"Calm down zombie." She picked up her drink, biting down on the straw. "Don't you want to try a sample of my potion first?"

"Depends what ingredients you've used."

"It's a *secret* formula," she whispered.

*

"What are we meant to do, Tancan!" Finn scouted the area. "We're trapped!"

Tancan pointed to the top corner of the room. "Aha, I know what this is. We're inside an escape room, and we must find a key. I bet Taylor set us up!" He waved at the invisible camera. "Hello, Taylor, give us our first clue!"

"Do you really think Taylor trapped us in here? I mean, she was the one who led us here."

"Exactly!" Tancan yanked books off the shelves, searching for a hidden lever. "She's been very sneaky recently, I think she's hiding a secret from us.

"Be careful! Those books must belong to whoever lives here." Finn crouched, peeking through the keyhole. "Umm, Tancan... Taylor is in the kitchen. This isn't an escape room. We've locked ourselves into a random person's house!"

He lifted a plant pot. "There must be a hidden key somewhere."

"Tancan, are you listening to me?"

"Maybe there is a murderer at this party. Maybe it's me. Because I was the person who murdered our mum, wasn't I, Finn?"

"Please stop! Tancan *stop!* You're scaring me!"

"Hey, Finn, what's your favourite scary movie?" He chuckled. "I'm just messing with you; an alien wouldn't be the best horror villain now, would it? Don't worry, I am going to save you. We are going to get out of here together, alright?"

"Tancan, are you feeling okay?"

"I'm feeling great! I haven't slept for 2 days, and I've never felt so energised in my life! When we escape, I need to try some of that cherry punch everyone's drinking!"

"I'm going to call Stephen to take us home."

"He can't save you; only I can save you. I need to *save* you this time." He began bashing his head against the brick wall, tears bawling from his eyes. "I need to save you, please let me save you! I should've *saved* you, Finn!"

"Tancan, stop! You're going to hurt yourself!" Finn twisted the doorknob.

The door opened.

"Abracadabra!" Tancan burst out laughing, an exaggerated laugh that didn't belong to him. "Congratulations, you've escaped!"

"This isn't funny! The door was never jammed, was it?"

He beamed a massive smile, as if he wasn't just screaming into a brick wall. "Everyone always picks treat, so I thought we should pick trick to be different."

"You're so annoying! You almost gave me a panic attack. Can we please go home now? I'm not meant to be here. I'm not even a teenager yet, and Dad said we have to be home before nine."

"That was only quest one. Now, the next task is to find Taylor."

*

Bella-Joules rubbed her hand over Taylor's lower arm.

Taylor pushed her hand off her. "I don't feel comfortable with the *touchy* parts."

"Oh, ok. Sorry if I make you uncomfortable."

"No, you don't... I like it when you touch me. I'm just *sensitive* in certain areas."

"Woah... Kinky," mumbled Tancan as he bombarded the kitchen area. He frowned. "Finn's being a party pooper and said we have to go home now."

Taylor swayed slightly as she stood. "Alright, *'Tinky-Winky'*, bet you've never seen two girls kissing before, huh?"

She formed a phone shape with her hands. "Bye, my gorgeous wife, don't forget to call me."

***

Tancan and Finn returned home with empty buckets, only five lollipops between them, and a very drunk Taylor sucking one of them in her mouth.

Felix curled up on the couch with Stephen, both watching a horror movie, and Melissa's pumpkin spice candle lit on the coffee table in front of them.

Felix jumped up, pausing the TV. "Did you guys have a nice time?"

Taylor, still sucking the lollipop, blurted out, "You should've partied with us; I'm gonna be so hungover in the morning!"

His eyebrows shot up. "*Party?*"

"Some kids Taylor knew threw this Halloween party. Sorry I should've texted you," said Finn. "It was only Taylor who had alcohol."

Tancan nodded. "I'm totally not *stoned* right now."

"I really hope you're joking, Tancan," Felix said. "I'm glad you guys had fun. I used to go to lots of Halloween parties back in Oklahoma." He leaned his head over Tancan's bucket. "So, what did you bring home for me?"

"Sorry, someone stole all the lollipops," Finn said, eyeing Taylor. "Do you think I could have a private chat with you and Stephen?"

"Yeah, sure. Is something wrong, Finn?"

He took them both into the kitchen. "Tancan didn't seem like himself today. He seemed overly energetic and told me he hadn't slept for two days. Then, he got really upset because he wanted to 'save' me. It wasn't like him at all."

They both froze.

Felix clawed his left hand onto his head.

"Dad, what's wrong?"

"There is something that I have kept from you and Tancan. Shortly after I married your mom, she got diagnosed with bipolar disorder. Tancan's new therapist told me it is possible he could've inherited it from her, but he wasn't certain. What you just described to me sounded like a manic episode. Your mother had a hypomanic episode just before she died."

35: Intruder

November 21st 2021 - 53 days before he destroyed himself.

Dear Star Diary,

Ever since Halloween, Taylor has kept disappearing. She tells me she's been going to the skatepark with Bella-Joules, and I believe her, but I doubt that's the only place she goes. She recently joined Bella-Joules' band, which are mainly boys, and practices with them a lot, staying far too late into the night to beat drums.

It didn't bother me too much to begin with, but then it became constant. Walking into my bedroom at whatever time she'd like. She suffers from insomnia most nights and tells me it's awkward staying awake whilst I'm fast asleep.

I messaged Bella-Joules asking why Taylor doesn't sleep over at her house instead of walking home alone in the middle of the night, but she told me Taylor walks home every day at 7:30. Something seemed off.

One night, I attempted to stay awake as long as possible, like I was waiting to catch Santa Claus delivering presents. At around three in the morning, I heard rattling, like a drawer was being shaken. I peeked my head out of my room, and my dad's door was open. He had never slept with the door open. Dad's loud snoring muted the rattling, but I still felt the motion.

There was someone else in his room.

Stephen had gone back to his place that night, so it wasn't him. They had their hood up, rummaging through Mum's vanity. My first thought was that we were being robbed, but I had to keep a low profile. I crept back into my room, picking up anything I could use as a weapon. I didn't want to hurt them, whoever they were, but I had to protect my family.

Dad's wallet always sat on top of his bedside table; they didn't seem to care. It was only the jewellery they wanted. They reached for her pendant, her favourite pendant. Now that I think about it, the necklace Taylor had on Halloween belonged to my mother. But this wasn't Taylor; she wasn't this tall, and her shoulders weren't broad at all. This was a man. Much younger than Dad and Stephen, but older than me.

My phone, which had charge for once, trembled in my hands. I had to call someone, anyone but the police. Whenever I felt scared, I would always go knock on Dad's door, but this guy was standing right over his face. What was I meant to do?

As I powered on my phone, the light shone out of my room and into the dark hallway. Then chimed the loudest ping like it was trying to get me killed. I threw it onto my bed. He must've heard me since he twisted his head around like an owl. I saw his eyes; nothing else.

In the morning, it still stung in my head. There was no way I could tell Dad what I saw, but I had no choice. That man could've walked into Finn or Sapphire's room. I told him everything, and I really thought he would believe me this time since it was too serious to lie about. I was wrong, of course.

"Tancan, I'm going to call the therapist," he said.

"What!" I exclaimed. "No, dad you have to listen to me. There was somebody in your room last night."

He placed his hand on the side of my shoulder. "Honey, you're not very well."

"The therapist is useless! He never tells me anything I want to hear, and whenever I try explaining things to him, he cuts me off, like whatever bullshit he has to say is more important."

"He's a lot more professional than your previous psychiatrist."

"I don't like him. He's mean. I want my old therapist back!"

"Calm down, you're scaring Sapphire."

"Please, listen to me! He stole Mum's green pendant!"

Dad checked her jewellery box; it was still there — untouched.

Was I really going crazy? Is anything I see real anymore?

When Stephen arrived, I told him everything that I told Dad. Someone had to believe me.

He placed his palm on my forehead and asked me if I was feeling hot.

"No." I shook my head, even though I was. "Can you and Dad just stop treating me like a psychiatric patient? You're meant to be the good one!" Words kept shooting out of my mouth, and it was like I had lost all control of my voice. "I always thought you loved me. I always thought you cared. You knew my dad was an alcoholic, and you did *nothing*. You have done nothing except lick my dad's face off!"

"Stop it!" he shouted. I can't believe Stephen yelled at me. He has never yelled at me. He used to love me. I made him crack. Something really was wrong with me.

Being honest, my head is getting worse, at least I think it is. Dad and Stephen told me to tell them when I feel upset, but then when I do, they tell me to stop overreacting, like I can control my emotions.

It's not like I can tell Finn either; I don't want to overload his young mind with my dark thoughts.

Taylor's hardly here anyway, so how is she meant to help? At least she's started to actually smile after getting all cutesy with Bella-Joules.

I might as well divert my thoughts into Fantasyland. I am getting to the point where I speak to the villagers more than my family.

I've spent the first fifteen years of my life wishing my dad could cradle me in his arms forever. Maybe I don't want that after all? I don't want him controlling me, telling me I'm too vulnerable to do things I know I'm capable of doing.

I want to go far, where he can't reach me, but I still want him to see me. I could zoom across space, soaring past radiant stars, and he could still see me through a telescope.

I need to climb out of my shell before it cracks even more.

— Love your favourite space nerd, Tancan :)

36: Wonderful Winter

December 14th 2021 - one month before he destroyed himself.

Taylor and Bella-Joules held hands as they walked through scenes straight out of the North Pole, with Tancan tagging along as the 'third wheel.'

By the entrance stood an ice-skating rink. Tancan had never skated before and never wanted to, but seeing how excited the girls were, he agreed to try it.

"You're taking too long," stated Taylor. "We're heading onto the ice, find us, just don't fall and die."

He nodded. Strapping his feet into the skates felt like squeezing into high heels and balancing on a tightrope at the same time.

He took a few shuffles, clinging to the railing for dear life as he watched the girls glide avidly into the mob of strangers whooshing past him. His gloves latched onto the railing tightly. "I need to get off," he murmured, as if the anxiety on his shoulder spoke for him.

*

He wandered through the smell of deep-frying doughnuts; everything was so magical. A unicorn backpack glistened brighter than the sizzling hot dogs. Stephen had it thrown over his shoulder, waiting in the hot chocolate line. Sapphire must have abandoned him with it.

Unaware that he was about to walk into a lamppost, Tancan's eyes fixed on the tallest ride in the park. He tapped Stephen on the shoulder. "Let's ride that!" he said, pointing almost to the sky.

Stephen scoffed, glancing up at the towering structure. "Nope, not in a million years." He shook his head. "Your dad was quite a daredevil back in the '90s. You could ask him?" he passed him a disposable cup. "Could you give this to Sapphire, please? Take the lid off and let it cool down before you give it to her—don't want her to burn her little mouth, do we?"

The steam curled through the small opening as he removed the lid. His mother's face skimmed up at him. Her features reflected in the piping liquid, as if someone had used a stencil to outline her head. He grabbed a wooden stirrer and swivelled it through the broth, corrupting her eyes, but her ashes still anchored to the bottom.

Finn, determined to win the most gigantic, cheaply made Axolotl, threw three balls and missed every can. But when Sapphire had a go, she took them all out in one shot!

Still shaken up, Tancan placed the cup on the wooden bench, eyes flicking towards his cheering dad. The sight made his chest tighten, warping an extra rubber band around his heart. *Why doesn't he ever look at me like that anymore?*

"Tancan!" Felix said, muffled by the half-eaten doughnut in his mouth. "I told you to stay close to Taylor. You can't wander around by yourself in a place like this."

"I don't know where she went."

Stephen took Sapphire on the carousel.

"Hey Dad," asked Tancan, holding Sapphire's axolotl. "Can you come on a ride with me?"

He raised an eyebrow, giving a thumbs-up whilst licking sugar from his fingers. "Alright, let's wait for these guys to get off first."

Finn trailed behind them, holding a penguin under his arms, half the size of Sapphire's prize. "Can I come on the ride too?" he asked.

"Sorry, I think it only has two seats," replied Tancan, "but I can go on with you after!"

"Don't worry." He gripped his penguin tighter, looking towards the floor. "I'll take Sapphire into the funhouse instead."

*

"You sure you want to do this, Tanks?" Felix asked, handing tokens into the booth.

He didn't reply. The ride looked like a rocket ship, and that was enough to seal his decision.

"This doesn't go upside down, does it?"

He smirked, holding a chuckle behind his teeth. It was too late to back away; they were already harnessed in.

"Tancan! You little—"

The ride rotated its mechanical arm, reeling like a propeller. Tancan pictured himself inside a space shuttle. The world blurred past. He was flying.

After about five loops around the solar system, he stopped at the top. Only a ball pit of festive lights beneath him.

Felix tightened his arms around his harness. "We're stuck!" he shrieked, scrunching his face.

"Dad, stop! You're going to shake it!"

Stephen shook his head, following them to the ride's exit gate. "You guys are both crazy."

"We survived!" said Tancan, hopping like a kangaroo and flapping his arms. "Dad was shitting himself at the top!"

"Woah, buddy, language!"

"Sorry!" He switched his attention to Felix, squeezing his waist. "Thanks, Dad!"

"Of course," he smiled, patting his back, "that ride was pretty rad!"

"'Rad?'" Taylor crept behind them. "Since when has your dad been a skater?" She grabbed Tancan's hand. "Bella–Joules is waiting for us at the Ferris wheel, and we need someone to hold our bags whilst we use the photo booth."

"Oh, okay. " He glared at the Polaroid picture of him and Taylor strapped underneath his phone case. "Are we going on the Ferris Wheel after?"

"We've already been on. I assumed you didn't like rides because of your anxieties and stuff."

"Oh... I thought we were going to spend time *together*."

"Bro, you're *not* my *girlfriend!* We aren't putting any labels on ourselves just yet, but I want to hang around with her, *alone*. Anyway, you're the one who ran off without us!"

"Yeah. Sorry."

"Anygay, since you *do* like rides, we were wondering if we could use your accessibility pass to skip the line for one of the coasters?"

"So first you use me as a bag holder, now you want to use me to jump the queues?" He teased, even though he knew exactly what she was doing. He wasn't as dumb as she thought he was.

"Yes, exactly!" she smiled. "I couldn't have worded it any better myself."

Dizziness clamped Tancan's head. The muffled chatter of crowds chuffed past him like a steam train. "Wait, Taylor, can we—"

She had already disappeared into the sea of bobble hats.

Bella-Joules stayed near the photo booth, tying her laces. "Tancan, are you alright?"

"Is it okay if I sit down for a minute?" he muttered, out of breath.

"Yeah, of course."

He sank onto a nearby bench, exhaling. "Sorry, I don't know if you already know this, but I'm autistic. I just get a bit overwhelmed in places like this."

"Don't worry." She smiled. "There's no need to apologise. My cousin is autistic too, but she's completely non-verbal."

He looked up at her, almost forcing eye contact. "Do you think you could do a favour for me?"

"Yeah, sure."

"Please look after Taylor. Make her feel... *loved* for once. She deserves it."

She placed a hand over her heart. "I *promise*."

**

"Hey, Felix?" Taylor said as they approached the exit gate.

"Yeah?"

"Is it okay if I go home with Bella-Joules?"

"Sure." He nodded. "I bet Tancan would love some privacy."

Tancan chased after her. "Taylor, wait!"

"What's wrong?"

"I have been wanting to talk to you about something."

"I'm too tired right now," she zipped up her coat. "I'll be back home tomorrow—tell me then."

"Dad, stop!" cried Finn. "Why are we leaving? The fireworks haven't started yet!"

Felix slipped off his gloves. "You know how your brother gets all triggered by the loud bangs they make. I don't want to 'set him off.'"

"Oh yeah, I forgot." He brushed past Tancan, whispering, "You ruin *everything*."

37: Wishlist

December 23rd 2021 - 3 weeks before he destroyed himself.

Dear Star Diary,

Finn's right. I do ruin everything. It's almost Christmas and I don't feel very festive. Each year I get reminded that I am approaching my final few childhood Christmases and each one is staring to be more of a chore. I have to practising socialising and masking reactions to literally everything.

It doesn't make sense that last Christmas was an entire year ago. I can remember it so vividly, like it was only a few months ago. That also means I first met Taylor nine months ago, which is weird since it feels like I have known her my entire life.

Anyway, guess what? Taylor lied. Maybe I don't know her as much as I thought I did. She didn't come home the day after the winter fair, and she hasn't come home once. She's spent every day with Bella-Joules and forgotten that

I even exist. I get she has a girlfriend now, but I wish she stopped ghosting me.

Yesterday, I got forced to go last-minute Christmas shopping, and Dad told me to take Sapphire to look at the decorations so he could shop freely without her wanting to buy every toy she picked up.

At the end of the aisle, Taylor and Bella-Joules were stood wearing tinsel around their necks like scarves. My sensory issues could never.

Taylor ran over to me, calling my name like she was actually excited to see me for once. She picked up this elf hat and said, "Would I be a sexy elf?"

"Yeah," I said, trying the hat on myself, "but not as hot as me."

"Wow," she scoffed, placing it back on the shelf. "If only I could dress like a witch every day." It was perfect. She had brought the topic up herself, so I finally had the opportunity to ask her about the one thing I had been seeking answers for.

I took her into an empty aisle, which was hard because it was literally Christmas in a few days, and the entire shop was packed. "Talking about the witch outfit," I said. "Do you remember the silver necklace you had in your pocket?"

"Yeah..." It was like her eyes popped out of her head.

"I think it belonged to my mum. Where did you find it?"

"Oh, yeah, it did. I saw it on the counter, and your dad said I could borrow it for my costume, as long as I put it back straight after."

I knew she was lying. She was talking way too fast, and it always stayed in the jewellery box. Someone must've moved it. Even if they did, Dad wouldn't have let her casually borrow the pendant necklace, marked with their wedding date. It wasn't a prop. Mum wore on the day that she died. "Why weren't you wearing it then?" I asked.

"I didn't want you to see it; I knew you probably would've reacted like this."

"Like *what*?"

"The voice you always use whenever you aren't in control of every little thing."

I had no idea what she was talking about. All I knew was that she was hiding something from me, but I wanted to get the stress of Christmas out of the way first.

"I wanted to ask you something too," she said. "Can you ask your dad if it is okay if I spend Christmas at your house since Bella-Joules is having relatives round and they don't know she's out yet?"

"Yeah, sure. Anyway, I have to go before Sapphire starts begging me for the six-foot inflatable Rudolph over there. I'll see you on Christmas Eve."

Taylor didn't seem as jolly as Bella-Joules was. Probably because she escaped her childhood before she let herself grow up.

I know I have a few years left of my childhood, but after every interaction, everyone always looks at me like I am a weirdo. I don't look like an innocent seven-year-old anymore, and I'm only going to get older. This will technically be my sixteenth Christmas, and I still can't walk past a toy store without getting excited. Toys were designed for kids, not for whatever I am.

There is nothing worse than trying to find your dad in a supermarket three days before Christmas. There were people down every aisle, and people are scary. I couldn't physically force myself down an aisle with over two people blocking the pathway; it was literally impossible.

It was ironic that I found Dad in the alcohol section, talking to someone he went to school with a hundred years ago.

"Ah," he said. "These are two of my kids."

They had been talking for fifty years, and I could already feel grey hairs poking through my scalp. Me and sapphire stood like awkward statues the entire time, and I was about to smash a bottle of wine over Dad's head.

Once the conversation stopped, I asked Dad if he had let Taylor borrow Mum's necklace on Halloween and he said, "Yeah, but she gave it back to me straight after."

I couldn't believe it. Taylor was telling the truth. He actually did. I couldn't react because we were in public, and I didn't want the entire shop thinking I was one of those kids throwing a tantrum over a lollipop. I peeked into Dad's trolley and stared at Sapphire's unicorn stocking fillers. If only I could be her. She's young, not autistic, and still feels the Christmas spirit. Living my dream.

I can already imagine Sapphire's face on Christmas morning, unboxing all her new toys and Dad will get me and Finn something more '*age appropriate.*' Don't get me wrong, I appreciate how thoughtful his gifts are, and at least he always tries to get me something space-related. I much prefer that to a unicorn slime kit, but it's not the actual present I care about; it's the joy.

I would much rather receive a piece of scrap paper with a hand-drawn alien on it than get a pair of branded trainers, and that's why many people don't understand me.

It's usually just me, Dad, Finn and Sapphire on Christmas day. Then, Stephen will arrive with a giant sack of presents. All of Dad's side of the family live in America and Mum cut off contact with her parents before I was born, so I've never got to experience the joy of grandparents either.

Last year, one of our neighbours died just before Christmas, and without telling me, my dad invited the neighbour's wife round for dinner. The first thing she did was approach me.

"Wow," she said. "Look how big you've grown. I remember when your mummy and daddy brought you home from the hospital." She spoke to me as if I were still a baby. I assume Dad already told her I was autistic.

I had no idea who this woman was, and suddenly she handed me this present, and told me the receipt was in the bag, and I could return it if I didn't like it.

I unwrapped an awful texture, the complete opposite of the soft polyester hoodies I always wore. On the back, the text read:

'I don't believe in aliens.'

I was about to scream, but I managed to mumble, "Thank you," before I did.

Later that night, I came downstairs and told Dad I wanted to return it, because I would not wear a tight, uncomfortable hoodie that says a complete lie on the back. It might just as well say:

'I am not autistic,' *or* ***'I am attracted to women.'***

He gave me *the look*, "Tancan, you're being ungrateful." I remember grring in his face and stomping upstairs. How was I being rude? She said I could return it. Humans are confusing creatures.

Mum would've understood that I wasn't trying to be ungrateful. Dad turned into the *Grinch* after she died. We used to go to church every Christmas morning, but now he refuses to go because it doesn't seem right without her.

— Love your favourite space nerd, Tancan :)

38: Merrily Mystery

December 25th 2021 - 19 days before he destroyed himself.

Tancan stayed up all night monitoring the Santa tracker on his phone. The screen showed him soaring over Paris. He couldn't fall asleep. He had to catch him.

A strange sound thumped on the roof, followed by bells jingling downstairs. He jumped upright as a tsunami of paranoia gripped his neck. What if the 'jewellery catcher' is back again?

He crept out of bed and tiptoed down the stairs, each step creaking his life away. He slowly pushed the door open. Apart from Taylor snoring on the sofa, the living room was empty and the Christmas tree still bare.

***

Sapphire dangled over Tancan's head, yelling, "Wake up! He's been!"

Taylor sat up on the couch. Three enormous sacks circled her, each embroidered with a child's name. In the corner, a slightly smaller pile had been set aside for her.

Unlike on his birthday, Tancan didn't mind opening Christmas presents with his family. The attention wasn't directly on him. Still, he couldn't bear the camera constantly landing on him and the crinkling sound of wrapping paper being shoved into a trash bag, but that was the least of his worries.

Felix handed Taylor her first present. "Here, this one's from us."

"Really? You shouldn't have."

"You've been family to us. It's the least we could do."

"Yeah," Stephen added. "You deserve this."

She leapt onto her feet before she could finish peeling the wrapper away. "No way! A new skateboard! Thank you so much, Dad—Felix!" she corrected.

Tancan's head shot around. *What did she just call him?*

Felix smiled. "You're welcome, sweetheart."

Sweetheart! Dad only calls me that! Tancan scrunched up a ball of wrapping paper, impulsively darting it at Taylor's head.

"What the heck, Tancan!" She exclaimed.

Felix hugged her, giving Tancan the same look as the previous year. It was always *his* fault.

Tears dripped down her cheek, not because she hurt, happy tears.

Felix ground his teeth. "Apologise to her right now!"

"Urgh!" Tancan groaned. "Leave me alone; it was just a soft bit of paper."

*

Stephen set a piping turkey in the centre of the table, next to a fresh bowl of pigs in blankets and roasted potatoes.

On the way to her seat, Taylor picked a Christmas cracker out of the empty Christmas tree box. She passed one side to Sapphire, counting, "Three... Two... One..."

Felix bolted across the room, "Stop!"

He was too late.

A sharp bang snapped through the air, followed by the whiff of gunpowder.

Tancan screamed across the entire dining room, clutching onto Finn's chair so tightly that it almost tipped. He pressed his forehead against the table. Then got up, letting all the food on his plate freeze along with everyone's faces. Dinner was ruined.

Taylor wasn't that hungry either, at least that's what she said after only eating the carrots on her plate. She cut into her turkey, checking if it was properly cooked. It wasn't pink, but she still didn't trust it.

"Ho, ho, ho, my little hoe." Taylor sat beside Tancan on the settee. "I'm really sorry about that. You know I'd never try to trigger you on purpose."

He nodded. "It's okay."

"So... Are you going to tell me why you launched a ball of wrapping paper at my face?"

"You won't understand."

"Bro, cheer up, it's Christmas! This is like the first Christmas in years where I am not sick and on my period at the same time. You should've seen Stephen nearly trip over my bag whilst putting the presents down. It was hilarious."

He froze, muttering, "He's not real?" He barged back into the kitchen and slammed his hand on the dining table, almost spilling water out of the glasses. "You *lied* to me!"

"About what?" asked Stephen.

He eyed his dad, "He's not *real*, is he?"

Felix swallowed his last potato. "Look, Tanks, we were planning to tell you this year."

Tanks? Where did Sweetheart go? Did he give that role to Taylor too? "So, you've been lying to Finn and Sapphire, too?"

"Finn knows," he said.

"Who's not real?" asked Sapphire.

"Nobody," assured Finn.

"You've all been lying to me for fifteen years!" Tancan screamed, slamming his head onto the kitchen table. "Why did Finn find out before me? I don't need to be babied my entire life!"

Felix gently moved him away from the table, where Sapphire couldn't hear. "Sweetheart, it's just a tradition. All parents make up his existence to make Christmas seem magical for their kids."

"I don't get. Why does everyone keeps hiding things from me? Your secret romance with Stephen, Taylor's weird obsession with Mum, the random man who broke into the house, and I still don't know the truth behind Mum's death!" Tancan dropped his head over his dad's shoulder, squeezing him tight as he sobbed down his back.

"I know, baby, I know..."

"But how?" He sniffled. "How did you afford all of this?"

"Stephen has helped me save up for months. I was hoping I could give you a good Christmas this year."

"Thanks for trying," he said, "but I'll never have a good Christmas without Mum."

39: Boxed

December 26th 2021 - 18 days before he destroyed himself.

Dear Star Diary,

My family are a bunch of liars.

I thought having Taylor over at Christmas would be fun, but she's just an invisible wall, blocking me out of my own home. Maybe I should abandon this messy family and go find a new one. It's not like they have already found a replacement, or anything. I think my battery is dying. Too bad my type got discontinued.

This morning, when I wasn't tripping over Sapphire's new toys, I sat next to Stephen.

"Oh, no!" he joked, mocking my height. "Looks like one of the elves escaped the North Pole," knowing full well I am like two inches away from towering over him. It was like he died and respawned as a completely different person. Last year, he was Dad's best friend, but now he's kissing Dad under the mistletoe, and is apparently Father Christmas as well. As much as I hate it, I know he has always been a part of my home.

A few months after Mum died, Dad started refurbishing the entire house. When I say everything moved around, I mean everything. He went on a spree, shifting around all the furniture. He ruined my safe space. The house I grew up in became a random building where I lived. It began after he tried covering a hole in the wall with a bookshelf, the same wall he had punched himself.

The only thing he kept in place was the photo of Stephen hugging me at my christening. Framed on the windowsill by Stephen himself, cherishing that moment like a trophy, and it's made me realise I don't appreciate that man as much as I'm supposed to.

I shuffled closer to Stephen. "I want to know the truth."

"About what?" he asked.

"Everything. I need to know more about my parents because I'm tired of all these secrets being kept from me."

"I know they hid a lot of things from you, buddy." He rested his hand on my shoulder. "They only wanted to protect you. You're still a kid; you don't need to worry about this sort of stuff yet."

By the tone in his voice, I was certain that he was about to admit my parents were aliens. "What stuff?" I asked.

"Do you remember when I used to take you and Finn to the park every Saturday and we would sit on the log bench and eat ice cream together?"

"Yeah, it was my favourite day of the week. How come?"

"When your mom announced she was pregnant with you, I was thrilled to the moon. However, your dad didn't react well at all. They argued for a while. He wanted nothing to do with you; he wasn't ready to be a dad, but she couldn't let you go."

"He wanted Mum to abort me? He had no right! It was her body; only she had control."

"You're right, buddy, she did. She wanted you. After you were born, your dad fell in love with your precious face and made him realize how much he loved you. As much as they both loved you, it was hard for them accept they were parents.

Your dad started heavily drinking shortly after she revealed she was pregnant with Finn. He only put his bottle down when he held you. Once Finn was born, your mom fell into this deep depression and started taking medication, but it wasn't enough for her; she needed more."

"Drugs? She wasn't an addict. She was the most religious woman I knew. You're making this up!"

"She wasn't very well, Tancan. You were too young to see what was happening. When her body was found, there were traces of heroin injected into her blood. I wanted to wait until you were older, but I think you're mature enough to understand.

Do you remember when your mum had to be hospitalised for her severe allergy? Me and you dad made that story up to cover the truth. Tancan, she wasn't allergic to nuts, she relapsed. How do you think we were meant to explain that to her children?"

Was he telling me she had killed herself? So, Dad was lying about her being murdered? I didn't understand. And if I didn't shoot her, which of us was lying? "Wait, how did she die then?" I asked.

"I don't know. Nobody knows."

All those words poured out of his mouth, and none of them sounded true, but I trusted him more than Dad.

"You were so young, I couldn't let you see how much pressure they were under. I've always wanted to be there for you and your siblings; I couldn't let you guys live like that. I *love* you so much, Tancan," he said, holding my hand. "I *love* your dad too; that's why I wanted to help him before it's too late. Just think, in a few months' time you can say that your dad has been sober for an entire year."

"But what if whatever happened to Mum will happen to him too?"

"I won't let that happen, I promise." He squeezed my hand tighter. "But if it did, I promise I'll always be here for you."

I hugged him and said, "Thank you for stepping into my life." I've always wanted to say that to him, but I never knew how to word it.

Before he could tell me anymore, Dad walked in. There were emotions splattered over his face, ones that I couldn't understand. He slid his phone into his pocket as if he had just ended a phone call and took Stephen into the freezing garden for a private conversation. It was weird. The kitchen's usually their private chat spot. Something was wrong.

I ran upstairs and carefully opened my bedroom window. I briefly heard Dad say something about me not being ready for something, then Stephen saying that it might be a good idea. Dad then whispered something about getting Christmas out of the way first. I had no clue what they were on about, but it didn't sound good.

— *Love your favourite space nerd, Tancan :)*

40: Girlhood

January 2nd 2022 - 11 days before he destroyed himself.

Dear Star Diary,

I cannot believe it is already 2022; it feels so strange. I am excited to see what new opportunities the new year brings but am truly horrified to turn sixteen in two months. I haven't made much progress since fourteen, and I want it all to stop. My legs are getting hairy. Ew. It is terrifying. I don't want to turn into a man unless my skin is as flawless as Stephen's. He never seems to age as fast as Dad does.

Talking of Stephen, him and Dad have been invading me most of the week. As much as I love them, it's frustrating when they knock on my door every ten minutes and ask if I'm feeling okay. They have been acting so abnormally lately, and some nights they will smother my forehead with kisses like I am their new kitten.

Am I dying or something?

This morning, Taylor went back to her place to drop off Sean's late Christmas card. I told her not to bother, as he didn't deserve a single letter she wrote to him, but she went anyway.

Twenty minutes later, she ran back to the house, frantically pounding on the door. It took me a while to answer since I was home alone and thought someone was trying to arrest me. Once I let her in, she grasped me and balanced her head on my shoulder. The hug was tight and very overwhelming, but I held on to her because she needed it.

"You were right," she sobbed. "I'm so dumb for going back!"

"No, you're not." I gently rested her head on a fluffy pillow and placed one of my alien plushies in her arms. "What happened?"

"Sean slapped me." She rolled her head to the side, holding her right cheek. "I wish you were my brother instead of that prick."

She started expressing some of her anxieties with me. She then paused, looking at my blank, zoned out face. "Are you even listening to me?" she spat. "Because it doesn't look like you are. People always say they care until they hear the voice of an emotionally unstable teenage girl, I'm so sick of it!"

I was listening to her; that's the truth. I could feel her voice rooted so deeply in my soul, but I couldn't react because my brain was trying to process every single sentence. Everything she said mattered so much, she just didn't realize that yet.

"Taylor," I said. "I love having you in my family, but I don't want you seeing my dad and Stephen as 'father-figures', it's hard enough sharing them with Finn and Sapphire." Why the hell did I say that! I was so dumb. Thinking of that moment is making me cringe.

She smiled and nodded.

I still felt like I had offended her in some way. I didn't mean to; I just didn't want to lie to her like my family had. "I care about you a lot, Taylor. I know it might sound corny or whatever, but it's the truth, and I'm so grateful for having the blessing of you in my life."

"Stop," she said, "you're going to make me cry."

"It's okay," I said. "You've already seen me cry plenty times before."

She went quiet for a while.

"Are you hungry?" I asked, trying to comfort her, but I think I said the wrong thing again.

"Of course I am!" she spat. "I'm starving. I am always starving, but I can't eat..."

"Why are you stopping yourself then?"

"Sean told me I had to stay beautiful, or nobody would like me. I must go to the toilet before I eat, to flush all the toxic crap out of me, and I still feel intoxicated. If I eat more than once a day, my body will feel so bloated that I will force myself to throw up.

"And then I will see girls, these gorgeous girls, who can start eating without washing their hands and still maintain the perfect weight, and it drives me insane.

"I used to try everything to fit in with the girls at school. I started wearing makeup, even though I could feel the awful texture clinging to my skin every time I opened my mouth. I hung around with multiple friend groups, and I always felt like the odd one out. Then, one day I just broke. I tried finding my own style and did the hobbies that I actually enjoyed because I didn't care what anyone had to say anymore.

"Even if my school life improved, I knew home would forever stay the same.

Some nights I would sit on the edge of my bed and just down a bottle of vodka. I knew I was harming myself, but it didn't make me overthink that some man in a van would pull over on the side of the road and grab me when I am pondering alone at night. I can't even tie my hair without a man watching me, and I'm sorry I'm ranting to you right now; I just can't deal with this anymore!"

That bastard. I had never felt that type of anger before, almost as if I could punch that man in the face. "Don't worry, Sean doesn't know you are here; you're safe."

"You don't understand; it's not just him; it's men in general. Even when Sean isn't near me, I still feel this parasite on my shoulder, constantly whispering into my ear and telling me all these terrible things will happen. You're like the only male I feel safe with."

I didn't know what to say. I brushed her hair out of her eyes and told her she is just as beautiful as all the other girls, but she must eat if she wants to remain healthy. Because at the end of the day she had a kind soul, and that's all that mattered.

She clung to my arm, stroking my baby hairs like the way I used to cling to Dad's arm. The sensation felt awful, but I was willing to go through anything to keep her regulated.

"Do you remember your parents much?" I asked.

"My dad was as evil man." She held on to her wrist. "Years ago, he was involved in a hit- and-run. She was a woman in her early 40s. She didn't survive. It took an entire month for him to be identified, even when he had already spent years abusing our family. He hated my mum and Sean but loved me. He used to call me 'cakepop' as a nickname, and I'm pretty sure that's why I broke down at your sister's birthday.

"Once he was arrested, Mum found a new partner and moved as far away as she could. We got put into foster homes, and then Sean started hanging out with gangs and got kicked out of every home. Once he turned eighteen, he stole me from my placement and made us live in an abandoned flat where his old druggie friend had lived before he had overdosed. That's when Sean started getting angry easily. I guess he had always had a bit of his dad in his heart."

"Do you know in what year your dad got arrested?" I asked.

"It was like 2014 because it was a few months before my eighth birthday."

I felt a shiver run up my spine. It was too much information to take in at once. Both Dad and Stephen's stories finally pieced together. Did Taylor's dad kill my mum too? But still nothing made sense. She told me her dad had been in prison since 2014, and Mum died in 2016. It couldn't have been him. Then who was it?

— Love your favourite space nerd, Tancan :)

41: Betrayed

January 9th 2022 - 4 days before he destroyed himself.

"WAKE UP!" Felix called into Tancan's room.

"I'm awake," Tancan moaned, half asleep.

"Don't worry, you're not going back to school today, but I need you to pack your bag with a few essentials."

Tancan shot out of bed and headed downstairs. Finn and Taylor were both in their school uniforms. He asked them if they knew what was happening, but they both shrugged. Surprises made his head buzz with stress, but this time was different. He was finally getting one-on-one time with his dad.

**

Tancan fastened his seatbelt. "It's been so long since it was just you and me," he said, voice bubbling with excitement. "Can you at least give me one hint of where we're going?"

Felix remained silent, eyes fixed on the road.

"Dad? Oh, I get it; you want me to guess. We must be going out of town—you told me to pack a bag, after all. Wait, stop! Are we going to Disneyland? I've seen videos like this online. You know how long I've waited to ride *Space Mountain!*"

The car slowed and pulled up outside the counselling building.

"Haha, nice try. I don't even have a session scheduled today." He leaned forward, trying to catch his dad's hidden smirk. He was good at this game. "Now can you tell me where we're going, or are you planning to ignore me the entire trip?"

Felix shuffled in his seat, gently placing his hand on top of Tancan's. "I love you, sweetheart."

"Dad?" His smile faltered. "Why are we here? What's going on?"

Without another word, Felix stepped out of the car and walked straight through the automatic doors.

*

"Hello again, Tancan," greeted the therapist. "Could you and your dad come with me into this room, please?"

He trailed behind his dad and clutched the back of his jumper, glancing towards the therapist's strut.

"Tancan," he began, "my team and I have been reviewing what you shared with me a few months ago. After much discussion, we've decided it would be best to section you for a little while."

Tancan drummed his fingers along the chair's armrest. "What does that mean?"

"It is where you get referred to stay at a special type of hospital."

"What? No!" He shot up in his seat and turned to Felix, panic flickering in his eyes. "Dad, you promised me he wouldn't hurt me!"

Felix's mouth was unreadable. He used only his hand to gesture him back into his seat.

"I don't understand! Maybe I have severe anxiety, or separation issues on top of my autism, but I don't need more therapy. I'll be okay!" His words tumbled out faster, rising with each sentence.

"We are aware of your diagnosis, but based on your most recent report, we believe you may be experiencing psychosis. However, we cannot diagnose you with anything else until you get assessed.

"The amount of detail you described to me about your mother's death is very alarming. We could be dealing with a handful of mental disorders." He softened his voice. "We want to monitor you only for a little while. That's all. If things go smoothly, you'll be back home before your sixteenth birthday."

Tancan blinked, shaking his head in disbelief. He rolled his eyes towards Felix. "You're not buying into all this crap, are you?"

Felix's face remained blank.

"You knew about this, didn't you? This is what you and Stephen were talking about on Boxing Day."

A heavy sigh escaped from Felix's chest.

"Do Taylor and Finn know?"

He shook his head. Still silent.

"To begin treatment, we'll need to confiscate any items that could pose a risk to your safety," the therapist instructed. "This includes any mobile devices or anything sharp like pins, jewellery or piercings."

"No," Tancan whispered, shrinking into himself. "I can't do this. I need to stay in my room. That's my safe space."

"I'm sorry, but there can be no negotiation. You'll need to follow the staff rules while you're there. Your father told us you prefer to stick to rules."

"No, not those rules!" he snapped. "*My* rules! The ones inside my head that I must follow or else I can't function properly. I've forced myself to follow the world's rules my entire life, and it's not fair!"

He reached out, grabbing Tancan's arm.

"DON'T TOUCH ME!" he screamed, jerking away. He dived onto the floor, wrapping his arms around his dad's legs. "Dad, please let me come home," he begged, burying his face into his knee. "I'll stop cutting myself. I'll do anything, I swear."

"Honey," said Felix, "you can't. You can't go home."

"Daddy, don't let me go! I'm your baby. They're going to hurt me. They're going to pump me full of meds and lock me in here forever!"

"Tancan, listen to me, we're only trying to help you."

"You're kidnapping me!" he spat. "Dad! Don't let them take me! You must save me!"

Felix's hands swallowed his face, tears streaming under his palms. "Look... My child is clearly distressed. I know this place could help him, but if he feels trapped in here, it's only going to cause more harm. I'll keep a close eye on him, and if the hallucinations get worse, I'll be the first to let you know."

"Mr. Milten, we strongly recommend keeping him—just for a month. If his condition escalates, it could lead to long-term dependence on medication. We are lucky we had the chance to intervene early."

Tancan glared at the wall behind him, plastered with fake posters. "What am I to you? A lab rat to experiment on? Is this some sort of episode of *Stranger Things?"* He turned to Felix, desperation etching the outline of his lips. "Dad... please. Get me out of here. I just want to go home."

He took a deep breath, placing his hand on Tancan's shoulder. "I've known my boy his entire life. If I force him to stay, he'll never trust me again. He'll never forgive me. I'm sorry, Doctor. He's not staying there." He grabbed Tancan's arm. "Don't worry, sweetheart, I've made a mistake."

Sweetheart meant nothing to him anymore. Still trembling, his fingers dug into his dad's coat as if letting go would mean disappearing.

"I'm going to prescribe Tancan with some lithium pills to stabilize his mood, but please stay alert for any changes in his diet."

*

Tancan curled up in the passenger seat, his sleeves pulled over his hands and eyes glued to the window. Outside, the weather was sharp, but his fingertips stung more inside the car, not knowing if he really was going home or dumped on the side of the road.

"I didn't want it to go like that," said Felix.

"Yeah, I know. You wanted them to take me away instead. I don't even care anymore. I'm sick of your shit. You're just a miserable man who drowns his feelings away. Stephen already told me all your dark secrets, you know? The way you behaved towards my mum and how you both became addicts before I even started school.

"And you think I'm the one who needs help?" he scoffed. "When will you take his tongue out of your mouth and tell me these things yourself? You're just a coward. Stephen's been a better dad than you've ever been. I'm sorry, but it's true. Going on a fair ride with me changed *nothing*. You were going to leave me there like I was broken."

"You're not broken, Tancan," his voice strained. "You're *hurting.* There's a difference. And you're right, sweetheart. I am a coward. I let your mom wander outside alone at night when I knew she wasn't stable."

"Did you murder her?"

"What?"

"I said, 'did you murder my mother?' You knew she was sick. You wanted to get rid of her, didn't you? Just how you tried to get rid of me. I'm not scared of you anymore, Dad."

"What has gotten into you lately, Tancan? You used to this kind, sensitive little boy, but ever since you've started hanging around with Taylor, you've had this sour attitude, and I'm not letting you carry on like this."

"Taylor hasn't done anything wrong; it's *you* that's the problem. You've made me feel like shit my entire life. I raised all your children because you just sat on your ass and drank beer all day. I'm disabled, and you've never wanted me, so I don't need some hairy ogre telling me to fix my attitude, *al-right?*" He opened the car door, exposing himself to the strong wind."

"Tancan, stop! Come back!"

He ran. He didn't look back. He was safer alone, and he knew his own way home.

***

Tancan bolted through the front door and dived onto the sofa, cuddling a pillow to his chest.

Stephen walked in, clattering his keys on the counter. "Tancan?"

"Oh, piss off, Stephen, I'm sick of your lies too. You must help me though. My dad wants to hurt me. Lock all the doors, quick!"

Tancan hid upstairs. The familiar space wrapped around him like a blanket. He sat on his bed, staring at his comfort items, but they weren't providing the comfort he needed.

He clasped his hands together, eyes shut. "Dear Lord, I don't understand why this happened today. I thought he *loved* me. I was getting better; I really was. *I haven't* had any hallucinations in weeks, and I've kind of separated from my fantasy world because I realised, I was separating myself from people like you. But anyway, I just wanted to thank you for always being there for me and believing in me, even though I have sinned more times this week than I have in my entire life. Please save me, God. Amen."

42: House Of Lies

January 12th 2022 - 24 hours before he destroyed himself.

Dear Star Diary,

I stopped taking my meds today. They made me feel weird. I feel fine, but I haven't told Dad because I know he'd probably freak out like he always does.

Sometimes I wish my eyes were cameras, recording everything I see. That way, I could edit out all the bad moments. Snip them away like nothing happened. I could change everything about myself, and nobody would notice. A brand-new life, one where I learn from my mistakes instead of them replaying in my head like a hamster wheel. But no matter how much I try to forget, I still see Dad's remorseless face, tormenting me like he wanted me trapped in that dungeon.

Dad and Stephen took Finn and Sapphire to the park, so Taylor and I had the house to ourselves today. "I have a new hyperfixation!" I announced.

"What is it?" She rolled her eyes. "Please don't tell me you're going to turn into one of those dinosaur-obsessed kids next."

"Well, I have started listening to true crime podcasts, and what if I investigate my mum's death myself? And if I finally find out how she died, then my dad will love me again!"

"Tancan—" she began, her voice much more serious than usual. "I need to tell you something, but you have to promise not to say a word to anyone. Especially not your dad."

I held out my pinkie. "I promise."

She sat on my bed, crossing her legs. "I know what happened to your mum."

"What?" I stepped back. "No, you don't. Nobody does."

She gripped her wrist. "I was *there*."

A lump rose in my throat, but I swallowed it. I didn't know what she meant, and part of me didn't want to hear any more.

"Look, I know it might seem like I'm lying," she said, "but I'm telling the truth. I've been keeping secrets from your family. I'm so sorry."

"What types of secrets?" I asked.

"The night before your tenth birthday, your mum showed up at my door. She'd been dealing with Sean for a couple of months. She asked him for a top-up, said she wanted to feel relaxed for your birthday. I don't remember anything after that.

"I only saw her step inside. Sean must've given her the wrong dose. I heard something crash in the kitchen, and when I got there... She was on the floor, still alive. Her chest was moving up and down, but Sean didn't check; he panicked and put on these yellow gloves and stuffed her into a black trash bag."

The lump in my throat reappeared. "So, you just stood there and watched?"

"Tancan, what was I supposed to do? I was a nine-year-old girl! He made me stay behind on lookout whilst he dumped the bag in some field."

I knew what field she was talking about.

"I assume she suffocated. When someone found her later that night, she was dead."

She could've lived. If he'd just left her alone, if someone had helped her, she might have been able to see the Mother's Day card I made her in year 6. Every word Taylor spat out was like a shovel, digging deep holes into the sandbox inside my mind, turning it into a pit I couldn't climb out of. I paced around my room. "We need to tell someone!"

"We can't! You don't know what Sean's capable of. He's dangerous." She unravelled the bandage around her arm, revealing what looked like a recording device. "Look."

"What is that?" I asked, leaning over her shoulder. This whole time she wasn't hiding scars; she was hiding whatever that was.

"I'm sorry, Tancan. I didn't want to record any conversation we've had. None of them, but I had to. If I hadn't, he would've hurt me."

Her bruises suddenly appeared much clearer.

"I know you've started becoming sceptical lately, and I hated hiding everything from you, but I couldn't risk both of us becoming his next victims. It started off last year when Sean paid Owen to pretend to date you."

"What? Owen was a part of the plan too?"

"The alley attack was just a hoax. None of it was real. Owen was never going to stab you, and I didn't break his arm either. Owen isn't the nicest of kids, but he never wanted to physically hurt you; it was Sean's idea. He only wanted to scare you enough to let me walk you home."

I stood there, frozen, trying to make sense of the mess unravelling like a fruit roll-up, but it was already stuck to the paper. She used me. The one person I thought might have understood me. I didn't know what to believe anymore. Dad probably paid her to be my friend, and I bet Noah never actually existed either.

"As each day passed, I realised what an amazing friend you truly are. You're funny, kind, and honestly, you're the only person in our class that had an actual personality."

She was making it about herself. It's never been about her. She's never had to put up with kids complaining every time she stepped foot in the classroom. "So you were just pretending to be my friend?" My voice cracked. "I thought you *liked* me?"

"I never lied to you, not about my feelings. I do care about you, and I love your family. This place feels safe. Safer from him. I never meant to hurt you, but Sean... He controls me. He's like my puppeteer. Most nights I snuck back to my place and uploaded the recordings to his laptop, but there were times when I forgot to hold the button down." She looked at the bruise on her arm. "And he would hear me talk about him."

My head was dizzy from the number of times I had paced. "I don't get it. Why did he even send you here? Mum died almost six years ago."

"He wanted me to search for anything that could tie him to your mum. Anything that would make him look guilty if any of this slipped out. I've been trying to find the necklace she was wearing when she died. The one with his fingerprint still marked on the chain."

"I... I saw someone in the middle of the night, rummaging through Mum's vanity."

"That was Sean," she admitted. "I let him in. He didn't believe I had searched enough."

Heat flushed into my forehead. "Are you insane? We let you into our home. We trusted you. Fed you, gave you gifts, a place to sleep, and this is how you repay us? Letting your psycho brother spy on my entire family?" I almost bashed my head against my wall but didn't. "You know how dangerous he is, and my little six-year-old sister lives here. S-I-X! If he had placed one hand on her, I would've ripped his head off!"

"Tancan," she stood against my door. "I meant what I said. I would never want Sapphire to get hurt; you know I would never have let that happen."

"My dad thought I was going mad, thinking I was seeing people break into our home. He tried locking me in a hospital, alone! And it was real! It was *all* real!"

"I'm sorry, okay? I didn't want any of this to go that far, but I still think you are emotionally unstable and maybe you do actually have the same disorder your mum had."

"Get out."

"Huh?"

"I said, get the *fuck* out of my room!" I shouted. I didn't mean to. Maybe I overreacted too much. I never shout at people. Maybe I was turning into my dad after all.

"I need space. Time to think, but before you go anywhere else, I want you to get the hammer from my dad's toolbox and crush that thing into bits," I commanded. "Then you're going to lock every single door once they get home from the park. You understand? And then we're calling the police. I'm not letting you go back to that *monster*."

"We can't call the police!"

"Why not?"

"If we do, he'll know I told. And if he finds a way in, your whole family could be in danger."

My chest tightened. Taylor, Sean, Owen, and my own parents trapped me in a house of lies. If only I had found the secret passageways sooner. I dropped my head onto a pillow. My room was spinning. Nothing was processing.

Taylor then sat next to me and pulled another device from her sock. "Here, he doesn't know I recorded this one."

I removed the usb stick and plugged it into my laptop, covered in space stickers, of course. I pressed play on the recording. It was Taylor and Sean arguing.

"Tell me the truth, Sean," Taylor's voice spoke. "I found an old news article in the Milten's house. Melissa's body was found covered in bruises. She wasn't bruised before you stuffed her into the bag."

"She woke up," he said. "She was screaming inside the bag, trying to claw her way out, so I kicked her in the rib. She then started whimpering like an animal, so I stomped on her head until she stopped."

"You're a monster. You could've let her go."

"Why would I do that? She would've told on me. Told people what I did to her, and that would've just exposed her other secrets, wouldn't it? If any of them ever, I mean *ever*, finds out about this, you are dead meat, Taylor Maxxie."

"Don't you carry any remorse in your body?"

"Shut your mouth! I did this for your sake. I lied so I could give you a place to live because nobody would want you in their home. Nobody would ever want you near them."

"Tancan did. He cared for me more than you ever could. I know this because you raised me and thank God I am nothing like *you*."

I pressed pause before the argument escalated. A sharp pain spiked my chest. "Taylor?" I asked. "What secrets is Sean talking about?"

She looked down as she spoke. "I think it's best if you find it yourself."

I felt something die inside of me after I heard the recording. I wanted to scream, shout and cry at the same time, but no emotions released.

Right now, I am still glued to my bed, trying to process everything I discovered today. Maybe I am dreaming. Maybe if I sleep, all this will disappear.

— Love your favourite space nerd, Tancan :)

43: The Idea

January 13th 2022 - the day he destroyed himself.

Tancan handed Taylor a fresh can of Monster. "Are you going to tell my dad you saw his wife get killed?"

"Shush! He's upstairs," she hissed. " You've seen how he reacts to things. I don't know if I ever will."

He shifted closer, whispering, "If you don't tell him, he'll end up finding out eventually, or worse, he might force me to drink your monster."

"Bro, shut up! You don't even like energy drinks."

"I just want to feel something. Anything. I crave the feeling you get when you drink, and now I'm ready. You and Bella-Joules always seem so happy when you're drunk. Maybe it'll make my fantasies feel real for once."

"No." She shook her head. "That's a terrible idea. It doesn't work the same for everyone. Look at your dad; he's an angry drunk."

"I read online it can make burnouts worse, but I need to escape this house. I'm trapped."

"There's this place I know, and the owner is one of Sean's dealers and sometimes lets me have a few free shots. I already broke the tracker. If we sneak out later, Sean and your dad won't know where we are."

"I mean, you owe me for lying to my face for almost a year. You really think going will be good for me?"

"Nope. Not at all. Everything you hate is there: loud music, overstimulating lights and drunk guys arguing over sports."

"Come on, I know my limits. I've spent fifteen years masking inside of this messed-up world, where everything keeps getting banned rather than fixed. I just want one night where I'm free."

"We should at least tell your dad where we're heading first, just in case something happens."

"Since when have you been the responsible one? No way am I talking to him or his little side chick, let's just go." He scattered through his wardrobe, pulling out the tightest, itchiest clothes he could find. Anything that would push him out of his comfort zone.

Finn poked his head into the room, raising his eyebrows. "Since when do you wear skinny jeans? You're so gay." .

Tancan ignored him, staring into the mirror. The reflection staring back didn't look like himself at all, as if he had switched bodies with an alien.

Before they left the house, Taylor asked, "Have you taken your pills today?"

"Yeah," he lied.

“Good. You sure you still want to do this?"

"Yes. I want to feel alive again!"

***

The club pulsed with chaotic fish, rippling through waves of pulsing beats.

Taylor snatched a tray of shots. "Here, try some!"

He looked down, dipping just the tip of his tongue into the glass. It burned. He recoiled, scraping his tongue with a napkin. "That tasted like bleach! How do people drink this?"

"I've gotten used to it over time," she said. “I’m going to the toilet. Don’t move.”

The disco lights tattooed across Tancan's face. Taylor was right; there were too many strangers. Everything was hurting more than it already did. Two minutes passed, then five. By fifteen, panic had bloomed across his chest. *Did she get lost? Did she leave? Did Sean find her?* He scanned the crowd again; the disoriented faces blurred together like some sort of fever dream.

He squeezed through the mosh pit, wandering into a deserted area of the club. The noise muffled behind the silent stairwell. As he looked around, a man roughly in his mid-thirties stopped half-way downstairs, passing a polite smile.

"Hey," the man greeted.

Tancan took a step back. "Hey... Sorry, I need to, uh, find my friend."

The man patted the side of his shoulder, an unlit cigarette between his index fingers. "No, stay here, lad."

"My friend went to the toilet, but I can't find her anywhere. She will worry if I don't go back."

His smirk widened. "I know where she is."

"Y-You do?"

"Yes, follow me."

The man led him further down the dimly lit, flickering hallway. The thumping music had now vanished. Every fire exit was the same, and none directed him outside.

"Excuse me, I don't think she's this way..."

The man stopped in the middle of the hallway, turning his head slowly. His smile hinged, looking behind. "So, what are you and your friend doing here tonight?" he asked.

"I—I wanted to escape and try new things like a lot of other kids my age. I know it's dumb. I wanted to feel better about myself, and being here makes me feel completely out of my comfort zone." He shifted back. "But back home, my family never wants to listen to me anymore."

His face softened, but his grin remained. "You can talk to me if you want; I'd love to listen."

"Thank you, but I think I should go back to see if my friend returned," Tancan muttered. The words had barely left his mouth before his thoughts went blank. The power switched off. He tried reaching his inner light switch, but the fuse was gone too. Tancan never destroyed himself; somebody had destroyed him.

44: Barriers

January 14th 2022 - 10 hours after being destroyed.

Dear Star Diary,

When I opened my eyes, I was home, sitting in my living room, surrounded by Dad, Stephen and a police officer. She had found me running down the street last night, but I didn't remember leaving the building.

After Dad saw the shattered look in my eyes, he reached out for a hug, but I pushed away. His fingernails were like razors, not the hands I knew. I felt fuzzy, but I've never felt this type of fuzzy before. Everything I looked at made me nauseous. Even right now, this diary is making something gurgle in my throat every time I press the pen down.

The police officer asked me some questions. I tried remembering some things, but nothing flowed. It didn't help that the entire time Dad was glancing at me like I was making up fake stories. After Taylor vanished, I didn't remember anything. I could only recall a man talking to me.

She asked for a description of him, but I had no clue what he looked like. The more I tried to recall his facial features, more vomit slithered up my throat. It burned like a trail of lava. No matter how much iced water I drank, the pain didn't go away. My wrists were in agony, and I could still feel hands clamping them.

She handed me a pencil and a sketchbook, then told me to draw the man. I started with the logo on his shoes; they were what I was looking at most of the time. Carefully, I drew an accurate scale of his hair and the clothes he wore, but then I reached the face. I had no control over my hands, as if he were still controlling them. They kept circulating the page until his head was completely squiggles.

She gave me a new sheet, but my hands did the same thing.

"Tancan," she said. "Did the man take any articles of clothing off of you or himself?"

My tight jeans and jacket were still strangling my skin. "No, I don't think he did."

"Did he hit you? Or touched you in areas where you felt uncomfortable? Did he try giving you any drugs?"

All the questions kept piling on top of each other. "I don't know. As I said, I don't remember any of it. When he first spoke to me, he asked if I was hungry, and I told him I had already eaten, but that seemed to make him mad."

She lifted her head from her notepad and looked directly at me. "Tancan Milten, you are a victim."

What? No, I wasn't. This wasn't true. My brain flickered through thoughts. What if I wanted him to hurt me? What if he had just stopped if I had said no? It felt like my head was about to explode.

Once she left the house, Dad left too.

Stephen handed me dinner. I scooped a spoonful of mac and cheese and pushed it into my mouth. It tasted wrong. I usually loved the texture of the one he makes, but I couldn't handle it this time. I couldn't eat anything. Something was stopping me. As I lowered the fork back down, I saw bruises wrapped around my lower arm. The man must've really hurt me, unless I did it to myself.

Dad came back half an hour later. I had no idea where he had been, but his mood still hadn't changed. He only pretended to act calm around the police officer. "You stupid boy! What the hell were you thinking? I have taught you about stranger danger your entire life," he said. "You know you're not meant to follow random men, especially not in a place like that. You idiot!"

"Felix. Go to bed!" commanded Stephen. It was like he was putting my dad in a time-out. I would've found it hilarious, but in that moment I didn't. "Nothing that happened was his fault, you know that. None of us knows what happened. You know how he exaggerates things. The man could've just yelled at him or something. He gets triggered and runs away; that's just how he is."

"Well, something must've made him scream down the street at three o'clock in the morning! Melissa always got herself caught up at those clubs and got into random men's cars. Those manic episodes led her to her death, and I'm not letting my son go down the same path as her!"

They argued for a while, but I felt like I had caused everything. Dad was right. I was an idiot. What was I thinking? But the main question that lingered on my mind was, what had happened to Taylor?

I took a shower and rinsed that man's scent off my body, but I could still smell him. He reeked of cigarettes and this earthy-scented cologne. I could still trace the stench of his tonsil stones huffing in my face. I kept cranking the knob until I felt my skin burn. It got to the point where my skin was turning red. I scrubbed and scrubbed, but bugs were still crawling up my arms. I changed into my pyjamas. They weren't as cosy as usual.

I couldn't sleep last night either. I could still hear my muffled screams as he blocked my mouth with his hand. I almost suffocated under my bed covers until Stephen walked in to say goodnight.

"I promise what happened to you wasn't your fault," he said.

"But what if it was?"

"He is an adult; you are a child. And your dad's right, you shouldn't be following random men in places like that. Tancan, I promise you're not in trouble. Trust me, I will find this man and make sure he is locked away for a very long time." He bent over to kiss me on the cheek, like he always did, but I barged my elbow into his face. I couldn't cope that night. "Okay." He faced the door. "I love you. Good-night."

I awoke, hearing a knock at the door. Outside, Taylor's face glared at my window. I galloped down the stairs. "Where were you?" I exhaled, opening the door.

"Good." She exhaled. "You got home safe. I am so sorry I—"

Dad walked up behind me and closed the door in her face. He told me to go upstairs, but I hid in the kitchen instead.

"I liked you," he said. "I was thrilled that my son finally had a friend who didn't judge him. I guess I was wrong. You directed him to a place that you knew was dangerous; you know how vulnerable he is! Then you abandoned him alone in an unfamiliar place. You should be ashamed of yourself. You are a *sick* kid and need help like the rest of your messed-up family!"

I peeked out the window to see her eyes shimmering with tears. It looked like she was about to say something, but she didn't.

"You are no longer allowed to contact my son, you hear me? I will pack all your belongings and drop them off later."

She walked away with tears drifting down her cheekbones. She always raged when she was upset, not sulked like that.

I wanted to talk to her myself, but Dad wouldn't let me. He insisted I hand him my phone so he could delete Taylor's number from my contacts. I gripped on with full strength. "Why do you always use my disability against me?" I yelled. I am sick of him constantly controlling me like I am his pet; I have a life too.

I left Taylor one last text, but she left me opened. She probably hated me now.

— Love your favourite space nerd, Tancan :)

45: Humiliation

January 16th 2022 - 3 days after he had been destroyed.

Every stranger that passed Tancan was an insect; his eyes scanned the street for any signs of danger. A creeping sensation crawled up his spine. There was a spider on his back, inching closer with every step. His speed quickened, causing his keychains to clash together, until the so-called venomous bug drifted past.

"Are you sure you are feeling well enough to go in?" Finn asked, catching up to him.

"I'm sure," he lied. "I already promised Dad I would go back after Christmas. Can I sit with you at lunch?"

"No." He smirked. "Just kidding, of course you can. I'm not that mean."

"Sorry, I'm meant to be your older brother, not the other way around."

"Stop apologising! You've been through a lot lately, and you're autistic; I'm not."

He stared at the lemon shark pin on Finn's bag. "Says the person with a shark obsession."

They both stepped into the humid school air. Finn approached his friend group, who were sitting at a wooden table, but his brother had vanished.

Tancan sat by Taylor's locker, hoping she would appear.

As soon as she spotted Tancan, she stormed down the corridor.

He chased after her. "Hey, Taylor, can we talk?"

She didn't glance back and kept walking towards the courtyard.

"I get that you're mad—"

"Mad? You think I'm *mad?* Your dad just sent me back to live with my convicted brother!" she turned her head towards him, revealing a swollen purple patch beneath her eye, lightly covered with concealer. "Yes, before you ask, Sean found out what I did."

"I'll talk to Dad, I promise. We can sort something out. But please don't be mad at me. It's not like I chose to avoid you."

"When is it ever your fault, huh?" she spat. "You need to learn to own up to your own actions."

A crowd of kids formed a loose circle around them.

"I didn't blame you! When I got home, I told my dad everything that had happened. He just automatically assumed you left me on purpose."

"And you let him blame me?" When you knew that wasn't true?"

"I panicked! I'm sorry he yelled at you like that." Guilt swam around his pupils. "But you did kind of abandon me."

The circle of kids tightened around them, drawing closer as if they were moths hogging a lightbulb.

Taylor's jaw clenched. "We promised the day that we met we would never *lie* to each other! I told you to stay there and wait. And you ignored me and followed some rando? I needed a *piss.* Can I not do that anymore? Are you that irresponsible to not just sit and wait?"

"Yeah, like you've never *lied* to me before." He scoffed. "You lied about nearly everything, plus the guy told me he knew where you were."

"Are you honestly that gullible? What do I tell you the most?"

"I don't know..."

"Don't. Trust. Men."

"I thought he would help me because I was just a lost kid."

"Tancan, he saw you were young and took advantage. That man wanted to *hurt* you. You're lucky you had the opportunity to run; otherwise, it could've been a lot worse. I was searching the entire building for you! Yes, I might have had a couple more shots after using the bathroom, but I would *never* abandon you. I always feel like I'm your carer whenever I'm with you. Like I'm responsible for looking after a toddler. It's embarrassing walking past other groups of *normal* teenagers."

Nearly the entire school had wrapped itself around the scene. Phones recording from a distance, whispers, smirks, and silent gasps rippled in waves.

The same ripples punctured his heart. "I do things for you too."

Her arms folded tightly across her chest. "Like what?"

"I crossed off the amount of calories on every single snack you ate, and that was the least I did for you."

"You don't know what it's like; you never will. You don't even dig the blade into your arm deep enough. Maybe next time you should pierce it deeper and see what real pain feels like."

That sentence alone hurt more than any blade could reach. "You're a *bitch*, Taylor."

"You're too sensitive; you need to learn the truth sometimes. Not everyone follows the stupid little rules in your head, and you need to accept that. Your family is just as messed up as mine. Your dad is a caitiff alcoholic, who is too worried to admit he is in love with another man and smothers you like a kitten."

"At least my dad doesn't force me to sell drugs!"

"At least I don't waste hours of my day watching space documentaries like a weirdo!"

"At least I didn't pretend to cut myself and use bandages to hide a recording device on my wrists."

Taylor's hand whipped across Tancan's face. A red mark splattered across his cheek.

She flinched, but it never came.

His eyes rolled to the ground. "I'm not *violent* like you," he muttered. "I don't *fight* people."

Over a hundred students raised their glowing screens, zooming in on their expressions and chanting, "Fight!"

"STOP RECORDING ME!" he yelled, ducking his head into his blazer.

Nobody listened.

A teacher stepped in, dragging Taylor away.

Before Tancan could even catch his breath, an unfamiliar male teacher with a serrated voice clamped a hand onto his shoulder. "Headmaster's office, now!"

A rocket ship launched in Tancan's skull, compressing the fuel into every single bone of his body. Roaring flames, then nothing. The surrounding faces blurred, their features dissolving as his weightless body crumpled to the grainy concrete.

46: The Dark Room

Tancan's heart pulsed awake before his eyes did. Suspended in the sound of strangers' voices drifting through the wind. Unaware of the blood dripping down his leg, he rolled onto his side.

The shadow of a tall, faceless male stood over him, pressing his foot on his chest and pinning him to the ground. He whispered over his head, each word nailing into his mind. He couldn't make it out, and he didn't want too either. But he knew he couldn't repeat it.

His eyes shuddered, emerging from whatever universe he had been stuck in. The man's foot lifted away, but something still anchored his body down.

"He's conscious!" A teacher shot his arm out like a barrier. "Kids, go back to class!"

Finn stepped forward, squeezing through mobs of laughing lions. "He's my *brother.*"

"We'll call your mum to pick him up."

"My mum's *dead,*" he mumbled before crouching down to Tancan, and placed his palm in his twitching hand. "I'm here; you'll be okay."

Tancan's face softened, a fragile smile fluttering across his lips, as the comfort of Finn unknotted the tangled wires in his chest.

Finn pulled his phone from inside his blazar pocket, unbothered by the teacher standing behind him. "I've texted Stephen; he's waiting inside reception for you. Go home and rest."

*

In the car, Tancan pinched one of the Polaroids out of his blazer pocket—the photo Finn had taken of him and Taylor. The moment frozen in time had unfrozen; it had become microwaved and fractured. His eyes latched onto the image for a moment, watching fake smiles corrupt as it slipped through his fingers. This whole time, he thought she was his friend, his *best* friend. He tore the photograph, ripping directly down the middle and shredding through the heart they had sculpted with their hands.

"She hates me now." His chest ached with something that felt like loss, but also tingled with something else, knowing that the pieces of his world would never fit back together. He blinked his tears away, but they continued to dribble onto his grazed knee. She lied to him. She slapped him. She used him, but everything that happened was still his fault.

"Nobody could hate you, Tancan," said Stephen. "Give her the space she needs to figure things out."

As they pulled onto the driveway, Tancan's eyes darted to the recycling bin, where a stack of empty beer cans leaned in a precarious position. His home wasn't any better than school. Something was wrong. His dad had been sober since last April. They didn't belong there.

Felix sat in his usual slouched position; eyes fixed on the TV and a can of beer clenched on top of his knee. "I got a call from the school. You got into a *fight?*"

Those liars. "It wasn't a fight," Tancan stated, holding his words together. "I don't *fight*!"

"I told you to stay away from that girl. Why do you never listen to me?"

"It's all your fault!" His scream almost ruptured the can out of Felix's hand. "I finally had a proper friend who noticed my existence in class. I was feeling happy for once in my life, and you ruined *everything*."

"I used to be just like you, but as you get older, you'll mature. In ten years' time, you'll be thanking me for everything I did for you."

"Mature? You clearly haven't. She needed me! You don't understand her, not how I did, and now I'll probably never see her again, all because of your loudmouth!"

His chair scraped across the floor as he rose. "I did you a favour. I got that *toxic* little shit out of your life."

"Don't talk about her like that! I was the only person she had, and she needed you too, and you just made everything worse!"

"I only did this because I *care* about you."

"Care about me?" He scoffed. "If you did, then you'd put that bloody can down! You've always been a dad, but you haven't been *my dad* for five years."

"I've spent months trying to get you the help you needed, so you didn't end up going through what your mom did!" He pulled a sandwich bag out of his pocket full of pills. "Can you explain what these were doing in the trash?"

Tancan sighed, clawing his head with his nails. "I couldn't cope. They made me feel weird. Dad, I'm sorry, please—"

"I've wasted almost sixteen years of my life dragging you to every appointment you needed. Do you have any idea how exhausting it is to look after someone like *you*?"

"Yeah, must have been difficult for you, otherwise you wouldn't have tried dumping me in a psychiatric hospital! I wish it were *you* instead of Mum; she would've known how to look after me."

“Don’t you dare bring her into this.”

“You’re so selfish, Dad. You let her wander outside shortly after she had a manic episode. Alone. In the dark. You were meant to be supervising her, but you stopped taking care of her and let her die.”

“Stop it!”

“If I’m making you angry, you should hit me. Go on, hit me! Make me feel all the pain Mum felt when she died alone hat night. Give me the bruises she had.”

“Stop it!”

“I’ve already been slapped across the face today. I’m not scared of pain anymore!”

“Stop it!” Felix's body vibrated like a controller and wobbled towards Tancan. He grasped his shoulders. His grip got tighter until the beer can crushed against his shoulder.

"D-Daddy, you're hurting me. Dad, stop! Stephen! Help!"

Stephen sprinted into the living room, attempting to pull his arms away, but that only resulted in him getting punched in the nose.

As Felix let go, he glared Tancan in the eye. "I wish I had a *normal* son; you're *too much!*"

"I'M AUTISTIC!" he roared. "I'm sorry that I'm 'too much' for you, but how am I able to change that? What don't you understand? Tell me. What don't you understand?"

Dropping to his knees whilst gripping his nose, Stephen wiped away the tear-streaks off Tancan's face. They weren't tears; they were remnants of beer splattered from Felix's mouth. He turned his gaze towards Felix. "You're *evil.*" He held onto Tancan's hand, leading him upstairs.

"I thought he was better," mumbled Tancan.

Stephen kissed his head. "I know, buddy. You can't be around him when he's like this. I need you to stay in your room whilst I go pick up Sapphire, okay?"

He nodded. "Your nose—"

"I'm okay. I promise. Are you okay? Does your shoulder hurt?"

"A little, but I'm fine."

Tancan sat on his bed, holding his shoulder as he listened to the argument beneath his feet.

"Look at you, trying to be the *'nice one'* again," hissed Felix. "You've messed up their lives!"

"Your kids were calling me in the middle of the night because they were scared of you. You think that's normal? Listen, you're lucky they're not separated in foster homes. I was this close to calling social services myself. I think it will benefit all of us if you move out until you can get yourself together."

"This is *my* house! *My wife* and I paid a deposit on this house."

"You're not well either, Felix; you're dangerous when you're like this."

It was like a nightmare Tancan couldn't escape from. He was trapped inside a UFO. The alien's downstairs weren't creatures from another planet; they were insecure men with lips that spat venom. He couldn't cry anymore; not even think clearly. The only thing he could do was empty his heart with *'I Bet on Losing Dogs'* by *Mitski* blasting through his headphones.

47: Reality

January 31st 2022 - 18 days after he had been destroyed.

Dear Star Diary,

I'm too much. I'm too much. I'm too much. I'm too much. I'm too much. I'm too much. I'm too much. I'm too much for everyone!

I don't understand why people are mean. I get it; not everyone is perfect, but I am talking about the people who don't have a single pea of remorse in their bodies. Everyone on earth has their own opinions, beliefs and appearances. Yet, most of them will probably get judged for one of those reasons at some point in their lives, and still nobody's stopping it.

I have been isolating myself in my room for about 2 weeks now. I can't tell what day it is anymore, and I feel like a slug. I've barely touched any of the safe foods that Stephen brought up to me. I think I might be losing too much weight. Whenever I lower my arm, I can feel my fingertips grazing past the outline of my bony pelvis.

My hair is as glossy as cooking oil, and I've felt light-headed. Most days, I can't get out of bed. No space documentaries; no internet. Alone with my thoughts. It's like the rest of my house is on fire and my room is made of ice. I'm stuck. The harrowing anxiety is like having a backpack full of rocks stuck to my back. It's painful. If I leave the room, they will crush me, and the fire will scold me.

The only achievement I completed this week was working out which person is climbing the stairs based on their footsteps — Dad sounds like a panting beast. I really believed he was a good person; how pathetic can I be? I remember him arguing with Mum after I first got diagnosed. It was only a mild argument, but I still caused it. I don't think he's ever really liked me.

I began to hate myself when I was nine. It was the age I realised something was different about me. Even after my diagnosis, I still felt like something was missing. If I had never existed, Mum would still be alive, and Dad wouldn't be an alcoholic. I destroyed my family.

I somehow tricked my brain into thinking I would have a successful life that isn't full of fake scenarios. In reality, being an astronaut would be impossible. Out of the eight billion people on this planet, only six hundred and seventy-eight people have gone to space, and nineteen never made it back. That means my chance of flying to space would be like 1/1,000,000. My fantasy land is designed with invisible ink; alcohol operates my dad's fantasy land. Why is everything so fake?

Everyone will view today differently. Some people will get married, and some people will try to protect their families from war, and there are other people like me who waste their precious life rotting in bed and scrolling on their phone. We will all be forgotten, eventually.

There will hardly be evidence that individuals ever existed on this planet. Bones will rot somewhere underneath a bunch of dirt. My favourite blanket will probably live longer than I will. Nobody can win in life, even if they are the richest or poorest in the world; they all get the same fate. My existence will become conspiracy theories — the same ones that I spent my life making up about aliens.

There will be a future of an entirely new population. New celebrities, movies, books, inventions and nobody I know will ever get to experience them.

The trouble is, nobody exactly knows how long they have left. I could have eighty years or a single hour. Some people die peacefully in their sleep surrounded by people they love; others spend their entire childhoods in hospitals and die before even starting school. Life isn't fair. A car could end someone's life; so can a single word.

All the money, all the fame, all the food, all of it are distractions to stop people from overthinking their fate. I've spent so much time engrossed in funny online videos just to avoid myself from hearing all the tragic events going on across the world.

All these celebrities dying, all these wars, all these debates about basic human rights. Why can't life be peaceful?

I am turning sixteen in less than two weeks, and I am nowhere near ready. Every month seems to fly through faster. I could take a selfie right now, and it would appear in my memories from five years ago. It's unreal. I will be old enough to work and earn my own money. It's so scary.

A lot happens at sixteen, like doing my GCSE exams and then starting college. I have so much potential to do something with my life, but anxiety makes me exhausted from doing literally anything.

Growing up, I always saw teenagers in series and books as teens who only ever worried about asking their crush out. I wish it were that simple. I was so stupid for wishing to be a teenager; I want to be him again. I want to be the child who was held in loving arms, the child who would only worry about upsetting my toys if I haven't played with them for a while, not whatever I am now.

People always assume that every autistic person isn't capable of holding emotions, but I am carrying about fifty on my back. Multiple variants of sadness that haven't been named yet.

I feel so maternal to every living creature on this planet, so much that I feel like crying after I see someone shoo off a pigeon or stomp on a spider. If any person shows me the tiniest bit of kindness, I will immediately fall in love with them because my brain attaches to people too easily.

That's how I damaged my friendship with Taylor. I got too close. I got too needy. I didn't give her the space she needed. I'm a terrible friend. Now I can see why it took so long to find one.

I'm tired, I'm hungry and I'm rotting away. Half the day is gone, and I'm still in bed. What am I doing with my life? I started this diary for fun to document my interest in space and alien conspiracy theories. I guess it turned out to be much more than that. What am I even saying? This is just a stupid-ass notebook I've written inside for an entire year. Who is this even for, anyway? Myself in ten years? I might write again in a few weeks when I have the motivation to do something, but for now, signing off.

- Your favourite space nerd, Tancan :/

48: Comfort Zone

After hurling his diary aside, Tancan unlocked his bedroom door, releasing the stuffy air.

As he stared into the bathroom mirror, he met a grim monster. Pimples speckled his skin like toppings on a greasy pepperoni pizza. Considering he'd always felt like a single segment of pineapple, it was a pleasant surprise.

A chill prickled across his spine. Someone was watching him.

Felix stood on the landing, silently monitoring his every move. And then ambled back downstairs.

Tancan sprinted into his room, pulling the brass door handle shut until he heard a click.

Tiny knuckles knocked on his door. "I think Daddy wants to talk to you," whispered Sapphire, a charm of innocence in her voice.

"I'm sorry, I just don't feel like talking right now."

"Do you want to play hide and seek later?"

"Maybe," he said, with no intention, but hearing her unicorn slippers stomp back downstairs made something inside of him hurt. That man was her dad too. He had to escape this cycle, for her. He had to protect Finn and Sapphire, no matter how depressed he felt.

*

"Is he still drinking?" Tancan's voice muffled through the door as Stephen placed a packet of alien crackers outside his room.

"He hasn't had a sip since you've been in your room. He feels awful."

"Do you think he meant what he said?"

"Buddy, of course he didn't. Sometimes people can say stupid things when they are upset, although I doubt I will ever be able to forgive him for this. It wouldn't be fair if I left him; I would be leaving my kids too."

"You don't know how he's actually feeling, do you?"

"Open the door," he commanded.

Tancan stepped out of his room.

Stephen hugged him. "You're right, I don't know. The alcohol is destroying him, and I don't know how to help him anymore."

Tancan's face was a chipped ceramic plate, barely held together by invisible cracks. He had already tried applying duct tape, but it wasn't strong enough.

Stephen's hands kneaded glue into his pores. "Look at you, buddy." He wiped Tancan's deep-fried hair. "You're making things worse for yourself. Do you think you could try showering today?"

Tancan nodded, looking down at Stephen's watch. "It's 4:45," he murmured. "I'll have to wait until 5:00."

*

After changing straight into his pyjamas, Tancan wrapped a towel around his head, holding wet strands of curtains out of his face. He was ready, though not mentally. He trudged down the creaking steps, glimpsing the shadow-creature in the artificial light.

The man he once called his dad sat in an armchair with a portrait of a five-year-old Tancan on his lap.

Tancan lingered in the doorway. His fingers brushed over his towel's rigid bristles, observing over silence between him and his dad.

Felix sighed. "Come sit down here for a minute."

His legs bounced with skittish energy. "What have I done wrong?"

"I know what I did was horrible—"

"No... what have I been doing wrong my entire life? No matter what I do, I'm always doing something wrong. Please tell me how I can fix myself. I'm trying, I'm really trying," he sobbed. "I just want you to *appreciate* me."

"Sweetheart," he began. Every mistake he had ever made with his first son had stained through his navy sweater. Tancan was now old enough to see what a wreck he was.

"I'm so sorry I failed you. My whole life I masked to be perfect for everyone, but I never seemed perfect enough for you. Sometimes I wish our brains spoke the same language. After some time in my room, I've realised that not everything is a fantasy. I have a higher chance of winning the lottery than going to space. I think it's time I accepted that, and I'm still waiting for you to accept *me*."

Felix shook his head slowly; his eyes puffed with tears. "Oh, my baby, I've always accepted you. You *saved* me. Since your mom died, I have been a wreck, and whenever I drank, all the pressure seemed to disappear. When I held you in my arms for the first time, I felt like I was holding a trophy. You are the buried treasure of my heart. Of all the babies in the world, I chose to love you. I believe in you, Tancan. I always have. If you want to fly into space, then you'd better practice your moonwalking."

Felix stood up, and pondered towards his vinyl rack, a playful glint in his eye as he sifted through each individual record. His fingers brushed against the disk as he steadily set the stylus down, filling the room's atmosphere with soft crackles that carried a sense of nostalgia.

"What are you doing?" asked Tancan, dabbing his sleeve over his face.

"Spending some quality time with my son."

The song had no lyrics, but somehow Felix could hear every word. He fluttered around the living room, mouthing imaginary words, before reaching out his hand towards his child.

"Nope."

Paused mid-dance, Felix raised his eyebrow, sketching a playful look of disappointment across his face.

Tancan stood like a penguin, rolling his eyes as he joined in, half smiling at his dad's sudden antics. "This is so embarrassing."

Felix gently placed a finger over his son's mouth, silencing him with a wink.

Tancan swayed in sync, tilting his head toward his dad. He couldn't let go, or else he would float away.

"I'm so sorry, my *precious* boy."

"It's okay. I *forgive* you, dad," he lied. He would never be able to forgive him for what he did.

49: Swings

February 5th 2022 - 23 days after he had been destroyed.

Tancan smiled, as if everything in his life was finally falling into place. He didn't have to apologise to every door he walked through or every space he occupied; he had no reason to. He finally felt his dad's love. The dance had healed him in ways he couldn't put into words. His childhood smile had returned.

"Here you go, Mum." He placed a pot of lavender on her grave. "I remember how much you loved that lavender perfume I got you for your birthday, so I thought you might like these."

He trotted through an arboretum, following birds' chirps towards his local library. His knitted gloves brushed against the oak trees, reminding him how beautiful nature really was. Most kids his age never acknowledged the small details around them, but he certainly did.

He blinked. Taylor's backpack was in front of him, strapped on somebody's back. His pace slowed as he followed them into the building.

They pulled their hood down.

It was her.

He looped around in a circle, camouflaging himself among the books.

She ducked down behind a row of shelves, but despite her attempt to hide, he caught up to her.

"What do you want?" she moaned, shrugging her shoulders.

"What are you doing in the library? You only read fanfiction."

"I saw you crossing the road and bolted: this was probably the worst place to hide from you." She smirked. "Or maybe I just miss our little adventures."

"Wait... I thought you *hated* me?"

"Huh? I thought you hated *me*?"

He looked over his shoulder to see the librarian giving them a death stare. "A library isn't the best place to chat; we should probably like go outside."

Taylor sat on a swing, rocking herself in swirls. "I'm sorry I slapped you. I don't know what came over me."

"It's okay. I've always wondered what it would feel like." He sat on the swing beside her. "Do you really feel embarrassed whenever you're with me in public?"

"Nah, I just spat out a bunch of things to upset you. I said some pretty messed-up things. Sorry, dude. I know our friendship got a bit crazy over the past few months, and I really want to start over without keeping any wild secrets from you this time, if you're willing to be my friend again?"

"Oh... I didn't realise we had *stopped* being friends. Did you mean what you said about me, like the good things?"

"Yeah, of course, I'm kinda glad I recorded our chats. You're the closest friend I've ever had, but If you ever meet Noah, don't tell him I said that." She paused, gazing at an empty crisp packet under her foot.

"Are you okay?" he asked.

"Yeah, I'm fine. I just missed you so much."

"You know... I'm here to talk whenever you need to because I *love* you, but not in *that* way, like a platonic friendship way, because I'm obviously not—"

"I know what you mean, dumbass. I love *you*, too."

"I also think you don't realize how beautiful you actually are."

"You're pretty too, Tancan."

He leaned back, lifting his feet as the words dissolved into his blood, smiling at the clouds with the surreal phrase *'I'm pretty'* moulded inside his head. He sat up again. "So, how's your relationship with your wife?"

"We broke up."

"No! Really? You guys were so cute together!"

"I'm just messing with ya! Bro, your gay ass is missing out on having such an amazing girlfriend as her. She's the best! Next Halloween, I'm dragging you back to that party to find a boyfriend because you can't third wheel us forever. Bella-Joules said If I keep making fun of her Irish accent, she'll make me dress as a leprechaun next year."

"Don't worry, I make fun of my dad's American accent all the time. I'm surprised he still loves me. It must've been hard for him moving here as an exchange student, all alone, when he was only three years older than us. Sometimes I forget he was once my age."

"I know, right? It's so weird to think about. Like we are now pretty much closer to being twenty than we are to ten, it's so scary. I always hear these girls in maths who are already planning their weddings and picking out baby names, and I don't want to think about any of that, ever."

"What do you mean?"

"I don't want to just be somebody's mum or wife; I want to be a free woman. There are always these expectations that this voice is telling me to follow, but my heart knows exactly what I want. It's always the same: go to school, get a job, get married, have kids, and at the end you just die. We all just work our entire lives to earn pieces of paper, and the only time we get a break is once we are too old to enjoy it.

"I can't live in this simulation anymore, putting myself under stress just to see some numbers pop up on a screen. I'm *done*, Tancan. I have these passions, these goals that I want to achieve, but wherever I go, there will always be men who won't take me seriously because all they see is my body, not my face.

"Then, once I'm gone, the cycle will continue. There will be new Taylors' who will go through all the same shit I did, and it will repeat itself over and over again. I'm not some fictional character in a book. I am a person who constantly gets *edited* by a *man*."

The elongated silhouette of his leg stretched across the rubber flooring. "You must've been born for a reason, and I think you should escape as soon as you can. I know I'm not a female and can never fully understand how you feel, but

I've always felt like a completely different species compared to other boys."

"That's why you're the only boy I've ever trusted." Taylor dragged her fingers over the ice-cold chain. “I just don’t feel *real*, Tancan,” she said, gazing at a church in the distance. “I’ve never felt like I’ve ever existed in the whole of my life.”

“But you are real. You’re real to *me.*”

“Yeah, I am real to you, but everyone else thinks I’m this angry, messed up teenage girl. I wish people could see who I really am. After five years, I’ve finally got my life together. I’ve got a beautiful girlfriend and I’m ready to explore the world with her, but I wouldn’t have gotten this far if I haven’t spent the past year with you; you’ve helped me find *myself.*”

“How did I do that?” he asked.

“I was scared. I was *so* scared. There had always been a confused little girl trapped somewhere in my heart, and you set her free. You found her answers, but you still haven’t found your own. You don’t need to mask in front of anyone, especially not me.”

“But it’s hard; you don’t get it. You’re not ‘*different*’ like I am.”

“I *do* get it. I can feel *everything* you feel, Tancan. You’re not going to feel any better unless you free yourself from your trauma." She glanced down at her shoes. "I'm autistic *too*."

He dragged his foot across the floor, stopping himself from swinging. "You are? Why didn't you ever tell me?"

"Because I didn't know if you'd believe me. I'm not diagnosed like you are."

"Of course I believe you. How long did it take you to figure it out?"

"I spent my whole childhood searching for answers the internet, wondering what was *wrong* with me. Everyone assumed I'd grow out of my traits, but I never did. I used to beg my mum not to send me to school because I didn't want anyone to find out and start treating me 'differently.' I saw how kids treated you, so I taught myself to mask my entire life just for people to *like* me and it is so *exhausting*. Then, I befriended you and realised I'm not so *worthless* after all."

"Don't you dare call yourself '*worthless*.' I wrote your name on almost every page of my diary just to prove how much you mean to me," he said. "I really like being around you. I've liked you since you called me a 'Creep' for complimenting your hair. I mean, it *does* make sense; I have noticed a few traits in you. You spent most of your time alone in my room, sitting on the exact same bean bag, and playing with my cat for as long as I can remember. So, how come you haven't received your diagnosis yet?"

"I've spent fifteen years yearning for it, but doctors only ever seem to diagnose boys because girls are 'too complicated.' That's why you got diagnosed at nine, and I'm still stuck *here*. I guess this whole time I was *jealous*. I was jealous because you have everything I've ever dreamed of: Parents who actual *love* you and siblings you *respect* you. I want it *all*, Tancan.

I've always craved for friendship with someone like you. Someone who finally *gets* me after everyone around me looks at me like I'm a robot and goes quiet as soon as I open my mouth. And whenever I try to socialise too much, the day will end with a migraine and a wave of fatigue. I'm trying to sort my life out and nothing is working!

I'm an autistic, queer teenage girl, surrounded by crime and violence. I can't even go one day without being judged for being myself. In year 7, I got told off for stimming in class. I've masked every day since then. 'I'll get over it on day,' I say to myself as I try to get along with my day, but that memory is fixed somewhere in my brain and is tormenting me every chance it can get.

I don't get what I'm doing wrong. I always try to be nice to people, yeah, I can sometimes lash out when I am so overwhelmed that I can feel every piece of clothing clinging to my skin, but I've never hurt anyone." She caught her tears with her sleeve. "I haven't hurt *anybody*. Why is everyone against *me*?""

He gripped onto the metal chain, tighter than he had ever before. "You *get* me. You actually *understand* me."

"I've always understood you; I just never knew how to tell you." She looked up at the sky. "I hate how early it gets dark in winter."

"Yeah, me too." He observed all the lampposts illuminating the road ahead. "I should probably get going, don't want to freak Dad out. Would you like to come back my place?"

"Nah, it's ok. I'd rather not interrupt your 'homo household,'" she teased, grinning back at him. "At least your dad hasn't banned me from using your Wi-Fi." She crouched, picking up her backpack. "It's alright being back at my place, at least when Sean's not there."

"Don't listen to a word he says. You're *perfect*, and you'll get away from him, I *promise*."

"I know I will. I'm going to run away tomorrow night, Tancan, I hope you know that, and I'm *not* coming back. So, this will be our last time together. Thanks for being there for me."

"What! No! Taylor, you can't leave me here. Please, take me with you!"

"I can't. I need to do this alone."

"What about Bella-Joules? You're just going to leave her too?

"That's easier than trying to explain this to her. I need to focus om my *own* life. I don't think I can handle a proper relationship. Please, tell her that I'm sorry. I need to escape this tragic world before it's too late."

"Okay, you do that; that's what you *want*, and I'm not going to stop you. I'm going to fly into space one day too." He stepped off the swing. "Before you leave, can I err... hug you?"

She nodded, pulling Herbert out of her pocket. "Do you think you can look after him whilst I'm gone?"

"What? Taylor, no... You carry him everywhere with you."

"You'll take better care of him than I will."

He waddled towards her, enveloping her in his arms. "Bye, Taylor." She still felt fragile, like bones wrapped in bubble wrap.

"*Bye*, T-N-T. I'll miss you." She learned into his ear. "You'll find out the truth about your mum eventually."

Before he could even ask what she meant by that, she had vanished into the night sky.

50: Derealisation

Dear Star Diary,

Hi, sorry. I'm back.

I feel so guilty. I regret every single time I felt jealous of Taylor. It all makes sense. Her being autistic makes so much sense. That's why we instantly clicked! Why has it taken me so long to realise that? She was going through much more trauma than me.

Why did I judge her for making inappropriate jokes as a way of healing herself. I feel awful. She just wanted me to like her.

After I spoke to her today, I felt a wave of relief flush over my head. She told me some things that really changed my perspective on life, and maybe she's right about a lot of those things. What if we are living in a simulation after all?

The first full day I spent with her, at the shopping centre, seemed only a week ago, but somehow it has almost been a year. Time has glitched. As I walked with her through town, I felt like a video game character, and everyone who blurred past me were NPCs. I remember the way Taylor looked at me as if she were yearning for something true in her life, and now I feel the same.

I remember playing a game called, '*What Remains Of Edith Finch,*' and one of the characters was boy obsessed with space, just like me, who tried to fly by looping around on the swing. I think about that scene a lot because he had the same ambition as me, but I don't know what I truly want anymore.

I often gaze into the mirror until my face morphs into weird shapes. Who is that person staring into my soul? I open my mouth. I see teeth and realise that there is an actual skeleton living inside of me, not just a Halloween prop, a doll stand that keeps my organs from crumbling. I'm just bones wrapped in flesh and anxiety, but I feel much more than that.

One day I will lose my sense of touch, and then my heart will stop beating. What even is a human? What even is life? I have so many questions, but I will disappear before they can be answered. Waiting patiently; watching everything around me perish. It's like I'm spectating myself from outside my own body.

When I try to remember previous interactions, all I see are my expressions from a third-person perspective, which is strange because I have only ever seen my reflection and not my actual face.

I don't even feel real at this point, like I'm watching this series about myself, and every birthday is the start of a new season. I'm quite surprised people find me entertaining enough to air fifteen seasons of me babbling on about aliens. Aren't people bored yet? Nothing really happens in each episode, and they all end with me crying.

I get this dizzy feeling, like I've discovered something that I wasn't supposed to know. When I overthink something too much, my brain feels sore. There are baby photos scattered across the place I call my home, so why don't I remember being that young? My parents lived years before I existed, which is odd because before I was born, I was trapped in an empty abyss.

Reproduction doesn't make sense. Everything seems unrealistic. The existence of the tooth fairy seems more realistic than my life. What do you mean I started off as a egg and sperm cell? Why are so many things in life so normalised when they shouldn't be.

Am I hallucinating everything? My whole life feels made up.

Jeez, I know mental illness runs in my family, but I'm not that ill, am I?

Even if I am not real, I'd like to think Taylor is. To handle my trauma, I fabricate scenarios in my mind; Taylor covers hers with sarcastic jokes, but eventually we will both crack. No matter how many times she embarrasses me in front of the entire school or keeps secrets from my family, I will always love her because she is my soulmate.

She's gorgeous. Her heart is gorgeous. Everything about her is gorgeous, and everything else around me looks so beautiful too. I just wish everyone viewed life the same way as I do.

Even in winter, I can still feel the sun beaming onto my face as I look out the passenger window and let maladaptive dreams flicker through my mind. Headphones on, blasting music through my eardrums as if I am in control, and escaping the human body I'm stuck in.

When my soul is floating through the solar system, I can still feel my dad's presence sitting next to me, but he only becomes visible once I open my eyes. I believe he is just as pretty as Taylor because I cannot understand how people can consider someone ugly, no matter how bitter their heart is.

Specks of Dad's hair are slowly greying, and he's not as energetic as he used to be, but his laugh has never changed. No matter how much he hides his feelings through his smile, I can tell how depressed he is. It began a few years before Mum died. I saw the exhaustion in his eyes, but my brain was too young to censor what was happening to him.

I should've stopped him and told him that we were going to be alright, instead of letting him arrange more play-dates with alcohol, but I'm not going to blame myself for that as it wasn't my responsibility. I am his offspring, and now he shares all his thoughts with me. Wow, thanks, Dad. I guess I'm really privileged that he is still around and hasn't abandoned me yet. I don't think there are many dads who would want me as their son. I'm too needy.

Taylor is aware of how needy I am, and that's why she liked to bully me. It's more like remarks about literally anything I do, but she called it bullying. I don't take it to heart because I know she didn't try to hurt my feelings like the kids did at school. She actually has a great sense of humour, and I'm glad she was my friend. No, she was my *best* friend, and I hope she knows that.

Whenever I went out with her, all my deep thoughts seem to go away. I just wish she were real.

— Love your favourite space nerd, Tancan :/

51: Photographic

The house was calm, calmer than it had been in years. Nobody was shouting or crying, at least not out loud.

Tancan tied his noodle-like arms around Stephen's semi-muscular shoulders, and whispered, "goodnight, *Dad.*" in his ear.

A close-lipped smile enlightened his face, crinkles forming around the corners of his eyes. "Did you just call me 'Dad?'" he asked.

"Maybe." He smirked, taking the other half of his heart towards his actual dad. This time, he leaned forward, pressing his lips against Felix's cheek.

"What is this for, sweetheart?"

"Nothing... I just wanted to say goodnight."

*

Tancan sank into his mattress and reached for the remote. He could've watched five episodes in the time he spent scrolling, before deciding to rewatch one of his favourites for the hundredth time.

The room was finally his again. No more Taylor sneaking around. No more masking in his quiet space. Just him and the half-deflated spaceman balloon—barely floating in the corner. But somehow distancing away made their friendship even stronger.

Something grazed his leg. Thinking it was his cat, he booted his foot, tumbling his alien plushies onto the floor. "Starla, get your big butt off my bed," he mumbled, but when he opened his eyes, Finn was curled beside him, pulling his own blanket over his shoulders.

Tancan sat up. "Hey, are you okay?"

Finn twitched beneath the covers. "I had a nightmare."

"Aw, no, what was it about?" He held Finn's hand. "Don't worry, I'm here. I'm *always* here."

He shifted his eyes between Tancan's door and wardrobe. "I was trapped in this weird, abandoned building. The walls surrounding me were enclosed. I don't know how I got in; I was just there. Then, I walked down this never-ending narrow hallway. It was pitch black until I saw a candle resting on top of this table, which was covered in Dad's empty beer cans."

Tancan's unblinking, immobile eyes could imagine everything. It sounded far too familiar, like he had lived through that same dream numerous times. "I don't think we belong in this family," he said.

"We wouldn't be understood in another one either," added Finn, cuddling one of Tancan's teddies. “Tancan... I keep feeling this pain in my chest and it really hurts.”

“You’ll be okay, Finn, it’s probably just anxiety.”

*

The wind howling at the window didn't wake them; the soft brush of their dad's fingers did.

"I'm going to the pharmacy to pick up some Selincro pills," Felix said, grinning like he was persuading his kids more than himself. "Daddy's going to get better."

Tancan sighed. "You were doing so well without them before, and they always gave you headaches. Can't you just get some sort of counselling instead?"

"I know, sweetheart. I need to be your dad again, to both of you. All your mom ever wanted was to see her little boys happy. That being said, I'm also going to get you some more lithium pills, and you can't waste them this time, okay? "

He nodded.

*

Finn raced back into Tancan's room with his camera strapped around his neck. "Want to come to the park with me, Stephen and Sapphire? I'm taking some winter photos for my journal!"

Tancan scoffed. "Are you kidding me? It's like minus fifty degrees out there!"

"You're the most boring person in the entire world. Can I at least take a portrait of you in front of the front door? Don't worry, it's to add to my winter project. I'm not taking random mugs of you."

"Fine. But you better not edit me getting eaten by a shark."

He grinned. "No promises!"

Finn captured Tancan standing between plant pots in front of a worn, faded doormat. The edges dulled over the years of shoes scraping against its rubber outline.

He gently tugged the photo from the slot. Still blank. He held it delicately by the glossy white border. The image slowly developed, bleeding colour onto his brother's clothes. A speck of white pigment appeared to be threaded across the left side of his face. "Oh... That's weird. My camera has never done this before." He stepped out the door. "I'll try to fix it when I get home."

Tancan loitered on the doorstep, observing Stephen spraying de-icer across the windscreen, then gazed back at Finn. "Okay *Max Caufield,* stop taking photos and get into the car."

"Have fun being a loner!" he yelled, stepping into the car.

Tancan's hand glided through the bittersweet air, shouting, "Bye!" as they disappeared into the misty morning.

He climbed upstairs and walked into the spare bedroom, full of his mum's belongings.

Three large boxes stacked on top of each other in the far corner. Tancan grabbed the top one, emptying piles of Melissa's clothes onto the floor and dragged them further into the corner. Once the floor was cleared, he moved the empty box to the centre of the room and sat inside.

He pulled a purple Sharpie out his pocket and scribbled control panels onto the flaps. He placed his headphones on as if they were a helmet, listening to sounds of a rocket getting prepared to blast into space. He closed his eyes, leaning backwards. He was ready to fly to the moon.

52: Family

Felix stood in the pharmacy, tapping his foot, as the people ahead shifted like snails. A sudden cramp tightened around the front of his head. He hadn't even received his pills yet; it just appeared. Not like a headache; it was a migraine. His head was a throbbing pressure plate, and only vomiting would relieve the tension.

Grabbing his prescription, he hurried outside, rubbing the heel of his hand across his forehead. Something was wrong.

*

On the other side of town, Stephen bundled up against the crisp winter air. His boots crunched over the icy grass. "Come on, Finn, it's too chilly out here!"

"Just five minutes, please, I'm almost done!"

He rubbed his numbed fingers together. "Okay, but I'm taking Sapphire to the c—ahhh!"

"Are you okay, Stephen?" asked Sapphire.

His hand clamped onto his back. "Yeah, I'm fine, princess." He huffed. "Just getting older, that's all."

*

Both cars had pulled up at the same time.

Finn leapt out with his camera strap slung over his shoulder and ran to Felix. "Look, Dad!" He pressed the triangle button. "What? This one's blurry and so is this one!" When he swiped to the fifteenth photo, the same white speck from earlier had sliced through the branches.

As all four of them stepped inside, the sound of crackling music greeted them, echoing down the hallway and into the kitchen. The living room was untouched, the place Tancan usually lounged when he had the house to himself. Someone had only tweaked the record player, which sat behind a Tiffany lamp.

Felix sighed. "TANCAN! HOW MANY TIMES DO TELL YOU NOT TO LEAVE THE RECORD PLAYER RUNNING DOWN HERE? YOU KNOW HOW VALUABLE THESE VINYLS ARE TO ME!"

Still holding his head, he climbed upstairs. "Do you realise how easy it is for Starla to jump on the platform and scratch the disk?" Before another word slipped out, a crying-like sound came from the top of the stairs. Looking up, Starla stared down at him.

Perched on the edge of the landing, she slumped low to the ground, her tail twitching faster, every breath Felix took. She hardly ever left Tancan's room, unless it involved food.

She led him towards the spare room. Its once-white paint panels faded to an off-grey. Faint scratches marred low beneath the tarnished doorknob, like claws had dug through the paint.

Felix knocked. "Tancan, sweetheart? Are you in there?" When no response came, he knocked harder. "Tancan! Open the door!" Still met with silence, his patience snapped, "OPEN THE FUCKING DOOR!" he shouted, broken up with a mixture of anger and fear as he continued to bash his shoulder into the locked door, yelling for Stephen at the top of his lungs.

Stephen jumped from his seat. "Finn, Sapphire, stay here."

"Why, what's wrong?" asked Finn, but didn't get a response.

"He's locked himself in here." Breathing unevenly, Felix stepped aside for Stephen, his eyes darting between the door and the stairs. After a few thuds, the door unlatched, naturally swinging open.

The inside was straight out of a horror movie.

Tancan laid inside the box with his arms dangling outside. His diary thrown across the floor. Blood pooled around him, streaming from the deep gashes of his exposed veins, staining the worn carpet a dark crimson colour.

Felix staggered forward towards his son. The metallic scent of blood charged up his nostrils. He dropped to his knees, his trembling hands hovering over him, too afraid to touch his face. "My baby..."

Stephen twitched beneath the doorway; his face froze pale, not even flinching after a hand nudged past his arm.

Finn had crept behind him. The moment his eyes landed on Tancan, he let out a piercing scream. He crouched beside his big brother, his legs wobbling as he wrapped his arms around Tancan's still body. "No," he mumbled, choking on each letter. He lifted Tancan's stiff hand into his sweltering palm, clutching it tightly as though his touch could somehow bring him back.

Every muscle in Tancan's face retracted. It was clear he had been deceased for at least twenty minutes before they arrived home. He was gone. Forever.

Felix pressed two of his fingers on his son's pulse, unwilling to accept his fate.

"Dad. He's *dead,*" sulked Finn.

"No, he's not. He can't be. He's alright. No, he's just hurt. We've got to get him out of here; he's hurt. Finn help me lift him! Now!"

"Dad! Stop it! He's *gone*."

He tilted his head slowly, pressing a kiss to his son's forehead. "I'm so sorry, my boy," he whispered, his voice cracking. "Stephen, call the paramedics, now!" His hand brushed through Tancan's thick chocolate hair, soothing him one last time. He lifted his head, gazing towards the doorway.

A confused six-year-old's eyes scanned the blurb before she stepped into the book, yet to grasp the concept of death. She knitted her brows together as she tilted her head. "Did Tancan hurt himself?" She asked with childlike innocence.

Unable to answer her, Felix sniffled, wiping his face with the back of his hand. He opened his arms. "Come here, sweetheart."

She sat on his lap, clinging to the edge of his clammy shirt.

"Tancan has gone to visit your mommy in heaven."

She pointed, a confused tone in her voice. "No, he's right there."

"I know... His spirit has gone to be with Mommy now. Baby..." He held her to his chest. "Your brother has passed away."

Her playful expression faded. She leaned forward, picking up a piece of paper, the bottom right corner dripping with blood, and handed it to Felix. "Daddy, what's this?"

Dear Star Diary,

If you are reading this, it means I am probably dead, and I want you to know it's not your fault. I've been planning my funeral since I was thirteen, and I guess it is finally time.

I am honoured to have been born into such a loving family, which is full of my favourite people:

I love my dad. I inherited my geekiness from him, and he gave everything he had, even if it left him with nothing.

I love Stephen. The only other man I loved as much as my dad.

I love Finn. The best brother I could ever ask for and the only person who could almost understand me.

I love Sapphire. She always found a way to make me laugh, even on days when I was completely drained.

I love Starla. The smartest cat in the entire universe.

I love my mum. The woman who sacrificed everything for me.

I love Taylor. My best friend, who didn't make me feel like the weird kid in town.

And finally, I hate Sean Maxxie. I hope your face gets mauled by a squirrel.

I would prefer to be cremated since I can't stand the thought of being trapped underground in a coffin, like I had already been for fifteen years, then you can sprinkle my ashes at my favourite places!

All I want is for everyone to remember me for who I was and not the person I masked myself to be. If I lived forever, I might've had time to understand things better. Life is brief and really complicated to navigate. As much as I know you love me, I know some days you hated me. And I accept that. I will always look down at you from the stars and see how many fresh memories get pinned in your heart. Don't blame yourself because I don't exactly know what made me end my life.

I was starting to feel human again, but then I went to that stupid club, and that stupid man was my final straw. I hope he's happy. I didn't feel like a person after that; I felt powerless. He destroyed me in ways I didn't think I could be.

I would also like to give my star diary to Finn, and I want him to continue taking photos and stick them across all the blank pages, so I could have the memories I never got to experience.

Please inform Taylor of my passing. I have no idea how she will react, but I feel guilty leaving her, and I'm sorry for leaving you too. Please don't forget me, lots of love, Tancan xxx

(P.S. Please don't throw away any of my things and don't look at my search history!)

Felix could barely read the words. The paper creased as he focused on the hurried handwriting, each word scraping off a layer of skin. As he read it aloud, he crumbled into sobs, clutching the only piece of Tancan he had left. It was a typed document, not a last-minute note. Felix flipped the page, revealing a list of funeral arrangements.

Tancan had planned it for a while, and nobody knew until it was too late to save him. In his note, he wrote humour, so nobody forgot the sound of his laugh, but everyone around him would never forget a single aspect of his personality.

Sapphire slid off her dad's lap and crept over to Tancan. Sitting cross-legged beside him. She began stroking his tender scalp as if he were one of the family's cats, shielding herself from the grim reality of life.

Fumbling with his phone, Felix's fingers twitched, taking several tries to unlock and dial emergency services. "My son... he's hurt himself. There's blood. He's not b-breathing," he blubbered. "Please hurry."

*

One paramedic crouched next to Tancan's body, shining a light into his pupils.

"No! Don't touch him!" Sapphire screamed.

"I'm sorry, Sapphire, I'm *so* sorry," Stephen cried as he pried her hands away.

"Let him go!" She reached out her arms. "You're hurting him!"

Finn clutched the wall, tightening his hands over his ears as he closed his eyes, distracting himself from the paramedics rolling his brother into a black cadaver pouch.

All the colours had been drained from the house. The once *Barbie dream house* had become a Victorian dollhouse. Familiar furnishings muted. Every shadow, every object faded into black-and-white.

The place Tancan once called home had become **Deep-faded.** Vibrant memories replaced by a void. Every channel on the television was static. Life had disconnected from the home alongside him.

*

Stephen stepped outside. The soreness led him down a back alley towards Taylor's house. His steps battled the breeze, gravity pushing the news further in his pocket. Inhaling, his hand hovered over the corrupted doorbell.

After hearing the many sirens dashing past, Taylor creaked the door open. Her face lit up, then noticed his expression. "Stephen? Is Tancan with you?" She asked. "What's wrong? Where's Tancan?"

"He... *Died.*" The words jammed in his throat. "We found him this morning. I'm sorry."

It took a while for his words to sink in. "Oh..." She tried to hold herself together but couldn't decide whether it would be appropriate to scream, cry or collapse into Stephen's arms. Instead, she turned and bolted out the door, her legs carrying her faster than ever before, passing house after house. She needed to escape.

She stumbled onto the grass, grazing her knees against the damp straw. "*Why*?" She yelped, tripping onto her back, and pounded her fists on the brick-solid mud. She gazed into the naked night sky, spotting only two single stars. "I'll miss you, T-N-T."

***

Felix sat on the edge of his rock-hard bed, snuggling the Alien his son had stuffed almost a year ago. Tancan's scent was still stained along the seamless stitches. He held his thumb over the small button stitched in the alien's hand. With a deep breath, he pressed down, pressing it again and again, whatever it took to hear his son's voice again. He let go, afraid that the sound would wear out.

*

Stephen stepped into the steaming shower, hoping the boiling water would scald away his emotions. Shampoo lathered his thick brown hair, but it hadn't soaked through the hole in his heart. As he stepped out, a mix of bubbles and tears drained down the sinkhole. He towelled off his hair, his eyes catching a pot by the sink.

Among the clutter, stood Tancan's toothbrush, all alone. It had no owner anymore. He left it nested, waiting for Tancan to come back, but he never did.

Toys, books, and shoes kicked off by the front door were all relics of a life once lived. The house itself felt like a museum, as though it belonged to some ancient ancestor rather than a young boy who had walked through it hours prior.

Stephen walked back into Felix's bedroom, with just a towel tightened around his waist and droplets of water slithering down his back.

The rest of the room was lit up by the dim bedside lamp and Felix's fiery eyes. Choking out between breaths, "My baby is *dead*," he announced.

Stephen stepped closer, firmly placing his moist hand on Felix's shoulder. "*Our* baby is dead," he corrected, using his towel to catch the waves splashing out of Felix's eyeballs.

"I could've *saved* him," sobbed Felix, sticking his head on Stephen's shoulders. "I should've stayed here. My wife and son are gone. When I stopped Melissa from swallowing five pills at once, I thought I had saved her too. I wanted us to grow old together, Stephen, and Tancan was meant to out-live both of us."

Stephen rubbed the back of Felix's head and said, "Life doesn't always go the way you planned it to be."

53: Finn

February 7th 2022 - 37 days after he had been destroyed.

Finn was adamant; he had to go to school. Deep down he wasn't ready, but the thought of being surrounded by his dead brother's alive belongings haunted him even more.

He walked through the gates alone; he was used to it by now. His brother wasn't skipping school because of his anxiety; his anxiety didn't exist anymore.

The usual banter was absent; only a few voices rippled through the crowd of silent mice.

"He's the brother of that year 11 who unalived himself," a voice whispered, not loud but loud enough for Finn to hear. Now, he wasn't the 'autistic kid's' brother; he was the 'dead kid's' brother.

A teacher tapped him on the shoulder. "You're welcome to come and sit in my office if you need some space." But he had no clue who the teacher was. Everyone finally started to notice him. It was like he was walking alone on a red carpet, surrounded by dozens of cameras. Manoeuvring through the maze of slamming lockers, he scurried into the library, escaping the many mobs of aliens his brother had dealt with.

Broken spines stood stiff along the shelves. Between the narrow gaps, two kids huddled down the aisle, their smirks full of cruel amusement.

"I heard that autistic kid in our year got jumped," one kid snickered. "He was such a *freak,* always staring off into space like a *weirdo.*"

"Stop! Honestly," the other kid bragged, "I think he had a brother in Year 8, probably just as strange as he was. Someone told me their dad was like super abusive and probably gave them both mental problems."

Finn's worm-like fingers slithered towards a bulky novel. His knuckles whitened as he unlatched the frisbee, letting it soar across the library like tubes in the London Underground, until the book smacked directly into one of the kids' heads.

Thanks to pricks like them, his brother was gone.

***

"I am aware of the tragic loss in your family, but violent outbursts like this are unacceptable," the principal said. "Throwing a book towards a peer, especially aiming at the head, shows a lack of control. We cannot allow this type of behaviour inside our premises. The most reasonable discipline we can put in place is permanent exclusion."

Felix thumped his wrist on the desk. "*'Permanent exclusion?'* Those kids mocked my dead child; he had every *right* to do what he did!"

"Mr Milten, please remain calm. You're lucky that the student's parents refused to press charges; this situation would've been dealt with much differently outside of school."

"He's just a twelve-year-old kid who's grieving his brother! This school has failed both my boys." He stood up. "Finn, let's go."

Finn kicked a loose pebble across the gravel, his hands buried deep in his pockets.

"Get in," Felix said, unlocking the car with a sharp click.

"Are you mad at me?" He glared out the tinted window, watching kids filter out of the school gates in their toxic friend groups. Nothing had changed for them; nothing had.

"Yes, I am mad," Felix stated, "but I'm not mad at *you*, sweetheart. Your brother would be as proud as I am. I love you Finn, you're one of the few people I still love." He placed his shaking hand on his lap. "You remind me so much of your mother." The car wasn't rolling, yet Felix was driving, smoothing his fingers around the wheel. "You don't *deserve* any of my features."

54: Aliens

February 28th 2022 - 46 days after he had been destroyed.

Tancan's casket rested on a raised platform, surrounded by signs that read: **Tancan Milten. March 21st, 2006 - February 6th, 2022.** Underneath marked: ***Forever 15.***

In his note, he specifically stated he wanted everyone to arrive in alien costumes, and that's all he wanted. No songs, no flowers, just aliens.

Stephen stood by the entrance, shooing away the people who arrived in plain suits and basic dresses. They didn't deserve to be there.

Arched clouds hovered over rows of painted faces as they all marched towards the church. The cheap fabric shimmered in the weak afternoon light, dribbling raindrops onto bulbous helmets.

Despite the recommendation to stay home, Finn slumped with his mask hung loosely around his neck. Sat in the corner, posing as something he wasn't. An icicle surfaced his lower eyelid, but the rest of his body remained still. It was a funeral, not a fancy dress party. He had chosen to wear Tancan's favourite hoodie because it was one of the few items that were still stained with his scent.

A group of bearers, wearing black topcoats, carried Tancan's coffin into the church, closely followed by Felix. He then sat down in the front row and squeezed Stephen's hand. Taylor sat next to them, holding Sapphire on her lap, but Finn remained stood in the back corner.

Silent aliens had invaded the church.

The priest adjusted his thin-rimmed glasses. "Today, we are here to remember the life of Tancan Milten. He was born in 2006 to Felix and Melissa Milten and known best for his obsession with space. You couldn't stand next to him for five minutes without him telling you one of his favourite facts. He loved a lot of things, but nothing bought him as much comfort as his star diary. Now, I invite the child's father, Felix Milten, to say a few words."

Trembling forward, Felix gripped the edges of the small wooden stand and cleared his throat. "Tancan... my son." He swallowed. "He embraced our planet more than us all. Maybe we never understood him enough, and I don't think he could ever understand us either." His vocal cords stung. "But if there is one thing I truly know, it is that he believed in something beyond this world. I hope he finally found it, wherever he is."

Stephen escorted him off the stage before the priest gave him a gentle nod. "If there is anyone else who would like to speak, please step forward."

Silence.

Finn raised his hand.

"Preferably anyone above the age of eighteen."

His arm shot up higher, his toes scrunching against the interior of his shoes.

The priest sighed, pointing towards him. "You there. Relation to Tancan Milten?"

"Uh... brother." His curved fingers brushed past his Polaroid camera, reaching deeper into his backpack, past crumpled pieces of paper and blunt pencils, until he pulled out miniature squares of mirrors.

He trod through the aisles, weaving past all the coiled antennas and placed the squares into the alien's palms. He climbed up the steps. "Now, I want all of you to look in the mirror. Hmm... you see an alien, right? That is what my brother was viewed as every single day of his life, and I promise every one of you, made him feel this way.

"My brother was *autistic*. He didn't have a disease; he had a disability." His eyes darted across the stained-glass windows. "I've never seen half of you in my life. I understand you are here to pay respect, but I know you would've refused to paint your face if he were still alive, wouldn't you? Why are you even here? If you respected him, you would know how much he would hate being surrounded by strangers. So just go home.

"I know so many things contributed to his death, but you just took him for granted." He glared over at Taylor, bouncing Sapphire on her knee. "Some of you made him feel loved, and I worship you for that, but the people who didn't, then you—" He took a massive breath, "You can all get lost."

"Okay," the priest said, reaching for the microphone. "That's enough now."

Finn gripped his fingers tightly around the microphone. "I'm still talking! Let me talk!" He opened Tancan's Star diary and turned to the last page.

Dear Tancan,

Do you remember when I accidentally scratched one of Dad's records and you took the entire blame yourself? You went out of your way to write an entire letter explaining how sorry you were and offered to use some of your own pocket money towards a new one, and that was just the type of person you were.

You were always there for me whenever Dad was too drunk to notice my existence. You raised me better than he could, despite you still being a disabled child yourself.

Most brothers fight; we never did because nothing scared you more than conflict.

All my life I grew up idolising you so much that I started to hate you, and I wish I could erase every single thought out of my head. But now it doesn't matter because I prayed so much that you would just disappear; now my wish came true, and I never once meant it like this.

You could destroy an entire city and Mum and Dad would still comfort you. All I ever wanted was for someone to take you away and place you into another family so that I could be seen for once, but if that had happened, I would've never have been able to experience the same nostalgia I had with you.

We still had years of gossip sessions left, and in two months, I will become a teenager, and you will never get to see me as one. You were the best brother I could ever ask for, and I hope nobody will judge you for being yourself in heaven. If you can hear me, all I wanted to say is that I love you because I feel like I never said it enough, even if you were the one who stole my last Kit Kat.

Love, Finn.

Before he left the podium, he placed ear defenders on top of Tancan's coffin. "Sorry," he whispered. "You would've hated the music they picked for you."

The curtains drew, trapping Tancan behind them.

"Stop!" Finn cried. "You can't... You can't *burn* my brother!"

Felix attempted to hug him, but Finn barged passed and yanked his backpack from the far corner. The camera inside jostled against his ribs as he swung the strap over his shoulder.

Keeping his head down, he strutted through the rows. He didn't stop. He didn't look back. No one called his name. Only Stephen's eyes followed him outside to the car parked beyond the ceremony, half-hidden behind a row of trees.

As soon as thunder rumbled, people tore away their costumes.

"Thank you for coming, Taylor," said Stephen, standing next to Tancan's alien-themed flower display. "I know you and Tancan had a strong bond."

She nodded. "Thank you for inviting me after everything that happened."

Felix approached her, eyes widened. "Thanks to you, somebody is going to take my *baby* away from me and burn him to ashes. Stay out of our life."

55: Taylor Maxxie

Taylor stood in front of the bathroom mirror, her hands gripping the sink as she used a flannel to wipe away the thick, slimy streaks of goo off her face. No matter how hard she scrubbed, it still clung to her hair like syrup.

"Why are you dressed like an alien?" Sean bickered from behind the doorway.

She scraped her face harder. "I'm not in the mood for this; I just got home from my best friend's *funeral*."

He scoffed. "I was worried he would turn you into one of those 'weird' kids if I made you stay at that house any longer."

Her head shot around like an owl. "He respected me more than you would ever think, you misogynistic cu—"

"What were you about to call me?" He hooked his fingers around hair, pulling her against the wall. "Don't you dare call me that again. Ever!" He slammed her cheek into the plasterboard.

Her hand dug into her pocket, pulling out her hidden pocketknife and darted it into his thigh, allowing her to push his hands away and run.

She ran.

And ran.

And ran until she made it to the same field where Sean had left Melissa Milten to suffocate.

Sean chased after her, slightly limping.

She tripped over a rock, but before she could get up, he had caught up. He dropped to his knees, pinning her shoulders to the damp grass. He tightened his hands around her neck.

Thunder rumbled.

Sean looked up, giving Taylor the opportunity to loosen her hands and wriggle the pocketknife back out of her trouser pocket. Gasping for air, she jammed the blade into his neck. Not once, not twice, but several times. Each stab for every woman he had ever hurt. The blood gurgled out of his mouth, smothering across her face.

"Rot in hell!" She screamed, pulling out her phone with her left hand, which wasn't covered in too much blood. She stared at herself through her front camera. "I'm sorry, Tan-can, I'm *really* sorry."

She gazed up at the stars, then back down at Sean's oozing body. Using her left thumb, she dialled 999. "My name is Taylor Maxxie, and I just *ended* my brother."

*

"Hands in the air! Let go of the weapon!" An officer pushed her to the floor, strapping the child's dripping hands into cuffs.

She didn't regret what she had done. She smiled as she got forced inro the police car, Yes, Sean was dead, but he had already destroyed her life a long time ago. She had ended it all. For good.

A small section of an old newspaper sat on the seat next to her, marked from: **March 21st 2016**

MARCH EDITION

The Audresbury Times

MARCH EDITION

Audresbury | Gloucestershire

Monday, March 21st 2016

THE TRAGIC MILTEN CASE

BY JASON MUNROE, SENIOR FEATURES CORRESPONDENT.

Man Charged with the murder of his wife and two young children.

In the early morning of Monday, March 21st, three bodies were found inside the property of Felix Milten.

Felix, 36, lived in the home with his wife, Melissa, 40, and their three children, Tancan, 10, Finnley, 6, and ten-month-old baby, Sapphire. In 2014, Felix was previously charged after assaulting a woman in a nightclub, and spent six months in custody.

At 2:35 AM, the police was informed of screaming inside of the residence down Cadesview Road. Officers arrived at the scene at 2:52 and discovered the bodies of Melissa, Finnley and Sapphire in the living room. Felix was detained into custody immediately.

After an hour of searching, Felix's oldest son, Tancan, was found alive, hiding in a bush at a field around the back of his house, covered in bruises. He was then taken to Audresbury Childrens Hospital.

RECORDINGS OF TANCAN MILTEN TALKING TO A FORENSIC PSYCHIATRIST IN 2016:

FP: Tancan, did you witness your father murdering your mother and siblings?

T: Yes.

FP: Did your father seem agitated before he murdered them?

T: Yes. Mum was arguing with him in the kitchen. She wanted to divorce him.

FP: Why did she want to get divorced?

T: He started drinking heavily after I got diagnosed with autism and became very aggressive towards my mum after she found out he cheated on her.

FP: Aggressive, how?

T: He threw plates at her a lot, or whatever he could reach. My mum also had bipolar disorder, so their arguments got out of hand a lot. I would always hide Finn and Sapphire in my room until they calmed down. I barricaded the door with my beanbag, but nowhere in the house was ever safe.

FP: Okay, you're doing very well, Tancan. You are very maturely spoken for a ten-year-old. Do you remember where you were when you witnessed the murders.

T: I was in my room. Me and Finn had just got into an argument because I wouldn't let him finish building my rocket ship. We heard Dad yelling at Mum, and then a plate smashed, so Finn rushed downstairs. I stayed upstairs because I was scared, until I heard Finn and Mum screaming. They were bleeding on the floor, I think Dad stabbed them with a kitchen knife, but I didn't see him holding one. Dad was stood over Sapphire's bassinet. He was strangling her with his bare hands to stop her from crying; it was like something had snapped inside of him. He had never physically hurt sapphire before.

FP: How did you escape?

T: I ran upstairs and he threw my rocket ship at me, but it missed. I ran back downstairs and straight out the front door. He started chasing me down the road. He was very drunk. It was so dark that I couldn't see where I was going, but I kept running as fast as I could. I ran through an alleyway and I'm not sure where I went after that. I know I just kept running, even though he had stopped chasing me at this point.

FP: Do you remember running down the road at Three in the morning and hiding in a field?

T: I don't know...

FP: You are very brave, Tancan. Thank you for giving me this information.

T: You're not going to tell him that I told on him, are you?

FP: Don't worry, you're safe. He's never going to hurt you ever again.

T: What's going to happen now?

FP: I'm not sure. You'll probably get placed in an emergency foster placement for the rest of the night.

Tancan never felt guilt for murdering his mother; he felt guilty because he left her and his siblings to die. He ran away like a coward, but if he stayed, he would've ended up like them.

After years of watching his mother put up with such inhumane treatment from his dad, it left him to develop multiple mental health problems later in life. The trauma damaged him so much that he created fake storylines and adventures to sugarcoat the truth that was far too aggressive to cope with.

In those stories, his dad was still an alcoholic, but he was recovering. He felt the love he never got from him. They wouldn't have been as realistic if everything disappeared. He had always been autistic; he couldn't change that.

He re-imagined what Finn and Sapphire would be like as they got older and wrote stories about them in his diary. at least in that universe he could watch his siblings grow up with him.

Finn was annoyed at Tancan before he died, so he got annoyed at Tancan easily in the stories. Every time Tancan wrote Finn's name, he started to cry at the fact Finn died thinking he was still upset with him.

As much as he wanted to imagine his mum alive, he couldn't. There had to be a way for him to write about his grief and express his emotions.

Stephen never existed outside of Tancan's mind. He was never a real person, someone who he wished he had in his life but didn't. Somebody who would keep him safe whenever his dad got angry.

He gave Stephen a romantic relationship with his dad to let out the anger he felt from his dad's previous affairs, this also gave him a reason for dad to accept his own identity crisis.

The relationship between Sean and Taylor was almost a metaphor for the way he saw Felix treat Melissa.

Some scenes happened, but most of them didn't. The Therapist and Space Dome worker were monsters made from his anxieties about what could happen if he tried asking for help. They would all think he was insane and punish him. That's why he made everyone else defend him.

Most of the school scenes actually did occur, without Taylor and Finn there to protect him, however, he never mentioned the times kids and teachers would avoid him for being the son of a criminal.

Bella-Joules was real too. She sat next him in class, but she never spoke to him. Taylor having a crush on her symbolised the way he wanted to be her friend and form a real friendship like he had with Taylor.

After being questioned by the forensic psychiatrist, Tancan stopped talking. He could only write for five years. He had nobody to talk to, even if he could. Everyone thought he was being difficult, but he couldn't process his emotions. It wasn't his fault; nobody gave him the help he deserved.

Tancan wasn't looking for Taylor in the club, he went in there hoping he could find someone to trust. That day his voice came back; the same day it shut off again. He only wanted help, but he received more trauma instead.

Tancan Milten took his life on February 6th, 2022, at fifteen years old, shortly after he wrote the scene where Taylor defeated Sean. It took two hours for a staff member to find him in his care home bedroom. He thought everyone hated him. He felt like everything was his fault.

When clearing his room, the staff member found: his mum's necklace, Finn's lemon shark pin, one of Sapphire's baby toys, a Sylvanian Families elephant figure and a sketch he drew of Taylor, all stuffed in a box underneath his bed.

Even though Taylor Maxxie was a part of Tancan Milten, her story didn't die with him. She was a real example of how neurodivergent girls get misunderstood on a daily basis. Millions of girls suffer through everything that she did every day of their lives, and it still hasn't stopped.

At the end of the day, nothing is ever going to be perfect, but I promise you there is somebody who cares about you, so live your life to the fullest because *you* matter. <3

IN LOVING MEMOMORY OF

AARON MCDONALD

And all the other precious lives lost too soon.

Exclusive bonus Chapters

March 2nd 2021 - 317 days before he destroyed himself.

An older staff worker knocked on Tancan's door. "Tancan, do you feel like talking today?" she called.

No Answer.

She opened the door to find Tancan doodling inside his diary. "What are you drawing there?" she asked.

In silence he closed the cover and glared at her.

"So... Your fifteenth birthday is in a few weeks, and I was wondering if you'd like to go anywhere to celebrate."

"I want to see *him*," he mumbled.

"I'm sorry, what was that? I haven't got my hearing-aid in."

He spoke louder but still mumbled the words, "I want to visit my Father in jail."

"That's not much of a celebration," she teased. "Tancan you've been through tremendous trauma and have barely spoken to anyone over the past five years. It really isn't a great idea."

"I was ten when it happened. I've matured a lot more since then. I've spent those five years terrified of him finding me again, but it would be much better if I found him first."

"I'll talk to some of the other staff members and see what we can do."

On Tancan's birthday, he never received the Alien hoodie he wrote about, the visit was the only thing he wanted.

A security guard assured Tancan that he would be safe, and his dad would be sat five foot away from him.

There he was. The serpent he once counted as family, sitting in an empty room, handcuffed to the table.

Felix gently opened his hand, hoping Tancan would hold it. "Hello, Tancan, I've missed you so much."

Tancan backed away. "Don't touch me, you sick bastard. Not after you laid your filthy hands on my mother. You strangled Sapphire to death. She was a baby. She couldn't even say no because she didn't know how to. You even killed Finn..."

"Jesus Christ, Tancan. You're acting like I *raped* them all too."

"I don't know what you did to them, but they were all your *victims*. So was Maxine Taylor. The girl in the bar, remember? That was her name, but you didn't even acknowledge that, did you? You just wanted to *fuck* a seventeen-year-old after you decided that Mum wasn't skinny enough for you.

"She only started binge eating after you constantly abused her for having a mental disorder and you probably gave her more of them. But no matter how much she ate, she was the most gorgeous woman I have ever seen. I really thought you would've matured after being arrested the first time, I guess I was wrong.

"I begged Mum to divorce you, but she was too *scared* of you. She knew you were capable of hurting *her* children. That's why she stayed. And you still *took* their lives away from them."

Tancan rolled up his sleeve. "Look. See all these cuts? I've tried draining your blood from my body, because that is how much I despise you. It sickens me how I was too young to see what a monster you were. I looked up to you. I hugged you. I even told you I loved you. If I had seen how you treated my mother, I would have never done any of those things.

"I never loved you; I never will. I hope you rot in here. I hope you die a very slow painful death and end up very far away from heaven. I hate you so much that I could kill you myself, right now with my bare hands, but I won't because I NOTHING like you.

"I also want to let you know that I'm an autistic gay feminist. I'm not ashamed, I'm very proud of being myself, the person you would've never let me be. I'm going to rewrite my life. I'm going to have friends and a dad who actually loves me. Don't worry, I'm not going to erase you from my life, I'm going to make you the person you would've *hated* to be."

Felix Milten died in jail on the 24th of December 2025.

An estimated 10-20 million people attempt to end their own life each year.

Suicide has become the third leading cause of death among 15–29-year-olds globally.

High masking autistic women are 13x more likely to take their life.

Up to 100,000 autistic girls could still be undiagnosed.

Around 13,400 autistic people died by suicide globally in 2021, accounting for 1.8% of all suicidal deaths.

Autistics relative risk of suicide is 2.85 times higher than the general population.

Sexual violence affects about 30% of women in the general population and between two to three times as much for autistic women.

One woman or girl is killed by someone in her own family every 11 minutes.

Teenagers remain the age group to most likely to be murdered with a knife. In 2024, 82% of homicides of kids aged 13-19 were the result of knife crime.

Half of all people who die by suicide may have major depressive disorder; having this or one of the other mood disorders such as bipolar disorder increases the risk of suicide x20.

A study in Britain found that at least half of suicides among young people are related to bullying.

35% of children aged 10-15 in England experienced in-person bullying.

The child being bullied may be seen as different due to characteristics like their appearance, race, religion, sexual orientation, disability, or even academic ability.

Only 1 out of 10 children facing domestic abuse receive support.

Now read that all again.

And again.

Global helplines:

Samaritans – UK: 0845 790 9090 (Rep. of Ireland: 116 123)

Childline – UK: 0800 1111

Lifeline – Northern Ireland: 0808 808 8000

Lifeline – Australia: 13 11 14

Kids Helpline – Australia: 1800 551 800

Youthline – New Zealand: 0800 37 66 33 or text 234

Childline – South Africa: 08000 55 555

Lifeline – South Africa: 0861 322 322

MHA – USA: 1 800 273 8255 or text 998

More Global Helplines: https://blog.opencounseling.com/suicide-hotlines/

ACKNOWLEDGMENTS

My writing journey:

My great-grandmother, Jean Florence Palmer, always dreamed of writing a book, but unfortunately, she never got around to that by the time of her passing in 2020. In 2021, at the age of thirteen, I decided I would carry her passion as one of my own.

Ironically, I always disliked reading throughout primary school and would always make my mum tick my reading planner to say that I had been reading as homework when I hadn't. Throughout the rest of primary, I realised something felt different about me. I started getting teased for still liking shows such as *Mickey Mouse*, and it made me feel very emotional to the point where I had to force myself to stop liking certain things to fit in with other kids my age.

I remember in 2019, when I was eleven years old, I was spinning in circles and a boy, not much younger than I was, asked me, "Are you autistic?"

"No," I said, "At least I don't think I am." As soon as I got home, I researched the symptoms of autism, assuming I wasn't. Almost all the symptoms matched up perfectly. I did a few online quizzes, and they all told me that I was 95% on the spectrum.

It took a lot of courage to tell some of my family members that I believe I may be neurodivergent, thinking they would think I'm just making things up, but some of them had already known for years. There were also a few older family members who were thought to be on the spectrum, but none of them had ever been diagnosed.

Just over a week after I turned twelve, lockdown happened. At first, I was happy that I got to stay home from school, but then I saw the negative impact it had on the world. I realised that I wanted to do something with my life and help other people.

Once school reopened, I spent most lunchtimes in the library looking at books. And that's when it clicked. I wanted to write my own fiction book about a character that I could relate to.

My mental health started getting worse, begging not to go into school. The only two things I found comfort in was writing and an actor and director I discovered at ten: *Bill Hader.* I really enjoyed his sense of humour and when I wasn't writing, I would spend time watching interviews where he talked a lot about anxiety. I had always been a massive movie buff who collected DVDs my entire life, so I decided to watch a lot of the movies he had been in. I stumbled across a movie called*: the skeleton twins*, where he starred alongside *Kristen Wiig.*

I continued watching sad drama movies as inspiration for my writing. As of the 25th of September 2025, when I am writing this, I have watched almost nine hundred films. Before I turned fourteen, I had already written an entire storyline about a few fictional characters I made with a lot of research.

Tancan isn't based on myself at all and is different from me in a lot of ways, but I wanted to make him relatable to other autistic individuals like me. By this point, I was on the waiting list, but certain I was neurodivergent. I looked for other books and movies about autistic characters, but my resources were limited. I really enjoyed: *A kind of spark* by *Elle McNicoll,* but I wanted to make my book aimed at a slightly older audience that tackles more adult themes.

I started reading more emotional books about teenagers like, *The Perks Of Being a Wallflower* by *Stephen Chbosky*, *All The Bright Places* by *Jennifer Niven,* and *Beautiful boy* by *David Sheff.* I loved the movies, so I knew I'd love the books, which also helped me improve my writing style.

2022 was when my favourite television series was released. *Heartbreak High* is an Australian *Netflix* original series which is an adaptation of a show of the same name that aired in the 90s. The modern version is very up to date with the current issues teens are struggling with. One character called *Quinni* is autistic and portrayed by autistic actress, *Chloe Hayden.* I remember screaming at the Tv, "That is literally me!" As soon as I finished the first season, I found out she was also an author and immediately purchased her book titled: *Different, not less.*

At fourteen, I decided to self-diagnose myself with autism. I knew it wasn't the best decision, but every sign was there. I started to make friends at school who understood me more than most teachers did, and I'd like to thank them for helping me through secondary school.

I created the character Taylor around the same time as Tancan, but she was more of a side character to begin with. Her dialogue was based on the way a lot of my friends and movie characters talked, but she didn't have much of her own storyline. I wanted to make her more realistic and give her problems that a lot of teenage girls go through so that some people could relate to her as well as Tancan.

As well as researching autistic traits, I researched female traits. As a male, I couldn't possibly know exactly how females feel. I didn't want to offend anyone, so I asked a lot of people how they felt growing up in female bodies. I needed

Taylor to be complex, not just a female character who yearns for love and happiness. I've always had a strong sense of Justice, anyway.

Before I turned fifteen, my entire first draft was completed, but my writing had no structure. The storyline was messy but had solid characters, so I started to dive deeper into structuring the book. I had always known the ending from the start. Tancan was going to die.

Halfway through my journey, I received devastating news that my friend's brother had taken his own life. Although I never got the opportunity to meet him, I knew how close they were, so I asked for permission to add a memoir at the end of the book.

Even though Tancan's character and storyline was fully fictional, I wanted to write a character to represent the way trauma and depression affected young individuals so people could see that they are not going through all of the pressure alone.

I had a lot of time off school because of a bullying incident and had online tutoring to make sure I didn't fail my GCSE exams. I also watched a lot of creative writing tutorials online and ended up passing my English literature and language exams.

During the summer of 2024, I started reading a lot of different genres. I liked psychological crime and thriller the most. I started doing a lot of research into psychology and mental illnesses and added more of a mystery element to the book which was mostly a coming-of-age story at that time. I spent most of my free time at college editing each chapter of *Deepfaded* until I had written an entire psychological thriller at sixteen.

Once I finished writing, I spent most of my time fixing grammar mistakes, formatting each page and designing the cover myself. I was an unemployed teenager who couldn't afford a professional editor, and I refused to use Ai. I wanted my book to be personal, and I was worried someone would delete parts I spent weeks rewriting.

March 4th, 2025, I officially got diagnosed with autism, two days after my seventeenth birthday.

I doubted my writing quite a lot, constantly researching pros and cons. I found Tancan's diary entries the easiest to write as I was able to put myself into Tancan's shoes and pretend I was a fifteen-year-old space nerd when I actually had no knowledge on his interests at all. I originally wanted to write the entire book in first-person narrative, but I felt like it would've messed the ending up.

July 12th, 2025, I had the opportunity to meet one of my biggest inspirations, *Holly Jackson*, who is most famous for writing the *Good Girls Guide To Murder* series. She seemed surprised when I told her I officially started writing Deepfaded when I was fourteen as she had written her first book at fifteen. I read her the first line of the prologue, and she really liked it which boosted my confidence a lot.

I started promoting *Deepfaded* on social media and joined online groups of other teen writers. A lot of people asked me how much money I wanted to make, but I told them it's not about the money since I wrote this entire book to help other struggling teenagers like myself. With the money I do make, I will donate it all to charities that support struggling women and children. However, I would love to do tours like some authors do and get to see how many people I've helped in real life.

I really enjoyed writing this and hope to keep writing books for the rest of my life and help lots of people. Let's see where the future takes me!

Thank you!

I'd like to thank everyone who believed in me throughout my journey so far, it means a lot to me!

And another thanks to the people who have taken time out of their precious day to read the book I spent years writing. I really appreciate it.

About the Author:

Craigson Palmer was born on March 2nd 2008, and aims to makes his audience feel understood and cared about.

Instagram: Craggle_Craigson

Tik Tok: Craggle_hader

Letterboxd: Craigson21

Email: Craigson.com@gmail.com

Printed in Dunstable, United Kingdom

78390691R00218